HIGHLAND BRAWN
The Band of Cousins, Book 8
Copyright © 2019 by Keira Montclair

Cover Design and Interior Format

HIGHLAND BRAWN

8 THE BAND OF COUSINS

KEIRA MONTCLAIR

The Grants and Ramsays

Family Tree (1280s)

GRANTS

LAIRD ALEXANDER GRANT and wife, MADDIE
John (Jake) and wife, Aline
James (Jamie) and wife, Gracie
Kyla and husband, Finlay
Connor
Elizabeth
Maeve

BRENNA GRANT and husband, QUADE RAMSAY
Torrian (Quade's son from his first marriage) and wife,
Heather—daughter, Nellie (Heather's daughter from a
previous relationship) and son, Lachlan
Lily (Quade's daughter from his first marriage) and hus-
band, Kyle—twin daughters, Lise and Liliana
Bethia and husband, Donnan—son, Drystan
Gregor
Jennet
Geva (adopted)
Emma (adopted)

ROBBIE GRANT and wife, CARALYN
Ashlyn (Caralyn's daughter from a previous relationship)
and husband, Magnus—daughter, X
Gracie (Caralyn's daughter from a previous relationship)
and husband, Jamie
Rodric (Roddy) and wife, Rose
Padraig

BRODIE GRANT and wife, CELESTINA
Loki (adopted) and wife, Arabella—sons, Kenzie (adopted) and Lucas, daughter, Ami (adopted)
Braden and wife, Cairstine—son, Steenie (Cairstine's son from previous relationship)
Catriona
Alison

JENNIE GRANT and husband, AEDAN CAMERON
Riley
Tara
Brin

RAMSAYS

QUADE RAMSAY and wife, BRENNA GRANT
Torrian (Quade's son from his first marriage) and wife, Heather—Nellie (Heather's daughter from a previous relationship) and son, Lachlan
Lily (Quade's daughter from his first marriage) and husband, Kyle—twin daughters, Lise and Liliana
Bethia and husband, Donnan
Gregor
Jennet

LOGAN RAMSAY and wife, GWYNETH
Molly (adopted) and husband, Tormod
Maggie (adopted)
Sorcha and husband, Cailean
Gavin
Brigid

MICHEIL RAMSAY and wife, DIANA
David
Daniel

AVELINA RAMSAY and DREW MENZIE
Elyse
Tad
Tomag
Maitland

To the reader

This is one of my favorites.
I hope it will be one of yours, too.

CHAPTER ONE

―◆―

"STOP THAT WOMAN!"

Connor Grant cursed because the small crowd in front of him ignored his plea. Hellfire, but he'd been searching for the woman with that white-blonde hair for the past day. He'd been up and down every street in South Berwick to no avail. Sela, it seemed, could be elusive when she wished.

He shoved the men out of his way, easy since he was at least a head taller than all of them. His sire had taught him that while it was best to keep a cool head, certain situations called for a show of strength. His height and bulk gave him an advantage, and he used it now, pushing bystanders out of the way in his haste to get to Sela. He was determined not to lose her this time.

Reaching the end of the street, he cursed again.

She had disappeared.

"Thorn!"

He spun around, searching for his wee friend or squire, as he preferred to be called. "Where the hell are you, Thorn?"

The small, dark-haired lad appeared out of the crowd and stared up at him with a worshipful look that humbled him. "What next, my lord?"

He hated it when the eight-year-old addressed him that way, but since he was in such haste, he allowed it. Nothing mattered as much as finding Sela. "Find the blonde woman. She was just ahead of us."

Thorn took a quick glance and immediately pointed to the left. "You mean that one?" She'd just darted out from behind a group of bystanders.

"God's blood, but she rankles me," he said, biting his tongue against a litany of curses. "Aye, that one. Follow her."

He took off toward Sela, knowing Thorn would be right behind him.

They ran and ran until Connor thought his chest would explode. She'd glanced back at them twice, hurrying her steps each time—which meant he and Thorn had needed to do the same. If only he could convince her to run toward him instead of away from him, but her expression was wary.

She moved around the corner of an alehouse, and he breathed a sigh of relief. If she intended to enter the building, he'd be able to catch up with her.

But she fooled him again. He stopped abruptly as he rounded the corner—the long alley next to the alehouse was empty. Before he could turn around, he was set upon from behind by five men. He kicked two of them and punched another two out cold, but there were too many and he couldn't unsheathe his sword fast enough. Five men wrestled him to the ground, and although he managed to stab two of them with the dagger from his boot, the weapon was knocked out of his hand as his face hit the ground. His hands were yanked behind him.

A moment later, tightly bound, he heard a young voice call out to him, "Master, they're kidnapping me. The Dubh men. I'm on a brown horse heading north." Thorn's voice fell away as the distance between them increased. "Help me, Connor!"

A sick feeling welled inside him, but he couldn't do anything. The men who'd ambushed him continued to punch and kick him, laughing as they did so. After a time, they walked off, one of them saying, "Not bad for one man, but you cannot fight a dozen, can you?"

The bastards could steal lads and lassies in the middle of town, and no one cared enough to stop them. They probably handed out gold coins to all the vendors who promised to keep their mouth shut about what they saw.

Their world had surely changed for the worse, and it was up to Connor and his cousins to set it to rights.

A rage set on him that he wished to let loose, but he thought of another piece of advice his sire had given him: "When you've gotten yourself in trouble, 'tis time to set the emotion far away." His sire was right. Forcing himself to tamp down his fury, he started working on the rope binding his hands.

To his delight, his outlook changed abruptly.

"What the hell have you gotten yourself into?" His cousin Roddy jumped off his horse and rushed to his side, pulling out a dagger to cut his bindings. His cousins had caught up. They'd all been patrolling the city together, looking for signs of unlawful activity, when Connor and Thorn had caught sight of Sela. She'd ducked into the market, making it impossible for him to follow her on horseback, and so they'd jumped down and gone off in pursuit of her. There'd been no time to inform the others. "Did not think I'd ever see the day you'd be beaten," Roddy continued.

"Save the taunting for later," he grumbled, rubbing his hands after the rope fell away.

Their cousin Braden rode up behind Roddy, his eyes wide with surprise when he caught sight of Connor's injuries.

"Stay on your horse, Braden. Channel men kidnapped Thorn," he said. "We have to get him back. *Now.*" A quick search of the area turned up his sword, and to his surprise, Midnight Moon trotted out from behind Braden.

"Many thanks to you, Braden," he said, knowing his loyal stallion would not have accompanied just anyone.

Once they were all mounted, Connor pointed north.

"He yelled out the direction they were taking him while they pounded on me."

"How many?" Braden asked.

"Around a dozen." They left the alley, entering the chaos of the main thoroughfare. It was market day, and everywhere Connor looked there were booths selling fresh fish, pastries, and ale, each of them crowded by customers.

"Your sire was right," Braden said, echoing his thoughts. "South Berwick is much busier than Edinburgh or Inverness. Out of my way!" he bellowed at the throng of people.

Connor's horse was such a magnificent beast that the onlookers stepped out of his way quickly, which pleased him because he didn't wish to worry about trampling bairns under the black horse's powerful hooves.

Accustomed to patrolling Grant land together, the cousins settled into their usual fast pace. Once they cleared the crowd, they soon caught up to the group of thieves. South Berwick drew many during market day, but once outside the busiest area, the crowd thinned quickly.

They were the only ones on this particular path, which made Connor wonder where they were taking Thorn. The Channel's quarters outside of Berwick must be well isolated.

"Kill the bastards," the one carrying Thorn yelled. The laddie whooped—the Grant war whoop, which Connor had taught him on the way to Berwick—and promptly bit the man's hand. "Ow, you wee bastard!" Unfortunately, the villain kept a tight hold on Thorn and maneuvered away from the Grants, putting several other men in front of him.

Braden, Roddy, and Connor spread out, quickly surrounding the group. All three of the cousins had learned from a young age to swing their swords from one side of the horse to the other, something their opponents could not do. The Grants fought hard, squeezing their horses forward, their method crushing their enemies. Metal clashed, blood flew, and bodies fell screaming off horses.

Finally, Connor made his way to Thorn's kidnapper, who'd retreated to the back of the group. The man took one look at him, hopped to the ground, and ran as fast as his legs would take him.

Connor plucked the lad off the horse and settled Thorn in front of him in the saddle. Once they had the lad, they galloped hard back toward Berwick. A couple of the thieves had recovered enough to follow them, but they couldn't match the pace of their war horses.

"You are the best fighter ever, my lord!" Thorn shouted, cheering the victory.

Connor couldn't help but grin at the lad's cheekiness. "'Tis not me alone, lad. My cousins and I were trained by our sires, and we've practiced many moons together. Now we fight like a team."

"Aye," Roddy said with a grin, "and those fools who kidnapped you did not even attempt to work together."

Braden chuckled. "'Tis proof the English have not yet learned how to fight."

Thorn asked, "Will you teach me someday?"

"Aye," Connor said, enjoying the lad's exuberance. "But you must work hard first."

"I will. I promise. As soon as I get my own sword, I'll practice with the three of you."

When they were no longer being followed, they turned into a clearing and dismounted to decide on their next activity.

"Thorn, you are hale?" Connor asked, still slightly out of breath from the battle. "No wounds?"

"Aye, my thanks for saving me. The Dubh men would have sold me. They..." he paused, finally taking a breath.

Connor put a hand on the boy's shoulder. "Slow down, lad. We'll not allow them to take you again. 'Twas my fault for leaving you alone."

Braden took a swig of ale from his skin, wiped his mouth with his sleeve, then asked, "Why'd you go off alone with the lad, Connor? I've not seen you move that quickly before, even in battle. I turned around and all I saw was your back."

Roddy nodded his agreement. "What could have been so important?"

"Not what," Braden said, "but whom? Who could make you leave without assistance? I think we know the answer."

Thorn, quick to defend his master, said, "But we saw her. We saw Sela. She looked back at us, then disappeared into a big crowd of people, right in the middle of the market vendors. We had to follow her."

"Thorn, did you ever see her when you were taken captive? Was she with any of those men?" Connor asked.

"Nay, she was not with us, but I heard them. I spied and I know where she is." The lad took on the self-important look he often wore when he thought of himself as his namesake—the son of Thor. An orphan, Thorn prided himself on his speed and deftness. He and his wee friend Nari had been living just outside of Edinburgh, hungry and destitute, when Connor and Gregor, another cousin, had stumbled upon them. The lads had quickly agreed to help them with their cause: ending the Channel of Dubh, the group of smugglers who stole lasses and lads and sent them across the waters.

The Grant and Ramsay cousins had been fighting the Channel for nearly a year now, and the end was finally nigh. In Edinburgh, they'd discovered one last shipment was being planned—a massive one—and it was going through Berwick. Gregor and Nari had stayed behind in Edinburgh, waiting for more help to arrive from the Band of Cousins, while Connor and the others had come straight to Berwick. Connor had also been driven by another motivation. It was an open secret among the cousins that he had a fascination with Sela. She'd been taken there under duress, and he'd followed.

Connor was convinced Sela knew the secrets of the

Channel, and although she had worked with them in the past, he suspected she had been coerced. The way she'd been brought to Berwick—bound—seemed to confirm it, although she was free now. She'd played a part in this ambush, but again, he doubted she'd been a willing participant. The looks she'd given him—which had clearly read *go away*—seemed to support that.

"Well done, lad. Where is she?" Connor got excited for a moment, then reminded himself this was a young boy, not an adult, so the explanation may not be as useful as he hoped.

"In a castle."

He groaned and massaged his forehead. How many castles were there in all of Scotland and England? Too many to search.

Thorn continued, "The big one by the water in Berwick."

Connor smiled because the lad had just helped their search tremendously. "Now that's helpful."

"Does he mean the castle that was built by King Edward?" Braden asked.

"Aye, they said he's letting them use it."

Surely the English king couldn't know what he was permitting, but Connor could not focus on that just yet. Had the lad learned the names of the leaders of the Channel of Dubh, the bastards who stole lads and lasses and sold them across the water?

Roddy spoke at the same time as Connor. "Them, who?"

Braden, apparently as anxious for the information as Roddy and Connor, said, "Out with it, lad, tell us exactly what you heard. Who'd they say was at the castle?"

"Those two bastards."

Sela sat in a chair in the solar, waiting for Guy and Dee, the leaders of the Channel of Dubh, to speak with her.

She'd been given strict instructions about what she was to do after she completed her assignment. There was to be no tarrying around the place where the lad had been taken. She was to return to the castle immediately once the men had accomplished their objective.

Guy and Dee wished to crush the band of Highlanders who'd successfully crushed their operation in Inverness and elsewhere in Scotland, and Connor Grant was the tallest, strongest member of the group. The most handsome, too, although Sela didn't wish to think of him that way. When he'd shown up in Berwick, Guy and Dee had been adamant that the time had come to stop him and the others.

Sela had hoped with all her heart that Connor and his wee friend would avoid the kidnapping scheme, which had been designed to lure Connor out of the city—and her heart had sunk when the lad had instead been captured.

And yet, according to the rumblings she'd heard, Connor had somehow come out ahead. He'd saved himself *and* the boy.

If only she trusted Connor Grant could save *her*.

She wanted no part of the Channel of Dubh, but they wielded an impossible power over her—one that meant they could coerce her to do anything.

Anything.

Although Guy and Dee had always been wicked men, they'd only developed their current operation—the Channel of Dubh—a year ago. Sela had been sent to Inverness to handle the women they'd taken captive, women who were forced to fight, or whore, for money they would never see. She'd been put in charge of the whole operation, and much to her shame, she'd excelled at convincing the lasses to do her bidding.

Men loved watching women fight, it turned out, and Sela had an uncanny eye for knowing which women were best suited to the practice. She'd used her heritage from her mother, the Norse beauty, as an intimidation tactic. Her voice and her looks had made her stand out, and it had worked to her advantage. Everyone feared the Ice Queen, though she knew not where the name had started.

She was so successful that Guy and Dee had bought her a new wardrobe in Inverness—a boon she'd neither asked for nor wanted—but she was also given better access to her *other* boon, the one she valued more than life itself.

She told herself that at least she'd helped the women. Ensured they had shelter and were fed. Arranged for their entertainment. That was all true, and it was much more than any of Guy and Dee's voluntary workers would have done, but it didn't take away from her guilt. She'd forced them to fight, turned her head when they were punished, and tolerated other things she preferred not to think about...

Then Connor Grant and his band of Highlanders had arrived in town. Connor unsettled her from the first. Usually she understood men's desires, their most base instincts.

But Connor was different.

He made the guilt she'd felt for years heavier, as did the mounting evidence that Guy and Dee were doing something much, much worse than collecting wagers and forcing women to whore. The scene she'd witnessed at the end of her time in Inverness—the Highlanders fighting the Channel men, pulling lasses out of crates...

The very thought of what Guy and Dee were doing, of what she was a party to, crushed her.

It was better not to know.

It was better not to ask for confirmation.

Already, she woke up screaming more nights than not, tormented by memories of the lasses abused by the Channel men.

She knew Connor must wonder why she stayed. Years ago, she'd tried to escape, but it was not possible anymore.

She was responsible for someone besides herself, and she kept that at the back of her mind at all times.

Finally, after what felt like hours of waiting, Guy came in and closed the door, one guard on either side of him. She stayed in her chair but did her best to stop kneading her hands. These men preyed on weakness. "Sela, I appreciate you following our instructions, but the venture failed."

"But I did exactly as you asked," she whimpered. She'd hoped she might get her boon early in exchange for her cooperation.

"You did, but the Grants got the lad back." He stepped closer to her and pulled her to standing. "Why does Connor Grant follow you? Why would he chase you?" His voice came out in that low, threatening tone she hated.

She squared her shoulders and looked Guy in the eye. "I don't know. I'd never seen him anywhere before he came to Inverness."

His arm reached out so fast she had no chance to protect herself. "You lie." He slapped her hard, but she didn't react other than to turn her face slightly from the blow.

How many slaps had she endured over the five years of her captivity? She didn't wish to count.

"I did as you asked. I told the truth about not knowing him before Inverness. The only other place I've seen him is in the whorehouse in Edinburgh. I know not why he follows me. I speak the truth, my lord." While she doubted his true heritage was noble, she knew how much Guy and Dee preferred to be addressed as if they were.

He gave her a scathing look but stepped back and indicated she was to sit down again.

Guy had brown hair that he kept rather short and a long beard he didn't trim. He was surprisingly fit for a man his age. He and Dee lived in England at a nobleman's castle, one much farther south, but their most recent venture had required them to travel more than usual.

After what had happened in Inverness, she had an inkling

of what that venture might be, but she chose not to face the truth of it. If she was right, she wasn't sure she could go on—and she needed to be strong.

For as much as she abhorred her assignment, she had no choice other than to cooperate.

"I've done all you asked. My boon mark is in another sennight. Have I met the requirements yet? I worked hard in Inverness."

He whirled around as if just realizing it was her boon time. How could he not know? Everyone knew when it was her boon time.

He paused, chewing on long hairs from his moustache while he stroked his beard. "You have a good start, but I think we'll have something else for you to do. We'll require your help in a new venture that will be unfolding in a matter of days. See that you do everything we ask. Or else…"

She shuddered involuntarily, because she knew exactly what "or else" meant.

CHAPTER TWO

CONNOR LED THE GROUP TO the castle on the water. It was a majestic sight, although it was evident it had deteriorated in places. The keep sat on a hill set back from the shoreline, distinctive for its four towers and deep turrets. Flags flew high in the wind, whipping freely. From its highest point, the view of the sea had to be spectacular from on high. Half a dozen guards surrounded the gates.

The castle wall traveled all the way to the sea, a most imposing picture. That wall would prevent anyone from strolling into the castle from the shoreline, instead forcing visitors to go through the gates or arrive by boat. If he were to guess, the design was purposeful—it allowed the castle dwellers to bypass the busy port of Berwick.

He considered the possibility of using the shoreline as a point of entry and decided against it—even if the guards couldn't properly watch it, it would be dangerous at night. If they needed to sneak inside, climbing the wall at the back would be a better alternative.

Based on the imposing fortress in front of him and the possibility that the Channel could send ships from inside the gates, it would be even more difficult for the Band of Cousins to stop this shipment from heading out to sea.

"What shall we do, my lord?" Thorn asked. "I know 'tis the castle they discussed. They were laughing about how close it was to town. They called it Berwick Castle."

"All in good time, Thorn. As long as we're this close to

the water, I want to check out the port. See how many berths there are for ships," Connor said. "My father told me this is one of the areas that earns Scotland the most money because it's the closest spot to France by ship. Many boats aim for this area, and a large amount of wool and other products leaves the port on a daily basis."

"I hope that all those in Berwick are not aware of the sale of bairns. Would be a sad testament to the value of coin, would it not?" Braden asked.

Roddy said, "I should hope not."

"Agreed," Connor said. "I'd like to search the town and see if anything looks familiar. In Inverness, the Channel men frequented alehouses and stored many crates in buildings near the docks in Inverness. Berwick looks much different than Inverness, so 'tis like starting over again. Where are the whorehouses? The most popular inns? The busiest alehouses?"

After leaving their horses in a safe place, they made their way to the center of town. The streets were still busy, bustling with a large number of people wandering about. Much like the other towns they'd visited in their quest to end the Channel, Berwick was dirty. The air smelled foul no matter where they went, and rats moved among the food stalls looking for scraps. Thorn informed them that he'd once had a job killing such varmints.

As they moved closer to the coastline, the salty scent of the sea wafted past them. Down near the center of the port, fishing boats lined the berths, and the smell of dead fish overpowered the other unsavory scents. Connor loved fish, but he had the sudden urge to heave. There were fewer vendors near the ship berths, mostly because they were teeming with activity. Boats of all sizes were lined up in berths, and still others were moored a bit farther out.

Connor stopped and stared out across the water, the others close behind him.

Thorn followed his gaze, then glanced up at him. "What

are you looking for?"

"A ship the size of the one we all saw in Inverness, but I don't see one."

"How big?" Braden asked. Neither he nor Roddy had been to Inverness.

"Double the size of any of these. These are mostly fishing boats. A few of these ships would be capable of carrying cargo, but human cargo weighs more than they can handle. I don't see any buildings close enough to hold the prisoners for a big shipment either. Nor is there an area to hide crates."

Roddy said, "I'm going for a meat pie while you look. Anyone care to join me?"

"Me!" Thorn yelled. "I'm starving."

Braden cocked his head. "I could use an ale."

The prospect of a rest was tempting, but Connor couldn't allow himself to be distracted. He would not stop until he found Sela again. She was here somewhere.

He could *feel* it.

"I'm going to keep looking for a while longer. Which alehouse are you going to?"

Braden pointed to the one at the end of the street they were on. "I think this one serves food."

"I'll see you there shortly," Connor said absentmindedly, waving his cousins off. He kept looking about, absorbing everything. It struck him again that this city was quite different than Inverness. Aye, they were different towns, but it went beyond that.

The reason for his reaction finally dawned on him.

He was surrounded by fishermen. There weren't many men strolling the docks looking for work or moving crates.

That was it.

Every time they'd visited the docks at Inverness, there had been men moving and lifting crates. Stacking them to the sides, loading them on the boats, grunting as they worked because the crates were so heavy. Not here. One boat was in the process of being loaded with small crates, but he suspected it was naught but wool or grain or perhaps an occasional crate of Scots liquid gold—whisky.

There were no crates large enough to fit a person.

His gaze carried over to the castle on the hill behind them. The castle had impenetrable walls around it, a fortress as strong as any he'd seen. When they'd approached from the other side, he had seen the wear on the stone, the crumbling edges. From here, it looked majestic and imposing.

A familiar voice caught his attention and he spun around, surprised to find himself staring into a pair of ice blue eyes.

Sela. She had two guards behind her. The woman was never left alone, another indication that she wasn't working for the Channel willingly.

Hell, she seemed to grow more beautiful each time he saw her. Her hair was pulled back into a plait that started at the crown of her head. It fell nearly to her hip, the whiteness of it so glaring in this environment that it had caught the attention of every man in the area, though the two guards behind her would make certain that no one stepped near her.

In Inverness and Edinburgh, she'd dressed in regal fashion, but today she wore a simple dark green wool gown, covered with a dark blue mantle. High cheekbones and a pair of luscious lips called to him, although he had to fight his natural reaction to her.

Beauty or not, she had a cold heart. She hadn't earned her nickname of "Ice Queen" for nothing. Although he suspected she wasn't working with the Channel of her own free will, there was no denying she *was* working with them. Had all the lasses who'd fought for her in Inverness been kidnapped? Had she given orders to the men who'd plucked them from their homes?

"Why do you follow me?" she asked, her lips pursed and unforgiving.

"I don't follow you," he replied with a smirk. "I think I was here first."

She chuckled, but the sound never reached her eyes or her lips. "Your homeland is deep in the Highlands. We passed Grant land on our journey here. And yet, here you are. First you showed up in Inverness, then Edinburgh, and now you've followed me to Berwick. I want you to leave me alone."

"Nay, I won't." He would get the answers to his questions before he left.

"What must I do to send you away? You cause trouble for me and it is unwelcome." Her gaze narrowed as she stepped closer to him, her chin lifting just a notch to meet his gaze.

He was certain she intended to intimidate him, but it wouldn't work. For some reason, having her step closer pleased him.

His gaze locked on hers, looking for any cracks in her icy mask. "Tell me why, and I'll go," he said.

"Why what?" Her stony glance told him he would have to do much more to break through to her.

He wanted to know what had frozen her heart as much as he wanted the names of the leaders of the Channel of Dubh. He believed she could lead him to them, but he had to come up with some leverage.

She wouldn't make it easy.

He took a step closer and leaned toward her. "Why would you take part in this operation? Have you no morals? No guilt?"

When he said that last word, he saw a glimmer of the woman beneath the ice. True, it had been fleeting, but he'd seen it nonetheless. She hadn't answered yet, so he pressed her. "I saw that."

"Saw what?"

He leaned in closer to whisper to her, and the sweet aroma of wildflowers and Sela washed over him, something he wished he could have avoided. He didn't need any more reminders of her to haunt his dreams at night. Avoiding the temptation to breathe in deeper, he held her gaze and said, "You flinched. You *do* feel guilty. Why do you do it?"

She surprised him by leaning in a wee bit closer, so close their lips nearly touched. "As I told you outside the whorehouse in Edinburgh, I have my reasons. You'll never know them."

The two were caught in a battle of wills of sorts, neither one moving. He was oblivious to all sounds around him, but intuition told him that he could speak low enough for her ears only. "Let me in and I'll help you."

The iciness melted away this time, revealing the woman trapped beneath it. Fear, hope, hatred, and love—all those emotions crossed her face in a moment that seemed to linger, but the most important one he saw was desperation.

He would never forget that look.

She pulled back and said, "Leave me alone. Please. You have no idea what trouble you cause."

She spun on her heel and left him, her steps not as strong and confident as usual. What he'd seen in her gaze had told him everything he needed to know. He would follow her until he conquered that look, forced it away forever.

Fear and desperation controlled this strong woman.

Sela held a fear so powerful, so all-consuming, that it drove everything she did.

He'd wipe that fear away if it was the last thing he did. If not, he'd probably die trying.

CHAPTER THREE

S ELA STALKED OFF, AFRAID TO say another word, afraid to be so close to that man.

Connor Grant stirred something inside her that she hadn't felt in years.

Hope.

Could he find some way to help her? No, if life had taught her one lesson, it was that hope was a foolish dream. Connor was one man against countless Englishmen. The two men who controlled her could call in a cluster of chain-mailed, armor-clad English knights at a moment's notice.

She'd played a part in ruining too many lives. Any more guilt would crush her. Although the Grants and their friends had won some battles against the Channel, they'd be foolish to make a stand against them here in Berwick.

Besides which, the mere act of talking to Connor was likely enough to bring more punishment down on her.

Oh, how she wished she were wrong. If she had her choice, she'd run away and live her life in peace, hidden deep in a forest where no one would bother her.

A man approached her from a crowd across the street.

"Sela!"

She froze, shocked to recognize him. Her entire body began to shake at the mere sight of him. The short man strode straight toward her, the two guards stepping back from her. "What are you doing out here? Have you been given permission to leave the castle? Who was that man you were speaking with?"

She backed up, her insides now churning with fear. How she hated this man, known as Hord, who delighted in inflicting punishments on the lasses forced to work for the Channel. He had a twisted mind, and his cruelty was beyond belief.

"Sela? I asked you a question. Must I see you punished?" he asked quietly, the smirk on his face proof of how much he enjoyed inflicting his odd forms of torture.

"Nay, Guy asked me to walk to the port to check on something. 'Tis why he sent two guards with me."

He moved forward. If he came any closer, she'd pass out for certain. She could feel her vision dimming at the edges.

"What were you sent to do?" The urge to cower overtook her, sickening her, as the small man with the paunch invaded her senses.

"He asked me to look for a ship. 'Tis supposed to arrive sometime today."

"Who was that?" he persisted, his beady eyes boring through her.

"I don't know what you're talking about..." she stammered, shaking her head in denial. He couldn't have seen her with Connor. She'd only allowed herself a moment to talk with him.

Hord grabbed her wrist in a tight vise and she gasped in fear, but the next sound almost caused her to crumple to the ground.

Connor Grant's voice echoed across town in a dull roar. "Unhand her."

———◆———

Connor had to fight the instinct to unsheathe his sword. He reached for the brute who'd grabbed Sela, but the man stood back and waved her guards forward to do their job. Those two weren't a challenge. He put his fist in the face of the first one and knocked him out cold, then grabbed the second one by the throat and punched him in the belly. When he fell back, Connor kicked him in the gut and he landed on the cobblestone street, his head snapping back and hitting the hard surface, knocking him out, also. Proud of himself for not killing anyone yet, Connor reached for the other man, who'd turned to run away.

He wasn't fast enough.

Connor grabbed him by the back of the neck and tossed him off to the side. He landed facedown on the street. "Who raised you? What gives you the right to hurt a woman?"

The man didn't look like much of a warrior—he'd lost most of his hair and had a small paunch—but he had the audacity to lift his head up and say, "I'll do as I like with the bitch." He placed his hands underneath him to lift himself back up.

The man apparently had a death wish, so Connor decided to oblige him. He bent over, rolled him over onto his back, picked him up by his tunic and lifted him into the air. "Say the word, Sela, and I'll twist his scrawny neck."

Sela ran toward him and grabbed his arm, "Nay, don't hurt him, please. Set him down. He didn't do anything to me."

He looked at Sela, barely able to speak. "You defend him? I saw him grab you. You'll be bruised on the morrow. One twist of his neck and he'll never touch you again."

He saw her glance down the street to a small group of horses headed their way. He still had the man in the air, and his face had turned a deep shade of red, but the look in his eyes was something Connor hadn't seen before. Despite the situation, which was very much in Connor's favor, the older man looked defiant.

"Put me down," he rasped.

"Sela? Do you need help? What goes on here?"

Three men approached them on horseback, one of

whom Connor recognized from Inverness, an older man with dark hair sprinkled with white.

"Vern, help us, please," Sela called out to the older man.

Connor set the fool down, glancing around him. "I'm defending a woman's honor. Someone ought to teach your friend how to treat a woman."

"Hord, what did you do?"

"I always do exactly as I wish." The man rubbed his neck where Connor had held him. "Sela, you'll pay for this."

"I didn't do anything wrong. Please."

The fear in Sela's face affected Connor, especially since she was usually so adept at hiding her emotions, but he was at a loss as to how to help her. He'd offered to twist the man's neck. Other than getting rid of him, what else could she want?

"Climb on and I'll take you back, Sela," Vern said. "Hord, behave yourself."

Sela glanced at Connor as she mounted the horse, but her gaze drifted back to Hord with a fear that brought out his every protective instinct. He would not forget the bastard, or the twisted grin he now wore as he stared after Sela. The expression on the daft man's face alone begged Connor to react.

He was outnumbered by far because another group of guards had come along to join them. Six men stepped toward him, but he turned and walked away. He wasn't ready to instigate another attack.

For now, he had no choice but to back down, but he knew he would face this man again. How had such a weakling turned the Ice Queen into a bowl of porridge?

———◆———

Connor bolted up in bed, wiping the sweat from his face.

He'd been dreaming about Sela, so real that he could smell her scent of wildflowers. She'd kissed him before running away and yelling over her shoulder, "Help me,

Connor. Please help me."

He moved over to the table in the middle of the chamber. They were staying at the inn on the edge of town, The Buck's Inn, an arrangement that ensured Gregor and the others could find them.

He poured himself a goblet of water from the ewer and swallowed it in one gulp. Hell, but the dream had seemed so real.

He had to get her to talk. Grabbing his sword, he left the chamber and headed down the staircase for a breath of fresh air. He heard snoring from behind one of the doors, and someone moving about in a chamber down the hall, but he doubted the inn was full. There hadn't been many people about earlier. He strode toward town until he could see the castle up on the hill, the mighty fortress he had to penetrate. In the dark of the night, it looked even more imposing. He had to get inside.

But how?

He guessed they would have a hundred guards or more, so he'd have to use subterfuge.

"My lord," a voice called out to him in the dark.

He glanced over his shoulder, surprised to see Thorn racing toward him. "What are you doing awake at this hour? 'Tis the middle of the night."

"But I will help you. I'll slip into the castle and find Mistress Sela. I can do it. I surely can!" His eyes were huge and luminescent in the dark of the night.

Connor thought the idea had merit, but only if he was certain she was inside.

"So you think you can sneak inside that fortress on the hill and get to Sela?"

"I can. You'd be surprised how well I can sneak around. Do not forget I am the son of Thor."

His cheeky comment nearly made Connor chuckle, but he controlled it because he could tell the lad meant every word.

"But some of the Dubh men would recognize you from earlier," he countered.

"If I put enough dirt on my face, they'll never see me in the dark. What do you wish for me to tell her?" The lad groped the ground in the dark to prove his point.

Connor pondered his proposition carefully, looking up at the half moon, the gray clouds passing over it every so often. His decision finally made, he nodded to Thorn. "You'll go inside, but you must accept one condition."

"What? I can do it," the lad said, hopping from one foot to the other.

"You will find out where she is—which window, which floor—then come back and tell me. Can you do that and return to me in less than an hour?"

"Aye, I will make you proud, my lord. You'll see." The scamp took off at a dead run only to be caught by Connor's whistle. He stopped and spun around. "What's wrong?"

"I'll go with you to find the best way in."

The lad paused, and he could see it was a difficult thing for him to do. He was anxious to take part in what he clearly saw as an adventure. Looking up at Connor, he whispered, "Shall we go now?"

Connor glanced around at the few drunks wandering the street and decided he saw no one threatening. Perhaps he should go back to get Braden or Roddy in case he needed assistance, but there was no point in waking them when he and Thorn could uncover what they needed and be back inside before they ever opened their eyes. Making his decision, he pointed. "Let's move. You stay with me until I give you instructions to go. Understood?"

"Aye!" The lad's enthusiasm reminded Connor of himself at a much younger age. He'd often tried to follow his twin brothers, Jamie and Jake, but more often than not they would send him back to the keep without any satisfaction.

Although he was now the tallest lad in his generation of

Grants, he'd been the runt for a good while. Even Braden and Roddy had been bigger, and Loki? He'd appeared to be a giant.

When he was a wee laddie, his sire would lift him up onto his shoulders and say, "There. Does it look any different from up there?"

Everything had looked better from atop his father's shoulders. "Someday you may be taller than me," he would tell Connor, "and if so, this would be your point-of-view. Use it wisely, lad. Because everyone will want to take the biggest man out."

How right his father had been.

He *was* taller than his father now, something he'd never expected to happen, but he still looked up to the man. Alexander Grant was the wisest man in the Highlands.

When they reached the outside of the castle walls, Connor found a hiding place and showed Thorn exactly where to climb the wall for the best footholds. The wall crumbled in spots, which made it easy.

"Thorn, promise me that you will only search for Sela's location. Understood?"

"Aye, my lord."

"And you're to come back if you run into too many guards. I'll not have you hurt. Are you listening?" he asked.

The lad nodded his head hard enough to give himself a neck ache.

"You have half an hour to get in and out. Return with her whereabouts and I'll buy you the biggest meat pie in all of Berwick on the morrow." Food still held as the best motivation for the lad.

"A lamb one? Could I have a lamb meat pie?" The lad's eyes were as big as the gems on Connor's sire's famous sword.

"Aye, if they have one. A lamb meat pie. Now go."

Thorn grinned at him as he started up the side of the wall with ease. Connor was surprised at how easily he found footholds. The lad slipped out of sight, and a few moments later, Connor let out the breath he hadn't realized he was holding. The lack of noise indicated Thorn had not been caught.

Connor's mind kept turning as he waited for news of Sela. She'd want to know why he'd followed her to the keep. He'd tell her that he needed information on the Dubh men, he decided. That much was true. His greater motivation was to help her—and to find out exactly what she feared.

He hadn't been waiting long when a noise from the top of the wall caught him. He hid in the small group of trees, surprised to see it was Thorn returning already.

The lad waited until he was next to him before blurting out, "I found her. I know where she is."

CHAPTER FOUR

———◆———

SELA FOLLOWED GUY INTO A chamber filled with many of the men in charge of this operation. Some she knew, some she did not.

Silence greeted her.

The group of men turned to stare at her. Hord, Dee, and Guy were all present, along with her only friend, Vern, and a few others. Dee pointed to a chair and said, "Sit, Sela."

She did as instructed, doing her best to ignore Hord, whose gaze was so unsettling it scrambled her thoughts.

The bastard's twisted grin always upset her.

"We have three big shipments arriving," Dee said. "One will be here in two days, the other two will be here the day after that. All of the shipments will be leaving the harbor five days from the morrow at the end of the day. Your job will be to care for the cargo until the ships go out of port. If this goes as planned, we'll have enough coin to slow our operation down, focus more on our whorehouses and fighting wagers again."

His words knifed into her. Although she felt stricken, she forced herself to look unmoved. "Will they be lasses or lads?" she asked, her voice unwavering. Her gaze shot to Vern, who looked equally disturbed by the news. She knew he would have left the Channel long ago were it not for her—and Guy and Dee's reputation for murdering anyone who did not agree with them.

"Mostly lasses between the ages of twelve and twenty, so

it shouldn't be a difficult situation for you to manage them with the assistance of several guards. You will be given an allotment of food for them. The last day the food will be laced with a sleep potion so there will be no problem getting them on the boat that night, though that could change. We haven't decided whether to put them asleep before or after they board the ship. It depends on the number of men and crates we will have. If there are enough of them, we'll not put them in crates. That information will be forthcoming when we have the true number of the cargo. Questions?"

"How many?"

"Between seventy-five and one hundred."

Sela almost fell off her chair. The mere thought made her want to weep. It was bad enough that they'd tried to send away her girls in Inverness—but one hundred lasses and lads?

"Do you not think the task could prove difficult with a group that large?" she asked Dee, refusing to look at anyone else.

"We will bind those who are troublesome," he said. "You must keep them inside the building and make sure they receive their rations."

"What happens if you don't lace their food with sleep potion the last day?" one of the men asked. He looked as if he hadn't had a bath in several moons.

"The alternative is to take them to a berth south of the port where they'll load themselves, Guy said.

"But witnesses will see them board, aye?" Hord asked. "Is that not a problem?"

"That location is far enough away for us to not to have to worry about witnesses." Guy scratched his beard, his usual indication of impatience. He then cast a long, weighing glance at the men assembled in front of him. "And I will remind all of you that we cannot have another instance like what happened at the other buildings in our possession. The guards at that location chose to imbibe rather than keep watch, and they paid for that mistake with their lives. This is a large operation and we must exercise the utmost caution."

"We cannot afford to lose any more of our captives or our guards," Dee said. "Do your jobs. You'll have plenty of days to drink yourself into oblivion once this is over. For those of you who choose not to work your hardest, we can easily find ways to make you work harder." He glanced from man to man, but most refused to look him in the eye. They'd clearly lost many men at the other holding.

Had the Grant warriors taken them out?

Although she was hesitant to engage in the discussion, Sela forced herself to ask a question. "Which building?"

She doubted she'd have the opportunity to use the information, but if she could do anything to stop this madness from unfolding, she would. If she saw Connor Grant again, what would he do with that information? Could he put a stop to the loading of the lasses on the ships, just as they'd done in Inverness?

"You'll find out in due time."

Sela played with the folds in her gown. "When may I receive my boon?" She held her breath and said a quick prayer.

"When this is finished in five days," Dee replied. "*If* it's successful."

She caught Hord tipping his head to Guy, who then asked, "Are you having problems with one of the Grants? I've heard he is in town. How do you know the man?"

"I met him in Inverness. He is part of that Band we've heard about. The Highlanders who fought our people near the port in Inverness." She kept her back as straight as possible, not wanting to let the bastard Hord know how he affected her.

"Get rid of him," Guy said to the others.

Hord asked, "Why don't we kill the fool and throw him

out to sea?"

Her gut clenched at the thought of them killing Connor. She hardly knew him, so why did she respond in such a way?

The answer came to her more quickly than she would have thought. He was the only truly honorable man she'd met since losing her parents. And even though the two men looked nothing alike, something about him reminded her of her sire.

The filthy man scoffed at Hord. "Are you out of your mind? Don't you know who you're dealing with? Connor Grant is Alex's son, and he's bigger than his sire. You won't take him down easily."

Another grinned and said, "My men took him down."

"Aye, I heard," Guy said. "But he still walks, and how many men did you lose? He's a formidable enemy, and we won't deal with him unless we're forced to."

Hord chuckled. "You have no backbone. Send him out to sea. I don't know why you don't get rid of him where he'll not be found."

Dee stood up, his eyes blazing. "Because he's from Clan Grant, you fool. Unless you care to call five hundred savage warriors down on us before the shipment, I'd leave him be. After the shipment is gone, do with him as you like. But do not kill him before that. We have enough men to handle Clan Ramsay, but not the Grants. I'm warning you, Hord, control yourself."

Hord grumbled for a time, but he didn't say anything else.

"That is all, Sela. Go to your chamber. We'll retrieve you on the day after the morrow as soon as the shipment arrives."

She wished to spit in his face. To yell. To scream. To run and run and run.

But she could not. They had the one and only piece of leverage that could keep her here.

She was powerless.

She nodded and left the solar, Vern trailing along behind her. "Do not worry. I will keep him at bay for now."

"Many thanks to you, Vern. I appreciate it. I need that boon." In this world of chaos, dirty deeds, coins, and cruelty, it was the only thing that kept her going. It was the last bit of goodness left to her.

"Do as you're told and all will be well."

She turned to face her friend as she reached her chamber. "My thanks for your help, Vern." The older man had become a protector for her, and for that, she was grateful.

He said, "Aye, you can rely on me."

Nodding, she entered the chamber and closed the door behind her. She leaned against the door for a moment, thinking about all that had happened, then pushed away from it and fell onto the bed, fully clothed. A dark-haired handsome Highlander dominated her thoughts.

By the saints above, she'd almost laughed hysterically when Connor had thrown Hord through the air. The fierce Highlander's defense of her "honor" had absolutely stunned her.

When had she ever had honor?

Five years ago, she'd lived a normal life. She'd been part of a loving family, but Dee and Guy had brought a group of men to her family's hut on the outskirts of Edinburgh. They'd restrained her father while they killed her mother in front of him, only to put a knife in his heart, too. She'd hidden in the corner and watched it all. They'd taken her away with them, and her life had been horrific ever since.

In the beginning, she'd wondered why they'd chosen her. Dee had told her the truth once. Guy had seen her white hair from afar and decided he had to have her. He'd offered to buy her, but her sire had refused. Apparently, they hadn't liked being turned away, so they'd returned to get what they wanted. Her sire had attempted to protect his family—he'd attacked the intruders so brutally Guy had thirsted for vengeance once he gained the upper hand.

How she missed her sweet mama Dyna with her pale blonde hair and her dancing blue eyes. She was a Norsewoman, so tall she could look Papa in the eye. The two had loved to dance in their small abode, Mama Dyna giggling shamelessly in delight.

There was no dancing anymore, and no singing either.

She forced herself to replay those memories every day so she'd never forget them. It was the most precious thing she had these days, well, other than the most precious thing of all.

As she lay there, alone in her bed, she found herself thinking of what it would be like to have a different life. To live in a small cottage in a forest with a big strong man who would cherish her and fight for her honor like Connor Grant had done. They'd love each other, raise their bairns together, and no one would ever, ever bother them.

She chastised herself for harboring such a foolish dream. It would never happen.

Nonetheless, she fell asleep dreaming of a dark-haired Highlander singing and dancing with her in his arms.

———◆———

Thorn had given Connor specific instructions on where to find Sela. The clever imp had been hiding at the end of a dark passageway when a man called Vern had escorted her to her chamber.

Connor had found her door with ease. The passageway was empty, and he planned to sneak inside to speak with Sela. If she was receptive to helping the Band of Cousins, he would try to convince her to come with him.

He just hoped he had the correct chamber.

Not wanting to make any noise at all, he decided against knocking and opened the door enough for him to see inside.

He released the breath he'd been holding. There she was,

sound asleep. He tiptoed inside, closing the door behind him, and made his way to her bed. Kneeling next to her, he had to use every bit of control he had not to touch her.

The one small torch cast a golden glow over her features. With her eyes closed, she appeared as serene as a nymph inside a chapel, her white hair fanned out behind her, her lithe form atop the covers. Every time he saw her, he was more taken with her. He could admit that to himself now. A small pert nose sat in the midst of high cheekbones, and long, pale lashes decorated her face like the finest icing on a pastry.

The ice that usually coated her had melted in slumber.

He could sit and stare at her for hours. To his surprise, her eyes opened, and she turned her head toward him, her fingers tentatively reaching up to touch his lips.

Puzzled by her touch—in the past she'd always pulled away, treated him with something like contempt—he froze, not wishing to break the spell. She cupped his cheek, pulling him closer until their noses nearly touched. Her gaze locked on his, full of something he'd never seen in her before. If he had to guess what she was thinking, he thought she was wishing.

Wishing for a different life, a different place.

Her lips touched his and he let her set the pace as she explored his mouth, her tongue darting between his lips. When he could no longer be a passive participant in the kiss, he slanted his mouth over hers, caressing her mouth as if it were the sweetest morsel he'd ever tasted. He groaned as their passion fueled, the pressure from her lips matching his own, their tongues dueling in an intense imitation of the mating ritual. Her hand reached for the back of his neck and anchored in his hair, tugging him closer, giving him greater access to her mouth.

His hand touched her hip, and too late, he recognized his mistake. Her eyes flew open as if she were seeing him for the first time. She shoved his shoulder, hard, then bolted out of the bed and cowered in the corner.

"How dare you touch me!" she whispered, her tone no less threatening than if she'd shouted from the top of the castle's tower.

"Sweetling, you touched me first. Were you asleep and unaware of your actions? Whether you wish to deny it or not, you were enjoying our kiss as much as I was."

"Never. I would never have kissed you."

He stood up, approaching her slowly, hands raised in a pledge that he meant no harm. "Sela, I'm not going to hurt you. I'm here to help you."

"Stay away from me. You'll only cause trouble. Get out. Please leave now." She wrapped her arms around herself in a hug, huddling in the corner with that awful look of desperation he recognized from earlier. "You don't understand how things are here."

He would have preferred a look of icy disdain to this show of fear.

"Sela, I don't know exactly what your relationship is with this group of cruel men, but I promise I will get you away. I'll never allow any of them to cause you pain again." He stepped closer, his hand coming up to brush her cheek briefly before she swatted it away.

"Nay, you cannot. There's naught you can do to help me except go away. Please, Connor," she whispered.

Connor was so befuddled he didn't know how to react. "Give me one good reason why I shouldn't whisk you away against your will. Why would you not wish to escape?" He kept his hands to himself, afraid to upset her anymore, but his purpose did not waver.

"I have my reasons."

"Are you Norse or Scottish? You are slipping into a Scots brogue," he asked. It was the first time he'd heard her do so. From her stature and icy beauty, he'd always assumed she was Norse. Until now, he'd never had reason to believe otherwise.

"My sire was Scottish. My mother Norse. I'm both."

"Come to the Highlands with me. They'll never come after you. They wouldn't dare attack Grant land."

"Nay, I cannot risk… You don't understand, but they hold a power over me you cannot fix."

"What is it you refuse to risk? Come now before we are discovered," he begged. He didn't know what he could do to convince her, only that he must. "They'll kill you when this is over. What could be more frightening than death?"

"There *is* a fate worse than death for me, 'tis all you need to know." Her hands trembled, convincing him that she believed what she said. What hold could they possibly have on her?

He reached for her arm, wishing to console her, but her reaction was swift.

"Don't touch me. Leave me be. Go away." The words were said without any bite. The ice had not yet returned, but the fear lingered.

It grew when the door suddenly opened.

"What goes here?"

CHAPTER FIVE

AS SOON AS A MAN appeared in the doorway, Connor had his hand on his weapon. He unsheathed his sword and took out two men with one blow. A bearded man stood at the back of the group, assessing the situation in a way that suggested he was one of the leaders of this group.

Connor fought hard, swinging his weapon over and over again until there were four men crumpled on the ground. "Your turn," Connor said as he advanced on the bearded bastard. He would like nothing better than to cut him down where he stood.

Unfortunately, that man whistled and another ten men came in from behind him. Connor fought with all the strength he had, but he was overpowered and held down by six men. Two of them stood over him, threatening him with his own sword.

Another two men entered, one of whom was the fool who'd dared to touch Sela in the middle of town. "Beat him but leave him alive," the bearded man said. "Deposit him far outside of town. Do not kill him, we don't need the entire slew of Grant warriors on us."

The short man, the one Sela feared most, said, "I'll take Sela. She lied. She said she had no interest in him, but he continues to show up."

Sela fell on her knees in front of the bearded man. "I'll do anything, but please don't send me with Hord. Please,

Guy."

The man she'd called Guy looked to the short man's companion, a man with a deep scar across his neck, who shook his head. "Sela, we need your compliance, and I don't like what I'm seeing. Hord will make sure you abide by our rules." He nodded to two men, who moved over and yanked her to her feet, dragging her behind him.

Connor heard her screams all the way down the passageway. When he had his chance, he'd kill that bastard, but it wasn't yet time.

Four men held him while the biggest of the group swung at him. Two blows later, he blacked out.

———◆———

Sela sat at the table, contemplating all that had happened. Hord had told her he'd be back, so she knew what was to come. She'd have to endure the worst possible form of torture.

Familiar with his tactics, she knew he'd left her alone to make her think about what was to come. How she wished she could have gone with Connor Grant, who was being beaten for trying to help her.

Why hadn't she told him the truth?

It was a simple answer. Fear. Fear of what her punishment would be, fear that her boon would be denied to her forever. Connor Grant couldn't possibly understand what drove her.

The door opened, and to her surprise, a wee red-haired lassie came straight for her, a doll clutched in one hand. "Mama! I've missed you so much. Where have you been?"

Sela closed her eyes and wrapped her arms around her daughter, Claray. Only three summers old, she was the one light in her dark life. She clutched her so tightly she feared she would hurt her. "Mama, why are you crying?" Her little hand came up and wiped the tear that slid down her cheek. "Don't cry, Mama. I'll stay with you forever."

How she wished that were true. She hugged her tightly again, inhaling her sweet fragrance. For the first two years of her life, Claray had lived with her, but then Guy and Dee had discovered they had a perfect method of controlling Sela: taking her daughter away from her. The first time had been when she tried to run away with Claray, but it had only been for a sennight. Then it had been over a fortnight when she tried to refuse a job in Inverness. The last two times had been a moon or more, once for escaping and the other for arguing. The separations were gut-wrenching, made worse by the fact that Sela did not trust the people who were watching her. "I missed you so, Claray. Forgive me for being gone so long? I love you. You are the sweetest thing I've ever seen."

She pulled her up onto her lap so she could sit back and look at her, memorizing everything there was about her. Those memories would help her get through the long days and nights she had to spend without her daughter. They'd help her do as she was told even though everything in her nature rebelled against it.

"I love you, too, Mama. Do you remember how you said Grandmama would keep watch over me? I saw a butterfly the other day, and I thought it might be her. It kept flying about my head. It even landed on my head once and it tickled. Do you think it was?"

"Aye, I'm sure 'twas Grandmama. Without a doubt, she was watching over you because she would adore you if she could be here with us. She would sing wonderful songs to you and plait your hair, put ribbons and flowers in it to make you even more beautiful."

"Look, Mama, is my doll not so lovely? Her eyes are blue, just as yours are," she said, looking at her with such adoration it humbled Sela. The doll was an old fabric creation she'd found for her, and it had been loved so much that she'd had to sew the holes closed many times. It didn't put an end to the allure the doll held for her daughter, something that pleased Sela.

"Blue eyes the same color as *yours*, my sweet," she said, kissing her daughter's forehead. How could she explain her daughter to someone like Connor Grant, who'd lived his whole life a free man? She'd given birth to the lassie about a year after she'd been stolen away from her home, forced to do her abusers' bidding. She'd hated every moment of her life until wee Claray, the most perfect being on the face of the earth, had come along.

But the bastards had turned her daughter into a weapon to be used against her.

If she didn't do as they ordered, they didn't just punish her—they threatened to punish Claray, something she could never allow. She would need to devise a way for them to escape someday, before her daughter grew into a woman, but none of her plans had worked thus far. After her last escape attempt went awry, Hord had unleashed his worst on her.

Every night she prayed that someone would come along and put an arrow into Hord's black heart. Guy and Dee, too.

It appalled her to think of the lives they'd ruined for coin and wealth and their own personal satisfaction.

It horrified her to know she'd played some small part in it.

The door opened and Hord stepped inside. His eyes had a way of looking *into* a person, as if assessing how best to hurt them. She held Claray close.

"Are you not going to thank Hord for your boon?"

Refusing to look at the twisted man's face, she said, "My thanks, Hord."

"Was this not a pleasant surprise for you?"

He spoke the truth—she'd expected punishment, not the boon, not her dearest daughter. Besides which, Hord didn't award boons, Guy and Dee did. She hadn't expected to be given her boon early, especially after what had happened.

"Well?"

"Aye, this was a most pleasant surprise and I am grateful," she lied. She'd never be grateful to the bastard.

"Come along," he said, spinning around to head out of the small chamber. Four guards stood outside, not a good sign, but she followed him with Claray. He led her down an unfamiliar passageway, then down a set of stairs. She had not spent much time in this castle, so she was unprepared for where they were going. Carrying her daughter, she tried to stay as calm as possible, hoping Claray would not sense her discomfort.

"Where are we going, Mama?" her wee lassie asked. Her daughter's innocence pleased her so much. How she prayed it would never be taken from her.

"I'm not sure, sweetling," she said.

They came to a door and Hord stood to the side, saying, "After you, my dear."

She stepped into the dark chamber, fear crawling up the back of her spine, but she reminded herself that she still had wee Claray with her, so she had not been brought here for punishment. Punishment always came to her alone.

The door slammed behind her and she spun on her heel, still clutching her daughter.

Nay, nay, nay!

"Mama, 'tis so dark in here."

She kissed her daughter's forehead, forcing herself to act calm. "Do not worry, Mama is here." Through the closed door, she pleaded, "Hord, please, not my daughter. Please?" Her voice cracked a wee bit, but Claray did not seem to notice.

The chamber was quite small and empty, not a stool or chest around. Hord did not reply for some time, but he finally said, "This should convince you to do as you are ordered. I have a surprise for you, my dear. I've sought out my favorite kind, the kind that like to bite."

A small movement caught her eye at the bottom of the

door—a smaller door was being opened. A familiar rustling sound forced her into action.

"Nay, nay, nay!!!" she shouted it out loud this time. Her daughter's eyes widened.

Spiders. The hoarder of spiders, as Hord was known, loved nothing better than to unleash the creatures on his victims. He spent hours searching in dark corners for them.

She screamed, but if she allowed fear to overwhelm her, Claray would pay the price.

How could she protect her? She held her now-squirming daughter with one arm and tore her own gown off, wrapping it around the wee lass as tightly as she could, covering every bit of skin.

Claray was crying now, but she could not let that stop her.

"Nay, nay! Please let us out! I'll not talk to him again. I promise!" She cried giant tears as hundreds of spiders invaded the chamber in a hideous wave. They immediately started crawling everywhere, including up her bare legs, her arms.

"Mama, what are those things?" Claray said between sobs.

Sela's feet stomped and stomped as she fought to keep the beasts off her precious daughter. "Close your eyes, Claray. Keep your mouth closed."

"Ow, Mama. They hurt. Ow…" The dress was not protecting her skin as much as Sela had hoped. She had to do something…the spiders were biting her legs, her arms, her neck, crawling up the walls all around her, but she had to think. She had to protect her daughter.

Lord above, help me. What do I do?

She crushed as many spiders as she could, then laid her daughter down on the ground, covering her with her body to protect her. "Put your face inside Mama's gown. Do not look out."

Sobs wracked her, but she covered her daughter, both

hands reaching out to crush and kill every spider that came near.

Kill them, kill them, kill them. Protect Claray, protect her. Help her.

She fought and fought, even when she thought she would surely pass out, forcing herself to stay awake to kill every last one. When the spiders' advance began to slow, she finally heard the eerie sound she hated most of all.

Hord laughed gleefully outside the chamber.

When she thought she'd nearly killed them all, she stood, looking at the walls, reaching out and killing more. Her skin burned with bites.

Claray cried against her chest. Peeking her head out, she asked, "Mama, are they gone? You saved me from them!"

Her daughter clung to her and began to hum a song, a balm to her soul. It was a song she oft sang to comfort Claray, and she knew her wee daughter was attempting to cheer her. The door opened and Vern came in, his eyes wide with alarm. "Och, lass. You did a fine job protecting her, but you…"

Her legs could no longer hold her up. She collapsed into Vern's arms, and the last thing she recalled was her friend saying, "Do not worry. I will take care of her. She's not hurt badly."

CHAPTER SIX

———

THORN WAITED AND WAITED. HE'D done good finding Sela, and he knew he'd given Connor the right directions.

So where the hell was he?

Unsure of what to do, he stood outside the curtain wall, looking about for signs of what might be happening inside, but all was quiet.

Oddly silent.

Until he heard the keening sound of a lass in pain, a horrible cry unlike anything he'd ever heard before.

Sela. It had to be Sela.

He must find Connor and tell him.

He scampered up the curtain wall, jumped down, and ran to the keep. There was no one about, and so he was able to sneak in through the back with ease. He found that odd because there'd been several guards before.

Once inside, the screams of the lass he thought to be Sela continued, a sound that scared him. What would make the Ice Queen scream like that?

He didn't wish to know. Connor could find her and help her, but first he needed to find *him*.

He crept down the passageway toward Sela's chamber just in time to see the door open. He hid in an alcove and waited. Ten guards came out chuckling about something.

"He was a fighter, was he not?"

"Hell, but he's a big bastard. I've not seen one that tall

before, and he's got some muscles."

They spoke of Connor! He wished he could thrash them, but they were too many. He knew what Connor would tell him—listen carefully and then find help—so that was exactly what he'd do.

"True. It took five of us to hold him down for you."

"He's not moving much now, is he?"

They all laughed until another scream echoed through the stone walls.

"God's bones, but that Hord is a sick man. I can't believe Guy and Dee keep him around. What if he turns on them?"

"He's too fat and lazy to hurt them. He prefers to torment women."

Another said, "He gives me nightmares."

"Poor laddie," his friend teased.

"What are we doing with this fool?"

He hefted something with both his arms, another man helping him. Thorn held back a gasp. They held Connor, and he wasn't moving.

"Take him down the path north of the Borderlands. Throw him into a clearing out of sight. Let the vultures and the animals at him. The Grants won't find him until it's too late."

A man came chasing down the passageway. "You have another passenger to take along."

"Who?" the one who appeared to be in charge asked.

"Sela. Hord wasn't kind. They think she'll be dead by morn."

Thorn thought his heart might beat right out of his chest. Poor Sela. When Connor got better—and Thorn knew he would—he'd kill them for hurting her.

"Why the hell would Hord do that? The man is demented. Guy and Dee won't be happy about this."

"He hadn't planned to hurt her this badly, but now he says we're to let her and her lover die together in a place where no one will see them. We're not to tell Guy and Dee just yet. He doesn't want them to know."

One man grumbled, "I don't like this."

"Hurry up," the new one said. "Guy and Dee will be back soon, and I, for one, don't wish to wake up to spiders in my bed."

"Fine, I'll get the cart. We can toss the two of them in it and cover them with plaids. We'll go out the back way."

Thorn was so excited that he nearly pished himself, but he figured he owed the bastards for hurting his friend, so he pished in the alcove instead.

Moving quietly, he crept back down the staircase and out the back. Just like before, there was no one about. He scaled the wall with no problem, then raced through the town. It was so late at night that no one was about.

He had to get back to The Buck's Inn and find Connor's cousins.

He ran so fast and hard that he tripped going up the stairs at the inn. When he stepped inside the chamber where Braden and Roddy were sleeping, he was surprised to see Braden sitting at a small table.

"Where've you been, lad?" Braden asked, jumping to his feet.

Thorn didn't have time to explain—he had to get them to move quickly. "Connor. They beat him and are leaving him in a clearing off the north path to Edinburgh. We have to save him. He wasn't moving. He's in really bad shape."

"Roddy, get your arse out of bed." Braden took a swig of ale and said, "Where did you two go?"

"After Sela. And she's in trouble, too. They're bringing her with Connor because she's nearly dead. I heard a lass screaming and I think 'twas her, but I had to see about Connor. Did I do good?"

Braden handed him a meat pie he'd hidden away. "You did good. Here, finish this. You look like you've earned it. Roddy, I'm leaving in one minute. We must find him before 'tis too late."

Connor groaned when he woke up, the bright clouds overhead telling him it was a new day. Every part of his body ached. Then the previous night's memories returned. The bastards had beat him to a pulp after finding him in Sela's chamber. They'd taken Sela away, but to where he didn't know.

He did his best to blink both lids, just realizing that one of his eyelids was swollen shut. He managed to roll onto his side so he could figure out exactly where they'd taken him. Fortunately, he was on a bed of leaves instead of a chamber in the cellars of the castle, a small consolation. But where was his horse?

Then he remembered. He and Thorn had gone to the castle on foot. His horse would still be at the stable.

As soon as he moved to his side, he froze. Sela lay next to him, barely breathing.

"God's teeth, lass. What did they do to you?" He'd never seen anything like it. She was dressed in just a shift under her mantle, and her skin was covered in lesions or bites of some type, her beautiful face marred horribly. He held his hand in front of her nose to see if he could feel her breathing.

Barely.

What the hell had she been forced to endure?

He cupped her face and brought his gaze close to hers. "Sela? Wake up, sweetling. They'll not hurt you again."

He pushed himself up to get a better look at their location, and her condition. Fortunately, a voice called to him.

"Grant, is that you?"

Connor breathed a sigh of relief, pleased to see his two cousins coming toward him, Thorn in front of Braden. The wee lad must have saved his arse. "How did you know where to find me? And where the hell are we?"

"You're north of Berwick, and you can thank wee Thorn,

or we'd never have known you were gone."

"I'm not wee," Thorn shouted. "I'm nearly as big as the both of you, but not Connor. He's the biggest of all."

Connor spat a stream of blood off to the side. "Aye, you must be big or you'd never have been able to scale the wall and follow me. My thanks to you, Thorn. Have you got anything to drink on you?" he asked his cousins.

The three of them dismounted, just then noticing Sela.

"What the hell?" Roddy whispered, stepping closer for a better look. "What happened to her?"

Braden asked, "Is she alive?"

"I heard her screaming last eve," Thorn said, his lip popping out. "I couldn't save her, I had to find Connor. I heard them say they thought she'd die soon."

Connor said, "Relax, lad. You did fine." He took a swig of ale from Roddy's skin and then moved closer to Sela. "She's alive, but barely. She needs to see a healer."

The other three moved closer, Thorn's gasp loud enough for all of them.

"What did that to her?" He took two steps back as if whatever she had could be caught.

Connor reached for her hands, opening one up that was clenched in a fist. "I'd say it was spiders. It looks like she killed ten with one hand." He brushed the dead creatures out of her hand, which was also covered with bites.

"They attacked her with spiders?" Thorn asked, his agitation growing in leaps and bounds. The lad shivered and brushed at his arm, as if he felt a phantom creature scurrying along it. "Don't let them get me, will you?"

"I think we just discovered how the Dubh men forced her to do their bidding," Connor said, running his hands gently over the mass of bites on one leg. "They tortured her, somehow unleashing a mass of insects on her in a small area. Mayhap they had her in a box or a small chamber." He pushed himself to a sitting position, knowing he had to get himself moving, as painful as it would be. He had aches or pains across every part of his body, including a pounding in his head that would not cease.

"Promise," Thorn said, his voice quaking. "I don't want that." He backed up until Connor wondered if he'd ever stop.

"Aye, I promise to protect you, lad." Connor held his hand up to Roddy. "Help me up, if you don't mind. They did a fine job on me, I must admit, though I made sure to take a few of them out first." Putting weight on his sore legs was not going to be easy, but it had to be done. Roddy helped him to his feet and he groaned, leaning over at the waist to absorb some of the pain. He'd have to ignore it in order to help Sela. His injuries were painful, but not life-threatening. Hers could be.

"How many?" Braden asked. "You look like you fought over twenty."

"I know," Thorn yelled. "At least ten. I saw them. They said you were big and muscular. They said five of them had to hold you down. We need to go after them."

Connor ruffled Thorn's hair. "My thanks, lad. But we'll be heading to Ramsay land first. "Roddy, help me get her on my horse. Glad you brought him along."

"But are we not going back?" Thorn asked.

"Nay. We need reinforcements. Will and Maggie were going to Edinburgh to assist Gregor, but who knows where they are at present."

Thorn interrupted him. "And Nari. Don't forget Nari. He's with them, too. I miss him."

"And Nari. Don't worry about your friend, lad. I'm sure they are all hale, but we cannot spare the time to look for them. According to Sela, the Channel men have hundreds of guards, even knights. We need a full contingent of warriors to defeat them. We're heading to Ramsay land. Aunt Brenna can tend to Sela's wounds, and we'll talk with Uncle Logan and come up with a plan for defeating these bastards. They should know where the others are, too."

They helped him mount and managed to get Sela in front of him, her back leaning against him. To their surprise, she never moved.

Roddy took a look at her up close and said, "We need to hurry. Many of those bites are festering already. I know what my mother would say. If they don't get treated, she'll not survive."

Connor couldn't help but hold her close. This was his fault.

He'd slay the men who'd done this to her. Of that much he was certain.

CHAPTER SEVEN

BY THE TIME THEY ARRIVED on Ramsay land, they had less than a sennight before the rumored shipment was to go out. They had much work to do in a short time. Sela hadn't awakened, and the longer they traveled, the more Connor worried.

Roddy said, "Keep giving her water. 'Tis what Mama and Aunt Brenna would say."

"I'm doing my best, but I can only get it to drizzle down into her throat."

When they reached the stables, Torrian, the chieftain of Clan Ramsay, came out to greet them. "What the hell? Connor, you don't look like you had a successful mission. And neither does she...who is she? And what attacked her? I've not seen anything like it."

"Spiders, we think. Or some kind of insect. Aunt Brenna is here?"

"Aye," Torrian replied after helping Sela down from the horse. "You'll be pleased to know that Gregor and Linet are also here, plus Gavin, Merewen, Will, and Maggie. They're all inside strategizing. The wee lad is in there as well," he said, his eyes darting to Thorn before they settled back on Connor. "I'm guessing you must have new information."

"I do, but first I must get Sela into Aunt Brenna's healing chamber."

If anyone could help her, it was Aunt Brenna, the best healer in the Highlands.

The expression on Torrian's face told him how shocked he was by the identity of the person he carried in his arms. Gregor must have told him about why Connor had left for Berwick when he did. He knew his cousins struggled to understand his interest in Sela.

Thorn called out from behind him. "I'll get the door for you, my lord." He hurried and opened the door to the keep, then shouted loud enough to wake Sela, though she didn't move, "Nari! Wait until you hear all I've done!" Once Connor stepped through, the laddie let the door slam shut and ran over to his wee friend, whose shock of red hair made him stand out from the rest of the group. "I'm a true guard. I saved Connor!"

Nari said, "Me, too! I saved Gregor. I had to find Maggie and send them after him."

"I had to find Connor's cousins after he was hurt." Thorn's eyes widened.

Maggie jumped up, but Connor kept walking, going directly past the two lads. He said, "Roddy and Braden will let you know what's happened. I need to get Sela into the healing chamber."

His cousins all stared at him, and he didn't need to ask why. His wounds looked far worse than they were, but Sela's were every bit as gruesome as they looked, her body now swollen in spots from the multiple bites.

When he opened the door to the healing chamber, he was pleased to see both Aunt Brenna and her daughter Jennet. His aunt turned as soon as she heard him.

"Oh my..." Aunt Brenna said. "Put her on that bed with the furs, Connor. She'll be mighty sore." His aunt had insisted on keeping a large bed in her healing chamber for those who needed it.

Jennet made her way over and peered at Sela's wounds, an odd expression on her face. "This is a most unusual case. Do you know her, Connor?"

"Aye, her name is Sela. She's the Norsewoman involved

with the Channel."

Jennet asked, "If she's with the Channel, then why bring her here?" She never took her gaze off Sela's wounds, scanning her arms, neck, and face. Always serious, Jennet was devoted to learning aught there was to know about healing from her mama.

His aunt said, "Jennet, we should be willing to help anyone who's hurt this badly and ask questions after they heal."

"What if..."

"I'll explain later, but of course, only if they did not hurt anyone we love."

Connor knew his cousin to be a persistent interrogator, always seeking answers for the quandaries of life.

Jennet then asked, "Connor, she did not get this way from hurting you, did she?"

"Nay. She was tortured for talking to me, because, as I suspected, she was forced into working with the Channel."

Aunt Brenna's lips drew down. "I think we can guess how they forced her to be compliant. What kind of insect bites, Connor? Have you any idea?"

"Some kind of spider. When I opened up her clenched fist, there were multiple dead spiders in her hand."

Aunt Brenna said, "Jennet, please get clean linen strips and a basin of water. Connor, I'll have you step out so I can examine her completely."

"I'd like to stay if you don't mind. She'll panic when she awakens."

His dear aunt patted his shoulder. "She won't wake up anytime soon. She's in a deep slumber, her body fighting for survival. Some spiders carry verra strong poison, causing the swelling. Go speak with your cousins. If she awakens, I'll come and get you."

Connor wished to kiss Sela's forehead, but he wouldn't do that when she was asleep. Nor was he ready to declare himself in front of his family.

He didn't understand his feelings for her, so it was much

too soon to publicly declare them.

Jennet, who'd come back with the things her mother had requested, came to a stop in front of him. "Here is some salve for your facial wounds. You will not want them festering as hers are. You may apply it yourself."

Connor peered at his serious cousin, not quite sure how to take the directive. But he thanked her for the salve and the linen square. Aunt Brenna said, "Why don't you wash your face over there?" She pointed to a small table where a pitcher of water and basin had been left out. "If not, Jennet will see to it." She did her best to hide her smirk.

"I'll do it," he said, taking the linen square and salve over to the table. He dipped the linen into the water and picked up the sliver of soap beside the basin. "You tend your patient, Jennet. She needs you far more than I do."

Once he finished, he headed back out to the great hall, anxious to see what the others in the Band of Cousins had to say about the Channel. He was particularly curious to hear how Gregor had fared, as he'd parted ways from his cousin to follow Sela. As he approached the trestle table, he stopped in his tracks.

His sire, Alex Grant, was descending the stairs to the great hall, followed by Uncle Logan. Connor had just seen his sire on Grant land, and nothing had been said about a visit. Nonetheless, it was a relief to see him—they needed all the help they could get, and no warrior was better suited to ride into battle than Alex Grant. Even now. The cousins all quieted as the elders sat down at one end of the table.

"We found Linet," Gregor said as Connor clasped his shoulder in greeting. His face split into a grin. "We've handfasted. She is with her parents at present, but we wish to hear what you've discovered. According to Linet, the count is now five days. A large shipment is due to leave the port at that point, but from where?"

Connor sank into a chair after congratulating Gregor on his good fortune, Maggie motioning for a serving lass to find him food and something to drink. "Greetings to you, Papa. I wasn't expecting to see you here, but it pleases me. We'll need your advice and assistance. Uncle Logan's, also."

"We need to know all of it, Connor," his sire said. "Who did this to you? To the lass?"

He filled them in on what he'd learned, which wasn't much more than they had already heard from Linet. "The only thing I can add is that their primary center is Berwick Castle. There are two Englishmen in charge, and they are operating out of the castle. 'Tis where the Dubh men are, and likely where the ships will berth. 'Tis well fortified."

As he finished, his mother entered the great hall, something that surprised him even more than seeing his father. He heard her slight gasp once her gaze settled on him. He didn't look his best, and he guessed he'd shocked his poor mother. Aunt Gwyneth followed her in. Connor greeted them both, then asked for the explanation his sire had been slow to give. "I'm happy to see you, Mama, Papa, but why are you both here?"

"Because this is finally about to come to an end," his sire said. "Three hundred Grant warriors are on their way to join us. Your brothers will stay at home to protect the clan, but your mother and I did not wish to sit comfortably at home while our son and our niece and nephews rode into battle. We came to help strategize. I see that was a wise decision, based on your condition and the woman's. I've heard but not seen her yet. These bastards need to be stopped."

Uncle Logan stood and paced behind the table, his stomps hard enough to wear a path in the stone. "Uncle Micheil and Uncle Drew are bringing fifty guards each. We'll be sending two hundred. The bastards aren't getting away this time. You've told us what you learned, now tell us what happened to you."

Connor shrugged. "I spoke with Sela in the port, but she was reprimanded for talking to me. After leaving my own impression on two of her guards, I left, but not before I saw her fearful reaction to one particular man. Thorn and I crept into Berwick Castle later last night to see if she would give me more information, but as you can see, they didn't appreciate my speaking with her."

"How did you get away, Thorn?" Uncle Logan asked.

"Who are you again?" the wee lad asked, staring up at the man pacing behind him. "Are you a Ramsay?" He paused, then added in a loud whisper, "Do you know the bollocks splitter?"

Uncle Logan stopped his pacing directly in front of Thorn, one brow quirked over the other. Only his mouth—the lips pressed a slight bit too tightly together—revealed he was on the verge of laughing. "The bollocks splitter? You're around lasses, lad. Not the most proper language, if you ask me."

Thorn glanced around him as if only just noticing all the women in the hall. "My apologies, but do you know her?"

"I think I do. What know you of her?"

"Did she pin a man to a tree by his...by his...was the arrow *between his legs*?" He looked up at Logan Ramsay, his hand going to the front of his trews.

"My name is Logan Ramsay, and the..."

"The *spy*? You're the spy? The one they call the Beast?" His hands shot out from his sides now, as if he wished to hug the man. When Connor and Gregor had first encountered Nari and Thorn, the lads had revealed their admiration for the Ramsay and Grant clans—they'd heard many stories about Logan and Gwyneth Ramsay, he imagined, as well as a few about his sire.

Uncle Logan grinned at this question, glancing at Connor's sire, his chest puffing out a wee bit. "Aye, I'm the Beast, but I plan on retiring that name. The woman you refer to is my wife. Everything you heard is true, and you'd better behave yourself around her. She's got a mighty good eye when she's got a bow in her hand."

Thorn stepped back quickly, until he stood just beside Connor's chair. He then leaned over and whispered, "Which one is she? And is it true?"

"She's sitting right over there," he pointed to where Aunt Gwyneth sat. "I'll introduce you a wee bit later. And aye, 'tis all true."

"Lad, if you've finished all your questions, I'm still waiting to hear how you rescued my son," Connor's sire said.

Thorn's eyes went wide. "Your sire is verra big," he whispered. "Is he as big as you?"

Connor whispered back, "Not quite. But close."

Thorn squared his shoulders and began his tale in a more confident tone. "I spied on her first, then Connor went inside, so I waited outside the wall, but when he didn't come back, I went back inside. I heard them talking about hurting Connor, so I went back for Braden and Roddy."

"Good job, lad," Alex said.

Connor added, "I tried to do it on my own. I know I shouldn't have, but I wanted to get her away from them. I knew she harbored a deep fear, and it seems to have been a valid one."

His father just arched his brow at him. "Her wounds?"

"From hundreds of spiders is my guess. I will be there when she awakens." He took three swigs of an ale and two bites of bread.

"Why?" His father wouldn't let it rest until he answered, that much he knew.

"Because she's been with the Dubh men. She can probably tell us exactly what they plan, when and where."

True, but it was not the answer his sire sought.

As if his sire could read his thoughts, he asked, "And what is she to you? I asked this of you before, and you were evasive. I think your feelings are stronger now. Am I wrong?"

Connor didn't know how to answer that question, so he paused, giving himself time to consider his answer.

Thorn chimed in. "I know what she is! 'Tis why the Dubh men said to leave them together."

Connor spun his head around to face Thorn.

"They said Hord nearly killed Sela so they'd have to leave the lovers out to die together." He nodded his head, apparently proud of his memory.

Connor shook his head and leaned forward, resting his elbows on his knees. "I was in her chamber searching for answers when they walked in and found the two of us together. They made an incorrect assumption. I was there for information."

"And now that you've brought her here, I'll ask you again how you feel about her," his father said.

Hell, but that man never did forget anything.

Connor wouldn't evade the question any longer. His answer would be honest. "I'm not sure. I'm driven to protect her." He glanced at his mother. "I saw her desperate fear and couldn't walk away."

The door to the healing chamber opened and Aunt Brenna came out. A hush settled over the group while they waited to hear what she had to say. Jennet followed her, paler than usual.

"I don't think we've ever seen a person in a more gruesome state. Connor, she is covered in bites. Everywhere. The only place that seems to have escaped is an area around her belly, as if she held something over herself."

"But she'll be fine, will she not? They're just bites…" Connor needed to hear that Sela would heal completely.

"Her body is fighting a fever and poison from some of the bites. If she were to awaken, I imagine the itching would be quite fierce. I can give her something to make her sleep, but I'll refrain if you wish to ask her some questions first."

"Is she awake now?"

"Nay, and… I'm not sure how to explain this, but you have to want to heal. If you think you can give her a reason to want to live, then perhaps you should sit with her. Talk to her. She may be able to hear you."

He nodded once, resolute. "I'll see if I can get her to awaken to answer a few questions. Do keep the potion handy. I don't want to see her in pain."

That statement was more telling than any other he could have said.

Sela opened her eyes, uncertain of where she was. The memories of her torture, of wee Claray's cries and screams, were fresh in her mind, so much so that when something brushed across her leg, she sat up, trying to kill it.

"There's naught there, Sela. I've been watching."

"But a spider...could have...maybe survived..." She glanced over at the speaker, surprised to see Connor Grant seated on a stool next to the bed. "Where am I?"

"You're in the Ramsay keep, tended by the best healer in all of Scotland."

"Nay, I have to get...where is she?" She tried to get herself out of bed, but her legs would not move. Glancing at her arms, she gasped when she saw the size of her arms, swollen with venom or whatever the spiders had carried. She was going nowhere. Vaguely, she recalled her dear friend Vern had promised to take care of Claray. She knew she could trust him so she fell back onto the bed, noticing the sweet aroma of heather coming from the mattress.

"How did I end up here? How did you get me away from the bastard?"

"The bastard?"

"Hord. The demented man with the spiders. I was sent to him for my punishment. 'Tis the last I remember. Where did you find me?"

"They apparently left us both for dead in a secluded place north of Berwick. Thorn said the man you called Hord feared he'd gone too far and nearly killed you. You're free of them."

Sela sighed and closed her eyes. "How I wish, but she's still with them, so I'll have to go back."

"Who is 'she?'" Connor asked, his gaze too shrewd by far. "What hold do they have over you besides the torture?"

An intense itching began in the middle of her head, then shot down to her hand. Scratching the many different spots proved fruitless, though she continued to try.

Connor moved to the side of the bed, sitting on the edge and tenderly reaching for her. "You cannot scratch, Sela," he said, holding her hands. "You'll only make it worse. My aunt has a sleeping potion she can give you, but I'd like to ask you some questions first. Are you willing?"

Sela stared at the handsome man beside her bed, wondering why he cared. He should hate her. Perhaps he only wanted news of the Channel. There *were* things she could tell him, but should she really tell him everything?

How could she bear it?

"I'll tell you all I know if you'll lie next to me and hold me." The intense urge to be comforted would not leave her. Her daughter comforted her, aye, but she was Claray's protector, not the other way around.

Inside her was a driving need to be close to someone who could kill both the spiders and Hord. Someone who could drive out some of the darkness that threatened to engulf her.

"All right. I would be pleased to do that."

She met his gaze and held it, the sincerity of his statement evident in his eyes. "Good," she whispered, "because I don't wish to see your face when you judge me."

CHAPTER EIGHT

SELA COULD BARELY MOVE, BUT Connor picked her up as if she weighed no more than a pine needle and settled her over to the side a bit. The bed was large enough for two. Clearly she'd lost her mind by inviting him to lay beside her, even if he was fully clothed.

"Are you comfortable enough there or would you like me to adjust you?" he asked, carefully arranging a plaid over her legs.

"Nay, I'm fine."

"There's that Scots brogue again." Laughter seemed to dance in his gaze at times. She'd noticed that from the first, although she'd tried not to care. Laughter, even in a gaze, had been so absent in her life these last five years.

"Aye. As I told you, my sire was Scottish. The Dubh men came to my home five years ago. They killed my parents in front of me, first my mother and then my father, and kidnapped me."

"Why? For no reason?" he asked, his hand holding hers lightly.

"Because they wanted me. That's the only reason I was given. They tried to purchase me from my sire and he refused. He did his best to fight them off, but he lost." Her eyes misted at the memory of how hard her sire had fought to protect her from the bastards, but they'd brought men with him, and he'd been helplessly outnumbered. "They dragged me along with them, although I kicked and scratched all I could."

"You must have been shocked. I'm so sorry you and your family were treated with such cruelty."

She watched his hand, moving ever so lightly over her skin, a caress unlike anything she'd ever experienced other than her mama's sweet touch. He was careful and gentle, something so rare for her that it stopped her thoughts, but then she wished to continue, to finish the horrid tale.

"They weren't known as the Dubh men yet, but the men known as Guy and Dee were the ones who began it, along with another man who was even nastier. That man is now dead.

"I'm sure you can guess how I had to serve the two men, and eventually I became with child. That was the best day of my imprisoned life because they both left me alone after that. I gave birth to a beautiful lass three years ago. I named her Claray."

She leaned her head down against his shoulder, his body cushioning hers so the pain of the wounds was not as severe. Had she ever known anyone as gentle as Connor Grant? He handled her as if she were a new babe in his arms. Closing her eyes for strength, she continued, "One of the men who started to work for them after I gave birth to Claray is known as Hord. He took a liking to me, and asked Guy and Dee for my hand in marriage. I refused because he frightened me, and he's hated me ever since. But I couldn't do it, I couldn't force myself and my bairn to have to answer to him.

"He was verra angry over my refusal. One day he discovered my fear of spiders, so he began to taunt me. He would collect them and set them free on me in the middle of the night. His obsession with me grew over time until it led to this." She waved her hand over her body. She paused again to gather strength.

"Once they brought the Channel to Inverness, they gave me the assignment to handle the women—fighting and whoring. I tried to run away with my daughter, and they... they took her from me. They said they'd only allow me to see her if I did as they bid. I soon learned there was another punishment for denying them—Hord's torment with the spiders. I did as they asked, doing my best to ignore the awful things I often had to do. I know it was wrong, but my wee lassie..."Tears choked her, threatening to soak Connor's shoulder, but she tried to contain them.

"This time was different?"

She nodded, even though she knew he couldn't see her. "Aye. My daughter was with me. I've never been so frightened in my life. Trying to protect her, to keep the spiders away from her..."

"Where did they do this?"

"Small chambers. He gathers bags and bags of spiders inside netting and releases them into the chamber. More spiders than you can imagine. They crawl all over you, and they bite if you move, if you swat them, if you do anything. I *hate* spiders. When it first happened, my reaction wasn't this severe, but the punishment was more than I could handle this time. The bastard put my daughter in with me."

Memories of Claray's screams blended with her own tormented her. She wept openly in Connor's arms, letting go of the pain she'd bottled up for so long. For the first time in five years, she felt safe and protected.

"Where is Claray now? She was not with you when I found you."

"Vern. He's become a protector of sorts to me, and he told me he'd take care of her, make sure she was hale. I trust him. He told me I'd done a fine job of protecting her. Connor, I tried, I took my gown off and wrapped her inside it as tightly as I could, but they still got through a bit, especially to her face." She hiccupped three times. "Then I put her underneath me on the floor to protect her. It was awful, so awful..."

"And where does this spineless bastard stand while you're

going through his torture?"

"He stands outside the door and watches through a small window, laughing, a sick sound that makes me ill all by itself."

He cupped her face the best he could and kissed her lightly, the merest of touches. "I don't wish to hurt you," he said as he kissed her again. "Tell me if I do, but I promise you on my honor as the son of Alexander Grant that I will find that bastard and kill him for what he's done to you and your daughter."

She met his gaze and held it. The determination she saw there awed her—but when it came to Claray, she was just as determined. "I have to go back. Many thanks for bringing me here, but I must go back for my daughter."

Whether he allowed it or not, she would find her way back.

Somehow.

Connor did all he could to tamp down his fury over the abuse and torture this poor woman had endured. And his anger toward that Hord bastard who'd dared to hurt a bairn of only three knew no bounds. Killing was too good for these men.

"Sela, you're in no shape to go back there. I cannot allow you to go back."

"True, not today, but I've been through this before. In another day or two, I'll be fine, and I *am* going back. You cannot stop me. I must go back for Claray."

"I'll get your daughter for you. If you tell me what you know of the castle, I'll find her."

"But she'll never come to you. She's afraid of men."

"Then I'll bring Thorn and Nari along."

"Who?"

"Thorn and Nari. Two young lads who help us. Surely she'll come to two laddies. They're but seven and eight winters."

"Connor Grant, I appreciate what you've done for me, but you're not my keeper. I will go back and you cannot stop me."

Connor could see how upsetting this was for her, so he decided to change the subject. He could see she had a strong character and an even stronger will. She'd not be stopped once she set her mind to something. He would have to discuss the matter with her later.

"All right. We'll talk about this on the morrow, but we need your help. We can put an end to the Channel if you can tell us where the shipments are going out, who's in charge, and where they are holding the bairns. We'll get them this eve and wee Claray could be among them."

She told him all she knew about the shipments, which didn't amount to much, but she knew the lads and lasses would be arriving in three shipments. "You cannot go this eve because they are not there yet."

"When will they be arriving?"

"The first shipment, from London, will arrive the day after the morrow. The other two will be arriving the next day."

"How many?"

"Between seventy-five and one hundred in total." Fear flashed in her eyes. "They have hundreds of English knights and warriors. They'll crush you."

"We are calling all our allies in, and my sire has over three hundred guards arriving by the morrow. We could number five hundred, if necessary. We'll take care of the bastards and save the young ones, too."

Aunt Brenna stepped inside the chamber as quietly as possible. "You're awake? How are you doing?"

"I have to go," Sela insisted. "Not today but on the morrow. I must go." She reached up to rake her hands her hair, wincing, then scratched her neck before reaching down quickly to touch her foot. "I appreciate all you've done for me, but once I can walk again, I must go." Her scratching became more persistent. "Please stop this itching. Please help me."

Connor nodded to his aunt to get her the sleeping potion. Then he did the only thing he could do. He held her while she swallowed the mixture, humming softly until she closed her eyes and fell against him.

Shortly after Sela fell asleep against his chest, the door opened and his parents entered the healing chamber.

"Mama, it seems I'm stuck for a wee bit. I don't wish to awaken her—she's so irritated by the bites that she had trouble falling asleep."

"I don't doubt it. I would suggest you relax and sleep a bit, too. Connor, you've got your own wounds to heal," his mother said, running her hand through the dark locks of hair that had fallen forward onto his brow. "You are so like your da."

His sire said, "She means you're stubborn, son."

Connor grinned. He always took it as a compliment when someone thought he was like his father.

"What can we do to help?" his mother asked.

"And what exactly is this woman to you?" his sire asked him again, expecting a different answer because they were alone. He knew the way his father's mind worked.

He could only be honest. "I'm not exactly sure. But I do need to tell you something more about her, something I didn't know until she informed me a few moments ago. She has a daughter."

"Is she married?"

"Nay, her mother and sire were killed, and the bastards who did it stole her away. Much like Braden's wife, she was abused and found herself with child. Mama, we have to get her daughter away from them. The bastard who did this to her," he motioned to Sela's skin, "set the spiders on both her and her wee daughter."

His mother gasped, her mouth falling open in shock.

"How old is the bairn?" His mother considered herself a protector of bairns, so he wasn't surprised the news had upset her.

Perhaps he shouldn't have spoken so openly.

"Her name is Claray, and she is three summers old. We have to get her away from them, and Sela will not rest until we do. In fact, she's insisted on going back as soon as she can travel because she won't risk losing her daughter. I don't doubt she'll do exactly that, but I can't allow her to return. 'Tis too risky. Do you not agree, Papa?"

His sire tipped his head. "Mayhap. But if she returns, she could spy for us." He nodded his head toward her sleeping form. "You say she's Norse?"

"Her sire was Scottish, her mother Norse. She's clearly not ready to return now, but she's hardier than you might think. She could be up and ready to go in a matter of hours."

Alex Grant shook his head. "Nay, she'll need days to recuperate from what she was subjected to, I'm certain. Does she know anything about the next shipment?"

Connor replied, "There are three shipments arriving. The first in two days, the other two the day after. I think she'll attempt to return before the first one arrives."

Connor's mother, her face like stone, shook her head. "Nay. She'll be after her bairn in less than a day. Husband, we must talk privately."

Connor's gaze shifted between his parents. He was not quite certain he knew the meaning of his mother's obstinate statement, but he finally gave in to his own need to heal.

He fell asleep with Sela in his arms.

CHAPTER NINE

"PLEASE, ALEX," MADDIE SAID, QUIETLY so as not to awaken their son. "This cannot wait."

Alex took her hand and led her out of the healing chamber. They passed through the great hall on their way back to the chamber they'd been using since their arrival. Logan tried to stop them, but Alex shook his head. "After I speak with my wife."

Logan nodded and stepped back, indicating his issue could indeed wait.

Once they were inside their chamber, Alex turned on his heel to look at her.

Maddie's belly churned inside, so much that she was powerless to ignore it. Everything told her she needed to take action, so she would. "Alex, you must take me to Berwick and bring that bairn to me."

Alex just quirked his brow at her, considering what she'd said. She wasn't sure how she would convince him, but she knew she must, because if he didn't escort her back to steal that child away, she'd have to go on her own. Sela wasn't well enough to make the journey, and Maddie wouldn't be able to relax until she knew that bairn was out of the clutches of those awful men.

She would get her way on this.

Apparently, her face had moved a wee bit, betraying her thoughts.

"Maddie, I know that look. You wish to save that child,

and we will, but the lass is surrounded by over a hundred English warriors. We cannot just walk in and demand they turn her over to us."

"Alex, we must protect the children."

"I understand your noble cause, but there are larger forces at work."

"The bastards subjected a bairn of three summers to torture. Those are the kind of memories that will stay with a child for decades. And who's caring for her while her mother is here healing? Is she being tortured even now?"

"You're not wrong, Maddie, but I must consider the operation as a whole. This is our chance to stop these men once and for all. We must do this for Scotland."

"I may operate on a much smaller scale than you," she said, meeting his gaze, "but it does not make my endeavor less important."

"What is this endeavor?"

"I must protect the bairns of our country. You consider everyone else, but I have purpose, too, and 'tis no less important."

"You would risk all to save this one child?"

"Aye, I would. The others will not be there for two to three days. We can save this child before that."

He stared at her, then ran his finger down her jawline. "This is important to you?"

"Every day she goes without safety and comfort is another day of torture for her. I cannot bear to think of her in such a situation. I was subjected to a similar situation, and I was much older. I cannot think how a lass of three summers would endure it."

He kissed her lips. She pressed herself closer to him but did not fall under his usual spell. This was too important to her. "Alex, I would prefer for you to help me, but if you cannot, I'll find another way."

Still cupping her face, he said, "All of Scotland places demands on me, but you have asked so little of me over the years."

Her voice cracked when she said, "Because I trust you, Alex."

"Then trust me when I say I will save both Claray and Sela when we go to battle with the English."

Her voice came out in the barest of whispers. "Nay. Claray must be saved on the morrow. Your men will be here by then to assist you. Those bastards don't need a wee bairn around to finish their deeds. Get her out. We'll fight them later."

"If I take three hundred of the warriors I've readied for this mission, I'll be telling the fools that we'll be attacking with that many in the future. I don't wish to reveal our strategy."

Maddie considered his point for a moment. Her husband was keen at coming up with the best tactics for battle, but she could not relent. "Perhaps you'll not need three hundred. A smaller number could handle the task. I see no reason to take all your warriors."

He reached back and massaged her neck. "You hide why you want this, but I know. 'Tis because our youngest son is asking you. You sense it, too. There's something between him and Sela. There is a possibility this wee bairn could become our granddaughter. Is that not part of your reasoning?"

Her heart could take no more, and so she fell against him sobbing. "Alex, we must stop those evil men."

"For you, anything," Alex said. He gave her a tender kiss, then mopped her tears away. "This might work. They'll not want to risk fighting us just yet. They cannot afford to lose men. I'll discuss the matter with Logan and our sons, but I think we can agree on a plan. If we decided to move forward, you will come with me on the morrow. Wee Claray will need more consoling than I can give."

She smiled at her dear husband, then leaned in for a kiss, though it was one of those times when he may not notice her. Sometimes her husband was so busy strategizing against a villain that he became engulfed in his own world.

Her lips met his, and he kissed her briefly, as absent-minded as she'd expected.

This time, she'd allow it.

The next time Sela awoke, she was alone in bed. Thoughts of Connor holding her while she fell asleep warmed her. She couldn't remember when she'd last felt precious to someone besides Claray. Pushing herself up on her elbows, she groaned at the pain and the itching, but it had definitely improved.

A sound told her that she was not alone after all. Glancing up, she noticed the woman seated across from her. Though her hair was as light as Connor's was dark, she could only be his mother. The striking beauty sat as though there were an arrow behind her straightening her back, and she wore a deep blue gown so striking that it appeared to have been designed just for her. Her blue eyes were filled with warmth and compassion. Of course they were. She was in awe of someone who would raise a son who was so fierce yet gentle.

"Good morn to you, Sela. I am Connor's mother. Once we finish our discussion, I'll send a maid with food and she can also help you clean up. May I have a few moments of your time?"

Sela didn't know how to react. Was she about to be lectured? Told to stay far away from her son? Accused of being a whore since she was an unmarried mother?

Out of respect for Connor, she nodded.

"My name is Madeline, but please call me Maddie. Connor has informed his father and me of the torture you were subjected to, and for this, you have my utmost sympathy. We were also told that your daughter of three summers was subjected to the same horrid treatment. Is this true?"

"Aye, my lady," Sela said, her eyes downcast.

"You need not refer to me as 'my lady.' I am no longer the mistress of the clan, but I do consider myself to be the mistress of the bairns. That your poor daughter was subjected to such treatment has upset me terribly. I have taken on the mission of retrieving her from the men who ran your life."

"But they'll not listen to you. They're cruel, evil monsters."

Raw fury filled Madeline Grant's kind eyes. "I *will* get that child away from them. You can count on it. My husband has nearly a thousand warriors at his disposal, and we have five other allies who will give us at least a hundred each. I think we can handle whatever men your monsters have hired to fight for them. They will go to battle, and the Scots will triumph, but before that happens, I will get your daughter away. Do not doubt my word."

Connor's mother spoke with such a passion that she could only admire her. She had no doubt that she meant what she said. Thinking about all the numbers she had offered, Sela became hopeful. Perhaps Connor and his family *did* have the might to crush out the Channel once and for all. If so, she could only help them.

"Many thanks to you, mistress. I fear Claray may not leave with you, so it will be best if I go with you."

"You are welcome, but I will warn you of two things."

Sela had never seen such a powerful woman, yet one who no one would suspect of such strength. Awe encompassed her. How would this woman feel about her son holding or kissing Sela? She suspected she knew the answer to that question. She was an unmarried woman with a young daughter.

"I know what you're thinking," Madeline said, her eyes warm again, "so allow me to tell you this before I give you my warnings. I judge people by what's in their heart and not their circumstances. You were forced into your life of servitude, and I understand how such a thing can happen. If my son chooses you, I will support him. But this brings me back to my two warnings for you."

"And they are?" She swallowed, a gulp much larger than she'd intended, but she couldn't help herself.

"First of all, please don't hurt my son. If he loves you, I hope you return his love, but if not, do not tease him with empty promises."

Sela nodded. "Agreed. I don't know what will happen after all of this, but I respect your son."

Her heart was in turmoil, but Connor had awakened something inside her. She could not think past the task that lay before her, yet she knew she wished to know him better.

"Second, I know you want to go to your daughter as soon as we get near Berwick Castle. You may feel driven to act without thinking, but I give you my word that I will do what is best for your daughter and I will see this done."

"That doesn't feel like a warning."

"'Tis not a warning...but this is. When we are in the position to gain your daughter back, do not get in my way."

Sela didn't say a word, her mouth agape and her eyes fixed on this wonderful, fearsome woman.

CHAPTER TEN

———◆———

CONNOR GLANCED OVER THE GROUP that was forming outside the Ramsay stables. His cousins, Braden, Roddy, Gavin, and Gregor, stood not far away from him, close enough for him to hear their conversation. Gavin's wife, Merewen, had wished to join them, but her sister, Linet, had convinced her to stay on Ramsay land. Both of them had been through enough of late.

Thorn raced up to Connor and said, "Godspeed with you, my lord." Then he leaned in close and whisper-shouted, "Kill those slimy bastards." It had been decided that Thorn and Nari were to stay back until the second group moved, but only the promise of unending fruit tarts and special training with Torrian had convinced them.

"And you are to make sure the women are protected, lad," Connor said.

"On my honor as a Highlander, my lord," he said quite seriously before running back to the keep.

Braden grinned after him, then turned to the others. "I still don't understand why we're not attacking right away. Kill the bastards now and we'll save the lasses and lads when their boats arrive in Berwick."

"I agree with Uncle Logan," Gregor said. "If we kill all involved, no one knows what will happen to those boats. The lasses and lads could be deserted, left somewhere to die."

"We could search for them," Gavin said. "But we know

not how they're arriving—by boat, cart, or horseback? We're lacking the basic information we need to be successful."

Roddy shook his head. "The risk is too great. "We cannot go all over Scotland searching for them."

Their cousins Daniel and David joined them. The Drummonds had arrived the previous eve to join the effort. "I overheard your conversation. 'Tis not just Scotland we would have to search, but all of England besides."

Connor joined the group. "You all have great ideas, but the reason we're not attacking right away is quite simple."

"What?" David asked.

"Because my mother insists that we go after Claray before the shipments arrive, and she thinks it would be safest to do so without a battle. Besides, we don't yet know where the lads and lasses will be kept."

"And Sela? How does she feel about all of this?" Gregor asked.

"She's agreed. She'll join my mother in case Claray refuses to go with her."

Daniel asked, "Why can't Sela be the one to collect her daughter? One look at our warriors, and the bastards are sure to hand her over."

Connor cleared his throat, then said, "Because I don't want her that close to those men. They left both of us to die, so they'll not be expecting to see her. I fear that Hord will go after Sela. He has a sick obsession with her."

Connor had his back to the keep, but his cousins' shocked expressions signaled he should turn around. He swiveled to face the keep and nearly fell on his face. His mother was walking toward them in leggings and a tunic, clothing usually worn by all the female archers in both clans.

His mother strode down the hill toward the stables, almost all eyes on her. She'd never paid much attention to what others thought, and this was no different. Her purpose mattered more to her than aught else.

Out of nowhere, Sela appeared at his side.

"Where did you come from?" he asked, surprised she'd been able to sneak up on them.

She smiled. "'Tis most easy to hide when your mother is commanding all the attention."

He grinned and said, "I like that."

"What? That your mother is coming?"

"Nay, that you smiled, and it's a real smile. I saw you smile in Inverness, but there was a tinge of nastiness behind it. I like this Sela better."

Some raw emotion glimmered in her eyes, but she averted her gaze.

Roddy said, "Lass, you must be mighty strong. Given the way you looked when we found you, I didn't think you would survive."

"I have someone who needs me," she said simply.

Daniel laughed. "Connor will be fine on his own after a bit."

Gavin snorted and said, "He's not as needy as you think, Sela."

Connor said, "You all know she speaks of her daughter, and I'm sure that my mother will be carrying Claray back to you before you know it. Do not doubt that she will do as she promises. My father will make sure she gets her way, or he'll take down half of England."

He saw the fleeting look of hope in Sela's eyes. He held his hand out to her and she mounted the horse with his assistance. She'd yet to regain her full strength, so he was grateful she'd agreed to ride with him. And the thought of her leaning against him was much more pleasing than riding Midnight Moon alone.

With the exception of Maggie and Will, all of the cousins were to be at the gates of Berwick Castle. The leaders of the Band of Cousins would meet them in Berwick after a quick stop in Edinburgh. They had a strong network of contacts there, and Maggie thought it might be worthwhile to glean what information they could before the final confrontation with the Channel men.

Once they were among their enemies, Connor's mother would be protected at all times, by a circle of people Alex trusted.

Uncle Logan seemed to be enjoying himself quite a bit as he rode back and forth, giving instructions to the various groups, telling them which area of the fields they would occupy. He came over to the cousins at last, leading his horse between Connor and Gavin. "You will take the front, Connor? You and the Band? 'Tis truly your operation, not ours. We're just here with the muscle."

"Aye, I'd be glad to be in front."

"And you'll remember that our goal this day is not to fight, agreed?"

Connor frowned. "I understand the focus of this mission. Why do you question me?"

Uncle Logan snorted. "I'd think that would be obvious. Because you're just like your sire, and you're presently driven for vengeance for grievances against this lass and her daughter." He nodded toward Sela. "I mean no offense, lass, but if he's anything like his father, he'll have them begging on their knees for doing you wrong."

"I appreciate that, but I can stand up for myself against those fools. However, I'll accept any assistance in getting my daughter away from them. Her safety comes first. Please remember that." She gave Connor and Logan each a pointed gaze before she faced front.

This time Gavin snorted, his bark of laughter much like his father's. "You don't know my aunt Maddie well, but if she said she'll get your daughter, you can count on it. I heard she said she'd stick a needle in the eye of the man who loves spiders, Hord. You can count on that, too, if he doesn't give the wee bairn up quickly. Uncle Alex will hold him down for her."

"She's quite a lady," Sela said. "I've not seen anyone stand up for bairns as she has." Her sideways glance at Maddie told Connor how impressed she was with his mother.

"She'll take care of Claray," he said.

Her voice came out in a whisper only he could hear. "I surely hope so."

———◆———

They'd stopped for the night in a meadow. The moon gave them plenty of light. Sela had made a point of climbing to the top of a small knoll just so she could look out over the lines of warriors brought by the Grants and their allies. They only brought a hundred men, leaving many of the Grant warriors on Ramsay land, where they would await further instruction from Alex Grant. They'd all agreed it was best not to reveal their full strength to the enemy.

Sela liked looking at the group because the sight of them gave her hope—hope that the hell she'd lived in for the past five years could be ending.

Hope that she could indeed have a sweet life with Claray.

But something else had come to life inside her. If she couldn't have a life with Claray, she wished for her daughter to have a mother like Madeline Grant and a father like Alex.

Or Connor.

After she finished her ablutions, she headed back to the group, adjusting the leggings Connor's Aunt Gwyneth had given her. The fierce woman had insisted they'd help her if she had to run.

Sela loved them because the bugs would have a tougher time finding her skin. She came under a large tree and stopped for a moment just to look up at the beauty of the sky through the bare branches. A broken twig behind her told her she was no longer alone.

Connor approached her, his white teeth shining in the moonlight. "I like you in leggings, Sela."

"My thanks. I'm quite fond of them." She ran her fingers

across the smooth fabric. If she had her way, she'd never wear another gown and she'd dress Claray the same way.

He stepped closer to her and she forced herself not to step back. Connor Grant was a good man. She'd tried to push him away, and still he'd sought to help her, to protect her and her daughter. He'd believed in her before he even knew the truth of her situation.

He leaned forward and kissed her forehead. "Your bites are looking much better."

She reached for his hand. "You mean I don't look quite so hideous anymore."

"You never did," he said, his hand sliding through the silky tresses she'd unbound for the night. "You're always beautiful to me."

"Connor, I wish for you to promise me something." She leaned into him, savoring his warm touch.

"Anything, if 'tis in my power," he said, cocooning her icy hand inside his two warm ones.

"If anything happens…"

"We will come out ahead. I promise you that."

Her other hand rested on his forearm. "Please? Hear my request?"

"Go ahead. I'm listening." He gave her his full attention, his straight hair hanging just below his shoulders while his gray eyes focused on hers intently.

When had she ever cared about a man this much? Other than her sire, she'd grown a fierce dislike of men, but this man had changed something inside her. When had she ever wished for a man's opinion or sought his warmth, his touch? When had she ever wished to run her fingers down a man's strong jawline, through the stubble of his beard and over to his lips?

Focus, Sela. Focus. The man drove her to distraction.

"If anything happens to me, will you ask your mother to raise Claray? Would you help her take care of my daughter?" She couldn't stop a tear from rolling down her cheek as her lips quivered.

He wrapped his arms around her, tucking her head against his shoulder. "You have my word. But you need not worry. You'll be coming back to Clan Ramsay with your daughter. You can choose to live a normal life there or at Clan Grant, though I would prefer for you to come to us. I wish to get to know you better. Much better."

Sela was already shaking her head. "We would never suit. I already have a daughter, and I was used..."

"Hush. You've done the best you could under difficult circumstances."

She leaned back to catch his gaze. "But I watched them beat lasses. I forced them to fight and allowed the men to force them to do other things..."

"You did those things to protect your wee bairn. Am I not correct?"

"Aye, but I have much to atone for." Her cheeks burned even in the cool of the night. If she escaped from this unscathed, she'd have to do much praying for forgiveness. "I fear I can never make things right."

"You can worry about that once you and Claray are safe."

She just nodded, not ready to share her thoughts.

He must have sensed her disquiet because he kissed her softly. His mouth tasted of the mint leaves he often chewed, and his kiss promised protection, caring, and so much more. When she was with Connor, she almost believed her dreams were still possible. He ended the kiss and she fell against him, her chin on his shoulder.

"Do you know what I fear will happen?"

"Tell me and I'll do what I can to banish that fear," he whispered into her ear, sending a shiver down her spine.

"That they'll only give up Claray if I return to them."

He stood back and said, "That's not a possibility. They do not need you."

"But once Hord knows I'm still alive, he will want me back. Or he'll try to hurt me."

He cupped her cheeks and said, "None of that is going to happen." He paused. "Is he Claray's sire? Pardon me if I'm being too personal, but is that his motivation? If so, we may have a harder time getting her away."

"Nay, 'tis Guy or Dee. I know not which one for sure." The palm of her hand came up to her mouth, but she forced the words out beyond it. His questions filled her with shame, but she recognized the importance of answering him honestly. "Do not be surprised when you see her. She has the red hair of my sire, George Seton."

"I'm sure she's beautiful," Connor said, his gaze catching hers.

"She *is* beautiful, especially her heart." She stifled the urge to cry, knowing she had to remain strong. Her daughter's life could depend on it.

She stared up at him. "Thank you for our promise. It comforts me to know she won't be alone if I cannot be with her. And promise me one more thing?" For so long, she'd avoided emotion, knowing all of her guilt and anger and grief were powerful enough to cripple her, but it was impossible to avoid it anymore. Impossible to avoid it around this man who brought everything to the surface. Tears flooded her cheeks.

"Anything, though 'tis not necessary," he said, his thumb brushing her cheek.

"Promise me you'll remember me."

———◆———

How had anyone ever thought her an Ice Queen? The woman who stood before him was all emotion. Warm and beautiful. Connor put his finger under her quivering chin to lift her gaze to his. "I will always remember you. You need not worry about that. From the moment I met you, you were burned into my mind. Naught will happen to you, but you have my word that should something go wrong I will always tell Claray about her mother."

"My thanks," she whispered, though her tears were so thick he doubted she could see the intent in his gaze.

"Come, you need to rest before we leave."

She just stared up at the sky, whether to hide her tears or to try to ignore him, he wasn't sure.

"You need rest if you're to heal, Sela. 'Twill help you be strong for Claray."

"I know that…"

"But?"

Her voice came out in the barest of whispers while her gaze searched the area to look for eavesdroppers, he guessed. "But I cannot."

"Why not?" The truth dawned on him. She'd had a nightmare when she'd been in the healing chamber. He'd seen her reach for bugs that weren't there. Now she was out in the open, exposed to the elements. How had he not guessed?

She averted her gaze, looking over his head as she might have in the days before, when she'd treated him as if he were nothing. Her way of defending herself, he realized. She'd been forced to arm herself against those around her. Her strength humbled him.

"Go to sleep and do not worry about me. I'll be fine," she said. But the dark circles under her eyes told him otherwise.

He stepped closer and whispered in her ear. "I'm going to set up a tent. I'll hold you through the night."

She shook her head and said, "Nay. Your mother and sire are here. What would they think of me?"

He reached up to trace the delicate slope of her jaw with one finger. "I'm not accepting that answer. We'll set the tent up away from the others so no one will see us. If you lie on top of me, no spiders can reach you from the ground. The tent over our heads will protect us from an attack from above."

"Oh, Connor," she said, swiping at her tears in embarrassment. "You need not…"

"I'll not allow you to refuse." He reached for her hand. "If you knew my parents better, you would not worry about it. They will not judge you."

He didn't wait for her answer but instead strode over to the packhorse to retrieve a tent. Most of them weren't in use because it was such a beautiful night.

Once he set the tent up, he held his hand out for her to climb inside. Her hesitance wrenched his gut. She couldn't stop scanning the material for any evidence of a creature in the night.

He climbed in next to her, lay flat on his back, and said, "Come. Face down on top of me. I'll act honorably, but you must sleep."

"I am exhausted," she admitted with a sigh.

She settled on him and all Connor could think was how wonderfully she fit against him.

"Close your eyes, lass. You need your sleep."

She slept the night through, not one nightmare.

CHAPTER ELEVEN

W RAPPED IN CONNOR'S ARMS, SELA had slept through the night, something that had not happened in a long time. She didn't understand the way he comforted her, when most men filled her with contempt and fear, but there was no denying it. They'd risen before the rest of the camp, and no one had commented on the tent.

They'd ridden toward Berwick Castle quietly, Sela in front of Connor. A small patrol had been sent out ahead of the group to check the area for any hidden factions. So far, nothing unusual had happened, but the closer they came to the castle, the more unsettled Sela felt. Connor rubbed her arm, attempting to calm her, but the thought of seeing Hord made her wish to vomit.

And what of Claray? Lady Brenna was the best healer in all the land, but her wee daughter wouldn't have had someone of equal talent to treat her bites. What if they still pained her?

What if Claray hated her because she had failed to save her from the spiders?

Stop! You must stop torturing yourself. Focus on Claray.

"Sweetling, I think it best that you ride behind me when we arrive outside the gates. I don't want Hord to see you right away. They can deal with my mother initially. If we must bring you into it, we will. My sire will judge that."

"Nay, Connor. I cannot hide. I must see Claray with my

own eyes. I need to stand strong in front of the bastards. I mustn't cower in front of them. If I hide, they'll think they still have me under their control."

"All right."

She almost told him what they had planned, but he would never allow it, and she could not allow him to stand in her way.

All she could do was hope he would forgive her.

———◆———

Connor heard sounds he recognized, glancing up in the sky right before they arrived at the gates. Will, Maggie's husband, was the former rover known as the Wild Falconer, his falcons rightly famous for their loyalty and ability to follow his direction.

If the falcons were near, Maggie and Will were almost upon them. Why would they change their minds? Or had they decided to stay at the back to observe?

The rest of the Band lined their horses up in a show of solidarity, his father in the middle with his mother in front of him. A guard was positioned in front of them, one on either side, and many behind them.

Two men, he guessed Guy and Dee, came out of the castle to greet them. "Greetings to the Highlanders. What brings you to England and why have you brought so many reinforcements? We have no desire for a battle."

Alex Grant spoke first. "You beat my son and left him for dead. Did you think we'd not retaliate? Be warned that we will if you don't agree to our demands today. We have no wish for battle now, and just so you're aware, you are indeed in Scotland. This land has gone back and forth, but Berwick is currently under Scots control. Mayhap you are lost?"

The man he guessed to be Guy laughed, a dark laugh that made Connor wish to throttle him.

"What is it you want? Speak and be done with this," the

other man, who had to be Dee, instructed, his eyes coming to settle on Sela.

Connor's mother was the first to speak. "You tell Hord that Madeline Grant, wife of Alexander Grant, wishes to see him now. And do not play foolish with me."

Dee's gaze panned over the group for a moment, as if he were assessing whether or not the request could be denied. Something like fear flashed in his eyes, and he turned back and spoke to a man behind him. "Get Hord and bring him here."

"Good, we will wait," Connor's mother said firmly.

If Connor were to guess, these men were nervous because they were not prepared for battle. They may have been promised a hundred guards, but that number had not yet arrived at Berwick Castle.

The foul man Connor recognized as Hord came through the cluster of horses—stringy dark hair, dark mantle, and an odd bag hanging from his waist. He had a sick grin on his face that made Connor wish to throttle him.

"Well, greetings to you, Sela. I'm so pleased you've returned to me. You have a tough constitution."

Uncle Logan and Aunt Gwyneth rode up to join Connor's mother, adding to the show of strength. It surprised no one in their group, except for Sela, whose eyes grew as large as coins, to see Aunt Gwyneth nock her bow and aim it at Hord.

The look Uncle Logan gave the wee man was a reminder of how he'd earned the title of Beast of the Highlands. "Where would you like her to aim? For your bollocks or straight for your eye? She can make the shot, as I'm sure you've heard. She's the best archer in all of Scotland and England."

"Are you Hord?" Connor's mother asked.

The man nodded briefly, but not with conviction. He was clearly afraid of the two women—and rightly so.

"You will bring me that bairn of three summers who

you dared to torture, and if you do not, I will have ten of my husband's men hold you down while I drive my sewing needle into both of your eyes."

Hord began to laugh, but it was a nervous sound void of humor. "I know not what child you speak of."

"Aye, you do, you bastard. I want my daughter," Sela shouted. So angry was she, Connor feared she'd vault off the horse. Connor's mother shot her a look that he recognized from childhood—although Madeline Grant was known for being kind and even-tempered, she could stop a rampaging boar with one glance. This was that kind of glance. Sela sagged back against him and did not speak again.

"You will bring me the lass named Claray," Connor's mother said, "or by the time I count to ten, those falcons over your head will be pecking your eyes out, while Gwyneth shoots her arrow and pins you to your horse. The last man who crossed her had his bollocks pinned to a tree. He did not live to tell the tale. Have I made myself clear?"

Hord nodded but didn't move, his gaze slowly raising overhead.

Will had clearly been giving lessons to others in the clan, for Maddie Grant whistled and two falcons dropped out of the sky, swooping around Hord's head, squawking as they did so. Hord bellowed and said, "Get her. Get Claray now."

Another whistle and the birds lifted back into the air, although they did not go far.

"Is that all you want?" Dee asked in apparent disbelief. "A lass of three summers?"

"'Tis what we came for, and I'll not leave without her."

A few moments later, a man emerged on horseback with a wee lass in his arms. Although she did indeed have red hair, her delicate features matched Sela's. This had to be Claray.

"Mama, is that you?" the wee lassie asked. "Take me away

with you. I don't like it here. Please?"

Sela moaned, and Connor had to wrap an arm around her to keep her from vaulting off the horse.

"Give me the bairn," Connor's mother insisted.

Hord said, "You'll get her, but we'll take Sela back. Sela, we need you. Come back and I'll send your daughter to safety with the Grants."

"Like hell. Let the child go," Connor barked.

"Mama, please!" Claray burst into a moaning, heart-wrenching cry.

Chaos erupted.

Hord reached for Claray, close enough to wrench her away from the man who held her, and she screamed. "Nay, nay, do not allow him to touch me. Please, Mama. Save me from him."

The man who held the lassie did his best to comfort her, but her eyes were wild with fear.

This time, Connor could not contain Sela. She jumped off Midnight Moon and raced to her daughter. No one stopped her when she grabbed the sobbing lassie. No one stopped her when she raced back to Connor's mother and handed the bairn to her.

"Go, please," she said, her voice hitching. "Get her away from here. Now."

Connor watched as his parents did just that. He expected Sela to come back to him then.

"Come here, Sela," Hord bellowed. "Or our men will start killing Highlanders."

Connor wanted to tell her it was an empty threat. The Channel bastards did not have the numbers to defeat them. But he didn't get the chance to speak.

"Nay, please," Sela said.

The wicked man grinned, his eyes sparkling with malice. "Come with me willingly, and I'll never go after your daughter again. If you fight, I'll kill your friends and see that Claray is thrown into a chamber full of spiders."

Still, Connor thought Sela would come to him. The threat was weak, they all knew it. So he felt equal parts surprise and horror when she glanced at him and mouthed the words, "Remember me."

Connor bellowed, his horse rearing, sending the other horses in different directions, as she raced back to the castle. Hord grabbed her in an instant and started dragging her back into the castle while Dee and Guy backed off, yelling, "Seal the gates."

The portcullis nearly caught Connor as he charged toward Sela. The heavy gate would have cut his neck off, but someone pulled him back.

The last thing he heard her say was, "I'm sorry, Connor."

CHAPTER TWELVE

CONNOR WAS WILD WITH FURY, but his cousins pulled their horses in front of him. "Calm down, Connor," someone said, although he was too agitated to register who'd spoken.

"You bastard, Hord," he bellowed. "If you touch her again, I'll kill you and put your head on a pike."

Uncle Logan and Aunt Gwyneth rounded on him next. "This is not the way," Logan said. "She can handle herself for two days. We'll get her back."

"He's right," Gregor said. "We have the lass, we'll get Sela later." He brought his horse even closer, then said in a lowered voice. "She's agreed to help us from the inside."

"What? You bastards went behind my back?" Connor thought he'd choke his cousin, but he said the words in a seething undertone. He would not do anything to endanger her. It would be best to ride a distance away before they spoke strategy.

He followed his parents and their guards out of Berwick until they reached a clearing at a safe distance. Connor dismounted and immediately went after Gregor. "You set this up? You told her to go back to spy?"

"Cease," Uncle Logan bellowed. "Sela made the suggestion herself, but she came to us, knowing you'd not support this. If you stop and use that mind of yours, you'll realize 'tis a brilliant plan she came up with. With Sela inside, we have a better chance of saving a hundred lads and lasses. When you can reason again, you'll understand why it needed to be done. We want them to think they stole her back, not that she went willingly. She played it beautifully, and so did you."

Connor stopped, pausing to process all he'd just heard.

"If it were anyone but Sela, you'd agree with the arrangement," Braden said from the group of cousins, all on their feet now. "Take your emotion out of this."

He stared at his cousin, not wanting to admit he was right. The sound of humming caught his ears. His mother's humming. He averted his gaze to the edge of the clearing, where his mama was holding a sweet lassie who was still asking for her mother.

He strode over to the bairn with the copper-colored hair and knelt down in front of her. "Claray, my name is Connor. I know you miss your mama right now, but I promise I'll bring her back to you. A couple of days from now, you'll see her again."

Her breath hitched twice and she leaned in closer to his mother. "Where are we going? I don't want to go back there. I don't like those men."

Connor's mother held her close, and the wee lassie's head rested on her shoulder. "We'll see your mama again, but first we're going to a magical castle full of lots of wee lassies for you to play with. You will love it there."

"Truly? Other lassies I can play with?"

"Aye," his mother said.

"Are there any spiders there? Please, no more spiders. They bite me." Fresh tears started rolling down her cheeks, and Connor wasn't surprised to see his sire walk in the opposite direction, clenching his fists like he wished to kill someone. He felt the same way.

His mother wiped Claray's tears away. "We'll protect you from the spiders," she said. "You'll get to sleep in a big fluffy bed filled with furs and pillows with two other wee lassies named Lise and Liliana. We could even put a netting around your bed to keep the spiders away." Her voice cracked, but she took a deep breath and continued, "There are even puppies for you to play with."

Connor had forgotten that Torrian's dog had just had a new litter of puppies. Lise and Liliana played with the wee pups so much they were exhausted by the attention come nightfall.

"What is a puppy? I've never seen one," Claray said, rubbing her eyes.

His mother said, "Wee furry animals who will kiss you and lay at your feet. And Cook makes the best fruit pies of anyone. You'll see."

"What is a fruit pie?"

Connor stared at the innocent lass, also noticing how everyone had quieted around him. Uncle Logan looked as if he were about to burst, but he, too, walked away, following his sire out of the clearing. Aunt Gwyneth swiped at her cheeks, doing everything she could to get rid of the evidence of her tears.

Hord and his partners were not going to die an easy death.

———— ◆ ————

Sela tore over to the stairs to the parapets, wanting to watch the Grants as they left. Wanting to see Claray...and also *him*. Connor looked furious enough to tear down the portcullis with his bare hands, but his family ushered him away. Her gaze quickly shifted to the wee lassie cradled on Madeline Grant's lap.

Claray had sobbed and tried to wriggle away as she handed her over to Maddie, but now she had her arms wrapped around the women's middle, and the dear woman held her close as they galloped away.

Hord's bellowing voice reached her, but she ignored him. What could he do to hurt her now? Claray was far away from his reach.

Dee's voice carried over the din. "*Now*, Sela. In the great hall."

Still, Sela followed the Grants with her gaze until she could no longer distinguish Maddie's horse from the others. Her daughter was safe.

If Sela did not survive this venture, Claray would be loved by Madeline Grant. What more could she hope for?

Connor Grant. The one man she was capable of loving.

That thought frightened her, but it comforted her, too. For years, she'd seen only greed and ugliness from the men in her life. Connor had reminded her that men could be honorable, too. They could be gentle and kind. That reminder had reawakened her goodness.

She feared Hord would never let her go, but at least she had her memories of the dark-haired Highlander's kisses.

"Sela, now!"

Guy's voice carried up to the parapets, so she made her way down the stairs to speak with him. She knew what he and Dee wanted. The first shipment was to arrive today from London, so they needed her right away.

But now she had another job. When she'd approached Connor's cousins secretly about returning to the Channel to find out where the lasses and lads would be held prior to the shipment, they'd been more than happy to go along with her suggestion.

Atonement. It was the sole reason she'd agreed to return. If she could save these young ones, maybe the Lord would consider forgiving her for her sins.

Maybe she could forgive herself.

She followed Dee and Guy across the hall, keeping her gaze far away from Hord. Guy grabbed her arm and shoved her ahead of him, forcing her into one of the small chambers off the hall. Hord stayed outside.

She used that point to her advantage, pleading with Dee, "If you keep him away from me, I'll do anything you ask of me. He nearly killed me."

"You don't give orders here, we do," Dee said. "It's con-venient you're back. The shipment is here from London. These are the older lasses, so they'll not need much care. Hord will not be anywhere near them."

"On the morrow, you'll change locations because there are two groups arriving. One holds younger lasses. Hord will not be allowed near the others either, so you will be safe until we get these shipments off." Dee and Guy both stared at her, waiting for her response.

"Where will I need to be on the morrow?" she asked. This was the information she would get to the Grants and Ramsays, if possible. Connor's cousins had sworn they'd send a young lad to her.

Guy grabbed her arms and pulled her close. "If you are considering getting information for your new friends, I suggest you forget it. Hord has been working on a new form of punishment. Just give us a reason to try it on you." He gave her a twisted smile and it took all of her will to turn her head away rather than cry out. "Your things have been moved to an inn. We no longer trust you to stay in the castle. Guards will escort you there later. We will watch your every move, Sela. I wouldn't try anything."

"Though if you sell us out," Dee added, "we'll kill you before Hord gets a hold of you. You can count on it."

CHAPTER THIRTEEN

CONNOR PACED IN A SMALL area outside the clearing that the guards had made their temporary home until all was settled, about two hours from Berwick. He hadn't had one moment's rest since leaving Castle Berwick.

Maggie and Will joined him, Uncle Logan not far behind them. Once they'd all settled, Maggie said, "I've indicated the others should join us. Connor, you've been pacing since we arrived. Why not sit on that log? I know this is difficult for you, but we thought Sela's assistance would be the best way to ensure we save every single lass and lad. Her suggestion was perfect."

"I understand the reasoning behind it, Maggie. I sincerely do, but Sela barely had time to heal from the spider attack. If that bastard puts her in danger again, I don't think she'll hold up. Had it been a sennight from now, she'd be better prepared."

"This couldn't wait," Maggie whispered.

Seething, Connor picked up a boulder and heaved it off as far as he could throw it.

Uncle Logan crossed his arms. "Or maybe she'd prefer that group. She had a child with Guy or Dee. Is that not what you said? Mayhap her loyalty is elsewhere."

Connor had heard enough. "The hell it is. She's not in love with any of those bastards, and she *will* help us. Uncle Logan, you've lost your ability to reason. You must have taken too many hits when they beat you."

No one said a word for a moment, though Braden and Roddy joined them quietly. Maggie and Will were watching her father closely, likely to see how he would react. Uncle Logan surprised them all by bursting into laughter. "I had to know. 'Tis as I suspected, aye, nephew? You're taken with the lass?"

Connor cursed under his breath. His uncle had caught him good. He wished to answer him, to deny what he was suggesting, but he could not. He stood and paced in a circle again, looking at the ground in front of him. "Aye, I suppose I am."

His uncle stopped his repetitive movement by clasping his shoulder. "Lad, love is the one thing a man cannot plan. When I met Gwynie, she threatened to cut my bollocks off, yet here I am."

"And you still have them both, aye, uncle?" Braden said.

Uncle Logan snorted and the rest of them chuckled. "When this is over, you should tell her exactly how you feel."

Connor scuffed the dirt with his boot. "She bears a great amount of guilt for all she's done. If she manages to put all of this behind her, do you think she would be accepted as part of our clan? We have some elderly curmudgeons who only get worse the older they get."

Maggie didn't hesitate to answer. "Not once has the Channel ever demonstrated any kindness toward a female. She was used as much as the others. There isn't anyone here who cannot attest to their cruelty." She motioned to herself and the other cousins. "We'll forgive her from her past, aye, but can you? If you doubt your ability to do so, then stay out of her life. She needs to heal and move on once this is over."

Connor ran his hand through his long locks, doing his best to untangle the mess the wind had made of them. "Do you truly believe we can put an end to the Channel?"

"Absolutely," Will said. "We're so close, it could be less

than a sennight before we see the end."

Uncle Logan clapped him on the back. "Your lass will be safe soon enough. We have close to one hundred warriors with us, another one hundred an hour away, and another three hundred gathering outside Ramsay land. They'll join us when we're ready, but I don't want these bastards knowing aught about our numbers. When the English knights move in, so will our reinforcements. We will win this one, especially now that we have your lass on the inside."

"I can do this," Connor said, rubbing his palms together, finally accepting what everyone else already had. Sela could be the key to putting an end to the Channel and stopping that shipment. "Tell me what to do."

"You're to take Thorn with you this night and see if you can get in touch with Sela. He and Nari have just arrived with the most recent small group of warriors. I don't know if they've freed Sela yet, but we advised her to watch for Thorn or Nari and tell them aught she's learned. She said to look for her near the Buck's Inn."

"Consider it done. Thorn and I will find her."

———◆———

Sela followed the men that evening into a large manor home north of the port of Berwick. Her insides tossed about, the same they always did when she was about to head into a situation that was totally unknown to her. Guy and Dee led the way, and just as she'd been promised, Hord was nowhere to be seen. When she entered the building, she was surprised to see a small group of ten lasses.

Why had she expected fifty?

Guy turned to her and whispered, "This is our most valuable group. Treat them kindly."

She wondered why they were considered more valuable than others. Perhaps Guy and Dee had simply secured a higher price to send them across the water.

They entered a small gathering hall furnished much like

a whorehouse, but she doubted any of the girls gathered by the hearth would make that connection. Odd tapestries hung on the wall, depicting some questionable activities, but she ignored them. The lasses sat around on large floor pillows, combing each other's hair and giggling, a most unusual activity considering they'd all been kidnapped.

"Greetings to you," Sela said, uncertain even what language they spoke.

"Greetings. Are you the maid? We've been waiting for our maid. We were promised one," the tallest lass asked.

"That will be at your new home," Dee said. "You'll be on your ship within two days. A short journey later and you'll be with your auntie in her castle in France."

"We've waited so long for this," the tall one said, turning to look at the others. "We had no idea it would be so easy to get there. Papa has promised us for many moons. Auntie will arrange all of our marriages. We'll be living with the wealthy men of France. You'll see, girls."

Sela was stunned. The girls were certainly in for a surprise when they reached the coast of France. True, they would possibly find themselves married, but not to any princes.

She lowered her gaze, embarrassed by their innocent excitement.

Guy said to her, "Come with me and I'll find food for them. They'll be treated better than the others, so do be wary of them. All you need to do is keep them here for a night, report to us every two hours across the street, and then you'll move along to the other building on the morrow. Understood?"

She nodded, following him back out for the food he'd promised the lasses.

This was to be a very long night.

———◆———

Connor rode his horse into Berwick that eve. This was

day three. Three more days to stop the Channel's plan. And yet, all of his thoughts were on Sela. Ever since he'd first set eyes upon the lass in Inverness, his heart had been floundering like a fish tossed onto shore. He couldn't make up his mind whether he loved her or not.

"What'll we do if she's not there?" Thorn asked. The wee lad sat in front of him on the saddle as he rode toward town.

"We must be patient, lad," Connor said. "If she doesn't come, we will need to find her. Somehow."

"Shouldn't be too hard. Sela's so pretty, people are bound to notice. Everyone's afraid of her, too."

"That may have been the way in Edinburgh, but I don't think it holds in Berwick."

"Her beauty would be legendary anywhere."

Connor wiped the sweat from his brow, the same sweat that materialized whenever he thought of the Norse beauty. He found he couldn't argue with the lad. Hadn't he acted like a lovesick fool over Sela these last weeks?

The pain that had ripped through him as he watched the portcullis drop between them still felt raw—not lessened by the knowledge that she'd agreed to spy for them. Or that it had been her idea.

She'd kept her decision from him, and that hurt, too.

One thing that he knew without question—he sure as hell wanted her. At first he'd felt naught but lust whenever he looked at her lips, those deep blue eyes, and the silky strands that fell down to her hips. That feeling had changed into a burning need to claim her. To protect her.

Mine.

He wanted to scream to the world that she belonged to him, that he wasn't afraid of having a powerful woman walk beside him. Together, they would be unstoppable.

Thoughts of Sela kept rolling through his head, persistent as the tide, as he dismounted on the edges of Berwick. He and Thorn tied Midnight Moon to a tree and made their way down the dark streets of the town. No moon showed behind the rolling clouds. The streets were bustling despite the hour.

Thorn whispered, "You could buy us each a meat pie, my lord."

"I told you not to call me that here. I don't want anyone knowing I'm of noble blood."

"Sorry, Connor. Now about those meat pies…"

Something odd called to Connor from behind them. He wasn't sure what his gut was telling him, but he sensed she was close. A smile lifted his lips when he realized what he was reacting to.

Quiet. The street had quieted, and he knew what had caused it. Thorn was right about Sela, after all—she'd be considered a fearsome beauty wherever she went. "Hush, lad," he whispered to Thorn. "She's coming. We need to head over to that copse of trees across from Buck's Inn." He grabbed Thorn's hand and hauled him over to the hidden area off the main path. If she had any guards with her, he didn't want them to see him.

Just as he'd expected, she came around the corner with two guards, one on either side of her. "Shite, you've got to distract her guards." They watched as the group came closer, but Sela and the guards came to a sudden stop outside a nearby alehouse and she motioned for the guards to go inside.

"Thorn, stand watch. Warn me when they return, then you'll get your meat pie," he said, handing a coin to the lad, who took off in a flash.

As soon as Sela was alone, Connor stepped away from the copse of trees, standing close enough to duck behind them if need be. "Sela, come to me," he whispered, though he feared she wouldn't. Had this short jaunt into her old life changed her?

She faced him, but the Ice Queen was back, her face like the covering of a loch in winter, unmoving and unreadable. Glancing over her shoulder, she took two steps toward him. She covered the next steps in a run.

Sela fell into his arms and he carried her behind the tree, his lips finding hers in the dark. He devoured her, his passion unbridled as he moved his mouth over hers. His breath coming out in a ragged whisper, he managed to ask, "They've not hurt you?"

"Nay," she replied, panting with the same need that possessed him. She kissed a line down his jaw. "Connor, will you take me away when this is over? Please?"

"Aye, I cannot stand being apart. I worry about you. It eats at my insides to know you're with them," he said. Unable to get enough of her, he cupped her breast through her gown, teasing her nipple until it peaked under the fabric.

She pulled away slightly, staring at him, and touched her finger to his lower lip. "You really do care for me, do you not? You're not just interested in bedding me?"

Her question, so bluntly phrased, caused all the uncertainty he'd felt about them to drain away. "Aye. I'll not lie, Sela, I want you, but I also care about you. I would like to *know* you. To have a future with you. I liked waking up with you in my arms."

"Will we ever be together?" Her eyes misted with the tears he couldn't bear for her to shed.

"Hush, know that I will fight for us to be together. What have you learned? Where are the youngest ones being held?"

"Only ten have arrived so far. They seem to be sisters and they think they're traveling to visit an aunt. 'Tis all I know. They are being held in a manor home north of the port. They would refuse to come with you at this point because they believe whatever tale they're being told. The others will be here on the morrow. One group in the morn, one late in the day. The ships leave mid-afternoon the following day. Three of them."

"Where?" he asked, kissing the hollow at the base of her

throat.

Her hands threaded through his hair, pulling him closer. "I don't know. They've not told me yet. They don't fully trust me."

Thorn ran up to them, his body thrumming with energy. "My lord, I mean Connor, they're coming!"

Connor gave her one last kiss. "High noon on the morrow. Same place."

The look she gave him, full of longing and not a single crystal of ice, humbled him. It made him desperate to carry her away from this place, to bring her somewhere she could be safe. But Sela left him before he could change his mind. She arrived in the middle of the path before her guards came out of the building, carrying fruit tarts and two ales.

Her icy look had returned.

"You like her, do you not, Connor?"

Connor sighed—Thorn was too perceptive by half—but he wouldn't lie to the lad. He knew how he felt. He didn't want to live without her. They belonged together. "Aye, I surely do like her, lad."

Thorn sighed, mimicking him. "But she's a *girl*."

"Get your meat pie," he said, giving him a small shove in the direction of the vendor.

That would give him the moment he needed because he had an important decision to make.

Should he stay or should he leave?

CHAPTER FOURTEEN

CONNOR STOOD IN THE SAME spot the next day, well after the sun was at its highest. Where the hell could she be?

Thorn said, "I think we should travel the path near the castle again, see if anything new is happening."

While Connor hated to leave the spot where he'd promised to meet Sela, he couldn't wait all day for her. If the group that had arrived was as large as they suspected, it was possible she wouldn't be able to break free.

It was in the Band's best interest for them to see what else they could learn around town. Maggie and Will were also in Berwick, gleaning information, but in a different area. The other cousins had remained back to guide the warriors.

Maggie had requested that the hundred warriors who'd set up camp an hour outside of the burgh join them at high noon just outside of Berwick. She wanted them at the ready for anything that could arise. All total, they now numbered nearly three hundred, with another two hundred ready to move forward.

But where was the Channel? Sela's failure to appear wasn't the only sign something was wrong. They hadn't seen any Dubh men out and about.

"Are you sure you'd recognize the Dubh men, lad?"

"Aye, they travel together, they speak to no one, they don't wear identifiable plaids. I don't see them here."

After a quick jaunt down near the port, they found Maggie and Will in the center of town. There weren't many about so they were easy to find.

"What have you learned?" Maggie asked. "Did Sela have any more information for you?"

Connor shrugged. "She never came. I know not what happened to her, but I suspect the next group arrived and she's been put in charge of them. Have you seen any unusual activity?"

"Nay, naught," Maggie confirmed. "And yet...something feels off."

He agreed and said so. They found their way to a vendor to purchase food, which allowed them the chance to chat with the two men behind the stand. "Things seem different this day," Connor said, speaking to the one who kept scanning the area. The man seemed far more interested in what was going on in town than in his present customers. "Something going to happen that we don't know about?"

The man leaned toward him, and in a whisper said, "Aye, I hear there's a large group of English knights headed this way."

"For what purpose?" Will asked, moving closer.

"I hear they're after the group of savage Highlanders that showed up at the castle gates the other day. They don't usually try to hide, so 'tis most unusual that they disappeared so quickly." He pointed to the man working next to him, who gave them a wide grin.

"We know most of what goes on in the town."

Connor was glad they'd dressed all in black to avoid being easily recognizable. "What are the knights planning?"

"We heard they're going to take over the town and keep the Highlanders out."

Thorn scampered off down the street, much to Connor's surprise. Usually he liked to be part of the conversations they intercepted. Then he noticed why. The lad did more pishing than anyone he knew.

He shifted his attention back to the men. "You're certain they're coming here?"

"Nay, not inside the town. They'll be on the periphery, keeping unwanteds out. Only those who live inside Berwick will be allowed in. That will keep the savages away."

As soon as they stepped away, Maggie said, "We must go back and advise the others of what we learned. We'll catch the knights off-guard."

"My lord!" Thorn rushed up to Connor and tugged on his tunic sleeve. "Guess what I heard? There's to be a game here in the town this day."

"Never mind, Thorn. We're mounting up and going off to fight the English knights. We need to be ready to do battle."

His words were clearly music to the lad's ears, for he jumped up and down in delight. "I'm coming, my lord."

———◆———

Sela scanned the area for the tenth time, still hoping they'd be discovered in the middle of this dastardly deed. The sixty lasses around her had arrived late the night before. This group was entirely different from the last. These lasses had been kidnapped and kept locked up overnight. They fought every step of the way. Since they were so difficult, Dee had decided to send them out first. The calm group would go on the second boat.

She wished to free the lasses, or to run as fast as she could to find Connor and tell them what was happening. Unfortunately, her behavior was intently scrutinized by Guy and Dee.

And Hord—the sick bastard.

She'd helped usher them to the top of the hill they'd just crested south of Berwick, surrounded by men with swords—men she'd never seen before. Hired hands. Many of them.

And there were more still to come.

Guy and Dee barked orders at everyone, their mood soured by the crying and squealing girls. The lasses clung to one another as they were forced down the hill, along the shoreline, and then ushered into the underbelly of a boat where they huddled together like criminals. Men shoved them along, hollering at them. She'd been told they were to be sent off in this boat originally intended for the smaller group, although she couldn't imagine how so many lasses would be able to sleep in the close space.

Hord trailed behind them, bellowing to Dee. "The next group will be here in an hour."

"Perfect. Send the knights to the north side of Berwick where the Highlanders are camped. Draw them out for three hours and we'll be done."

Sela couldn't believe her ears. Had she heard them right? Did they truly mean to do battle with the Highlanders?

Connor, where are you?

"Sela," Guy said, "move them into the boat faster. Tell them to stop their crying or we'll send spiders after them."

"Where did you get so many?" Sela asked, surprised at the number and their obvious innocence. Their language was not Scots or Gaelic, but a form of English unfamiliar to her.

"They all came from an abbey in England. We promised to ship them to an abbey in France. They wish to do the Lord's work in Europe." Guy made his statement as boldly as if it were truthful.

"Aye," Hord said with a snort, "they'll be doing the Lord's work, will they not?" He stepped closer to Sela. "Did you know that I will be escorting these lasses to France? Aye, I've got a wonderful berth just for me. I'm going along to be certain they'll behave." He lifted his jacket to expose the bag he carried.

The kind he used to hold spiders.

She wouldn't wish such a fate upon anyone, although a small, still-selfish part of her couldn't help but cheer that she would finally be free of him.

"I am allowed one companion. Guess who I'm choosing?" he said, leaning close enough to touch her jaw. "*You.*"

CHAPTER FIFTEEN

CONNOR STOOD IN THE MIDDLE of the cousins back in the Grant camp, now over one hundred and fifty strong. The Highlanders continued to dribble in— Menzies, Camerons, Grants. His confidence was waning. True, they had the numbers to take on many warriors, but what were the Dubh men planning? Where *were* they?

And where the hell was Sela?

They'd turned up nothing in Berwick. They'd even sent Thorn into Berwick Castle, but it had appeared deserted.

A sentry came racing toward them. "A large group of chain-mailed knights is headed this way. Reportedly an hour south of here."

Maggie spoke to the heads of the groups—Uncle Logan, Connor's sire, Uncle Drew, and Uncle Micheil. "Prepare your warriors. But do not slay Guy or Dee. We need them for information. 'Tis a long coastline and the lasses could be anywhere."

The men each moved to their groups. Connor turned around to cast his gaze over the gathered warriors. It was quite impressive. Braden and Roddy came up behind him. "Hard to believe we have such a group," Roddy said, clasping his shoulder. "With another hundred or more Grant warriors joining us soon. We'll put a quick end to this, aye?"

Connor was uneasy. Something wasn't right.

"Connor, you don't look convinced. What is it?" Braden

asked.

"I can't put it into words. A group of English knights is coming for us, but are they part of the Channel or were they just hired by the Dubh men? It doesn't feel right—especially because we couldn't uncover any of the Channel's tracks in Berwick. 'Tis as if they've disappeared."

Roddy said, "Then we must find them after we defeat this group. The numbers will be in our favor then, and if we must take the entire town as ransom, we'll do it."

Braden said, "Aye, someone must know something."

Connor quirked his brow, more uncertain than ever.

———◆———

Thorn was so excited that he would probably pish himself. He was going to be part of a big battle with the Grants of the Highlands. Everyone had heard of Alexander Grant and his prowess at the Battle of Largs. Thorn had eaten in his hall and even spoken to him, and now he'd see him in action. Gwyneth Ramsay would join the fighting, too. Everyone had heard the tales of how she could pin a man's bollocks to a tree with her arrows.

He giggled at the thought. Lasses could be quite fierce. Much like Sela.

It had surprised him to see Connor kissing Sela last eve. Although he'd gone off to spy on the guards, he'd looked back to see them wrapped around each other. What kind of devil's curse had the Ice Queen cast over him? Connor was the strongest and biggest lad he'd ever met, yet he wasn't safe from the beauty.

Thorn didn't understand why men got so foolish over lasses, though he knew his mother would have been the sweetest mama ever if she hadn't died birthing him. In fact, his sire used to tell him his mother always watched over him.

He wondered if his sire did, too, now that he was dead. If so, he hoped his father was watching how good he was doing. He wished to make him proud.

After seeing Connor and Sela together like that, he'd turned back toward the guards in the ale house, quick as he could. They'd been whispering and laughing to each other. He heard them say something about knights coming to attack the savages. He didn't know if that meant the Highlanders or not. Then he heard some words he didn't understand. One called it all a ruse and the other said it was a wily ploy on Guy's part.

He didn't know what any of that meant, but now that he thought about it, he'd heard much the same from the men he'd listened to while he was pishing in the town. They'd been talking about a ruse of knights.

What was a ruse? Did it mean a huge number? Or perhaps the "ruse" knights were the very meanest? Aye, that must be what they'd meant. It was a cruel group of knights coming. A ruse group.

See, he'd tell Nari. They could figure things out if they thought hard enough. He squared his shoulders at his clever findings and stepped closer to the group of cousins.

He listened to them talking, waiting for them to talk more of the battle.

"I fear 'tis a ruse," Connor said, shaking his head.

There it was, that word again!

Thorn tugged on Connor's tunic, trying to explain everything to him, but Connor shushed him with the wave of his hand. He tugged harder on Connor's tunic, again and again, until the great warrior finally looked down. "We're about to go to battle. What is so important that you must interrupt me?"

Thorn looked up at him, his neck tipping way back, and said, "What does that word mean? 'Tis the same word the men with Sela used."

Braden made a motion to silence the lad, but Connor stopped him. "What word, lad?" He knelt down so he was face to face with him. "What word?"

"Ruse."

"Tell me exactly what they said, and you'll never be without a meat pie if you want one."

"One man said the knights were a ruse, but I didn't know what that meant. The other man called them a wily ploy. Does that mean anything special? Does it mean they are extra cruel? Or something else?"

Connor grinned and lifted Thorn into the air, tossing him over his head. Although he didn't understand what had Connor so excited, he squealed with delight. "Aye, it does mean something else. Go get Nari and have him bring Gregor and Gavin." He called out to some of his cousins, the ones called Maggie and Will, waving them over. Thorn passed along the message, quick as he could, then dragged Nari back toward Connor. The great Alexander Grant had joined him, along with Logan Ramsay, the Beast of the Highlands. The two were quite impressive together.

But not as impressive as Connor. He was the biggest and the best.

Had anything more exciting ever happened?

"What is it?" Maggie asked.

"'Tis a ruse," Connor said. "The knights are a ruse to keep us busy while they load the ships and set sail early. 'Tis exactly as I suspected, and Thorn overheard the men with Sela discussing it. They didn't tell her they were planning to leave early because they don't trust her."

"Take your cousins and go down to shore," Alex said. "Forget the castle but examine the entire coastline. We'll stay here and fight the English fools, keep them busy so they'll not bother you."

Another couple of men walked over—two more of the cousins. Thorn was shocked and fascinated to see one of them lacked a hand. They were with another, older man, who looked a wee bit like Logan. "Change of strategy?" the man asked.

"Aye," Logan said. "The cousins are going to the coastline in case there is a ship ready to sail. We'll stay and handle the knights."

Connor turned to Thorn, who was hopping up and down as he listened, unable to stay still in his excitement. "This will be the big battle. Would you and Nari like to stay to watch the Highlanders take the English knights down?"

Thorn grabbed a hold of Nari's hand. "We may?"

"Aye, but you're to keep on eye on each other. No separating. We'll be back later."

Alex Grant looked at the two lads, fearsome enough that Thorn nearly pished himself, then crooked a finger at them. He tossed them both onto the back of his destrier, the biggest animal Thorn had ever seen. Although he could hardly think for excitement, he glanced back at his friend.

Connor was looking at his cousins, all of whom were gathered before him. Connor said, "Head for the coastline and the port. Will, Maggie, and I will take the south end. Gavin, Gregor, and Roddy, you take the middle. Braden, Daniel, and David take the north end. This is our one chance. We mustn't waste it."

And the cousins, all eight of them, were off.

———◆———

Sela's mind was barely functioning because her fear had overtaken everything. Her actions were rote as she helped herd the lasses onto the ship.

Her mind was busy planning her escape. She had to get away from Hord. She had to let the cousins know the location of the ship. But there was one problem—a big problem.

She couldn't swim.

Every thought she had of escaping involved jumping over the side of the ship. Jumping over or waiting until they were far out before she crept down the rope ladder on the side and swam back. Both plans had merit. It would probably be dark before they sailed away, and she wouldn't be seen in the murky waters.

But she couldn't swim.

What the hell was she to do now?

CHAPTER SIXTEEN

———◆———

CONNOR HAD BEEN STARTING TO think they'd never find the lasses in time, but they heard sounds of activity as they approached a small turn in the coastline. From behind a copse of trees, they watched the activity in the small cove. Screaming, crying, wailing lasses were being loaded into a ship.

They'd found them.

He scanned the area for a lass with white-blonde hair, and there she was on the deck, though she shouldn't be able to see them yet. His first instinct was to bellow with joy because the bastards hadn't gotten away with their ruse. They hadn't spirited off Sela and the other lasses. Then he saw two bastards he recognized—the leaders of the Channel.

When he pointed them out to the others, Maggie's jaw went slack and the color leached from her face. Will put his hand on her back. "Maggie? What is it?"

"I recognize those two men."

"You do? Where have you seen them before?" Connor asked, shocked that she knew them.

"They worked for Randall Baines, the Earl of Wingate. One is Gerold deVere and the other is Lawrence Granville. One was his marshal and the other his seneschal."

Randall Baines was the one who'd begun it all. Maggie and her sister Molly had lived with him and his mother as servants when they were lassies. His cruelty had left marks on both of them. Maggie had gone off in search of him, wanting to face her past, and in so doing she'd discovered he was involved in shipping lasses across the sea. Baines was dead, but his work had deeper roots. They'd discovered the Channel after he died.

Connor nodded. "Dee would be deVere. Guy is probably Granville."

Maggie dropped her head into her hands. "Why did I not think of this before? His men continued it. Of course. They've been in charge this whole time."

"Do not fault yourself, lass," Will said, rubbing the small of her back. "We had no way of knowing his men would continue the horrific venture."

Connor patted her shoulder. "My guess is they waited a while before they started the group up again, waiting to see if there were any repercussions coming their way. Had you gone after them back then, you'd have found naught."

Maggie's eyes teared up. "They fooled me completely."

"And what does my wife plan to do about it?" Will asked, wiping the tears from her cheeks. "Is this not your chance to pay them back?"

"You're right," she said, her tone fierce. "I want that bastard deVere myself. I remember him well."

Connor said, "He's all yours. I'd like to twist Hord's thick neck, but first we must ensure that boat doesn't leave."

Gavin, Gregor, and Roddy rode up, their horses huffing from exertion. "We found naught in the middle of the port, but I see why," said Gavin. "How shall we do this?"

"I wish we had our horses, but they'd be of no help in this landscape. The terrain is rocky coming down the slope, part of the reason the lasses are screaming. They keep losing their footing."

Maggie looked to Gavin and Gregor. "Are the men clear enough targets for your bows? We cannot risk hitting the lasses."

"Aye," Gregor said without hesitation. "With your help,

we can take out half of them while the rest of the cousins charge them with hand-to-hand combat."

Gavin's gaze scanned the area. "One of us up here, two of us above the beach in those trees halfway down the hill. Give us one moment to place ourselves and then the rest is in your hands, Grants and Drummonds."

Maggie stayed while Gavin and Gregor descended to find perches above the beach. "Godspeed," she said to the others. "Finishing this group will end the Channel. I'm certain of it."

After giving Gavin and Gregor time to find their positions, Connor, Braden, and Roddy let out their Grant war whoop and went after the Dubh men.

Connor's gaze searched the area, finally settling on Sela down near the ship. He only allowed himself to look at her for a moment before he charged at Guy. Better known as Granville. The man was so surprised he couldn't even get his sword out of its sheath. Connor drove his sword into his black heart and said, "Give my greetings to Baines in hell, you bastard."

He turned to search for others to fight, pleased to see many men dropping from his cousins' arrows. The lasses' screams filled the air as they ran to the boat for shelter. They didn't know the cousins had come to save them, not hurt them.

Much to Connor's shock, Dee dragged Maggie down from the hill. He must have caught sight of her in the trees or followed the path of her arrows, most of which had made their mark, to her hiding spot. Yanking on her hair, he pulled her along, slapping and beating her like a man turned daft.

"You bitch! This is all your fault." He swung his fist and hit her square in the jaw. "You should have died in that crate in Inverness."

Maggie kicked him and pulled out a dagger tucked inside her boot. She swung it at him but only left a shallow slice across his belly. It bled profusely but was not a mortal wound.

"I'll teach you to touch me," he growled, grabbing her weapon and twisting her arm behind her back.

Connor raced toward her and bellowed, "Will!" Her husband hadn't noticed the attack yet, but as soon as he heard Connor shouting his name, he took off at a dead run straight for Maggie, whistling for his falcons.

Although Will was closer, Connor fell in behind him, cursing when Dee slapped his cousin again. The falcons swooped down to peck him just as Will reached the two. From the way the bastard shrieked, Connor was pleased to see the birds were doing their best to frighten him. Will allowed the show to go on for a short time, but as soon as Dee—DeVere—let go of Maggie, he grabbed the man's tunic and nailed him with two punches. When Dee fell to the ground, Will put his foot on the bastard's chest and nodded to his wife. Maggie grasped her dagger with tears in her eyes then swung it over her head with a growl, stabbing him through the heart. Will assisted her, using enough force that he made sure the bastard took his last breath.

Guy was dead. Dee was dead. Most of the Channel appeared to be dead on the ground, though there were still some near the shoreline. Enough so they could question one of them about the final shipment. Or mayhap Sela would know where the lads and lasses were being kept.

Was it almost over?

Will picked Maggie up and held her close.

Connor turned around to check on the ship, and shock raced through him, nearly buckling his knees. Sela was aboard the boat—and Hord was releasing the final ties holding them to the posts.

"Get off the ship!" Connor yelled at the top of his lungs. "Sela, get the hell off the ship. He's pulling the ropes."

But moments after the words left his mouth, the ship started drifting away from shore. Connor killed another five men trying to get to the ship, but there was suddenly an endless supply of guards. The more he fought, the farther the ship moved.

"Sela, jump!"

———◆———

Sela had watched all in shock. Connor killing Guy. Dee attacking Maggie. Maggie killing Dee.

She couldn't believe they were both dead.

"Get off the ship!" Connor yelled. "Sela, get the hell off the ship. He's pulling the ropes."

The words jolted her out of her passive state. When she turned to see what he meant, she saw Hord untying the ropes on the posts, setting them out to sea.

The confused lasses kept climbing onto the ship, thinking they were climbing to safety.

"Nay, nay! Go back. These men are evil!"

Many of them ignored her, some shoving and pushing to get aboard the ship while others ran back to the shore. This was probably her last chance to jump and land in the water shallow enough for her to walk to safety, but she'd have to leave the lasses. When she looked at their innocent faces, she knew she couldn't do it.

Every one of them looked like her daughter.

She went to the ladder, knocking the girls climbing up back into the water. "Go back. Those men in black won't hurt you. They're here to save you."

She pulled the ladder up into the boat so no one else could get in. Then she did what she had to do.

She grabbed the two closest to her and pushed them back over the side of the boat, one by one. The other girls who'd climbed aboard looked at her questioningly. She said, "Go, they're planning to sell you. Get off now." Many of the lasses jumped overboard, but a few stayed.

Hord screamed at her, threatening to hurt her again, but she ignored him, shoving one more lass into the waist-deep water. When words wouldn't sway her, he grabbed her by her long plait, yanking her backward toward the end of the boat. "Leave them be. I must have a few to sell. And you are coming with me!" he bellowed, yanking even harder. He tugged her up against him until she heard the crunch of the spider bag, which caused her throat to fill with an awful liquid and her heartbeat to speed up uncontrollably.

Swinging her arms, she did what she could to fight the bastard, but he wouldn't let go. She watched the shoreline grow more and more distant. After witnessing her attack, all but one of the remaining girls jumped overboard. The one who stayed stared at her with a sick look she couldn't interpret.

Hord held her close and started to fumble with his bag. He said, "I'll stuff them in your mouth if I must, but you'll do as I say."

Sela jutted both of her elbows into his mid-section, hitting him with a big "oof," much to her delight. Then she stomped on his foot with all her strength.

"Bitch!" he shouted, but he didn't release her. She stomped on his feet two more times until he finally let go. She raced to the other end of the ship, grabbing the last girl by the hand and shouting, "Come. We must go now."

Maggie and Will waited at the shoreline, helping the girls out of the water and over to a place where they could huddle together.

Sela stood on the edge of the ship, the lass fighting her a bit, which puzzled her, but she refused to leave her behind. "Come, we must go now."

She looked down into the churning sea, wondering how deep it was. Why did the girl continue to fight her? Then she knew. She turned her head to her and said, "Now."

The poor girl looked at her, eyes full of desperation, and said, "I can't swim."

"I can't either, so we'll go together."

Even if they died, it would be a better fate than what

Hord would give them.

Hord said, "Sela, if you climb up there, I'll set the spiders lose on you, I swear."

She glanced back over her shoulder, taking the girl's hand in hers, preparing to jump.

Just before she leaped over the side of the boat, she saw Connor wading out toward them. She caught his gaze and yelled, "I can't swim."

And then she jumped over the lip of the boat, taking the squealing lass with her.

The last thing she heard before she hit the water was Connor. "Kick your feet!"

CHAPTER SEVENTEEN

———◆———

CONNOR HAD THOUGHT ALL WOULD be well. Guy and Dee were both dead. Many of the guards were dead, others had run off, and Sela had wisely begun to push the lasses over the side of the ship. They landed safely in water that wasn't over their heads—or at least they did until the boat was nearly empty. The remaining girls were jumping into deep water. *Sela* would have to jump into deep water. He swam out, Gavin and Gregor joining him to assist the lasses who were being dragged down by their heavy skirts.

Then Sela yelled something that nearly stopped his heart. She couldn't swim.

Hellfire, how could anyone not learn to swim?

"Kick your feet when you land," he yelled, swimming as hard as he could for her.

Gavin had also heard her declaration so he headed to the same area.

Sela and the lass whose hand she held went under together, and they were under for so long that Connor felt sure he would vomit.

"Gavin, where are they? Look for air bubbles. Do you see anything?"

He ducked underwater to see what he could find, but all the lasses had stirred up the bottom enough to keep him from seeing. He came up just in time to see Sela's head come above water, her one hand reaching for him.

He grabbed her, pulling her close, just as she pulled on her other hand. Her companion sputtered above water. Gavin grabbed the lass, who latched on to him eagerly, almost taking him underwater, but Connor yelled, "Stay calm or we'll go back under."

Only then did he let himself focus on the lass in his arms. It felt impossibly right to hold her. "You're hale, love?"

She nodded, choking up a bit of water.

"Why did you stay on the boat so long? Have you a death wish?"

Sela shook her head, tears flooding her cheeks. "I couldn't leave any of them with Hord. And the other men ignored us. They were just there to work the oars."

"Don't look back," Connor said, "He's still on board, staring over, but something tells me he won't be back for a while."

They'd finally reached a spot in the water where he could touch the bottom and stand up. As soon as she could, she threw her arms around him and said, "Connor Grant, take me far, far away from here."

He stopped briefly to confer with his cousins. Maggie and Will had three men tied up. They planned to bring them back to her sire and his father for questioning.

"Sela, what know you of the other boats and shipments?" Maggie asked.

She said, "There are about twenty lasses being held in the manor home at the end of the main street in the village. If you don't know it, I can take you there. The other shipment will be arriving at the same home in two hours."

Will said, "I know exactly where she's talking about. We'll go there, free the lasses they have, and await the third shipment. Anything else you can tell us?"

She shook her head, but then she thought for a moment. "Just that they supposedly have English knights here to keep the Highlanders from entering the village. Clearly, you managed to get past them."

"We need confirmation that this ends the Channel."

Sela nodded. "If Guy and Dee are dead, the Channel is dead. They didn't wish to share their power with anyone else. I've heard them arguing about it with Hord and others. The rest of their workers only collected small coin."

Maggie smiled. "I can only hope you're right. We'll check out our sources and free the lasses in the manor home."

"I'm taking Sela to get her things, then we'll see you back at camp." As he walked away, he glanced back over his shoulder. "Tell Thorn I'll be there by this eve."

Connor led Sela back up the hill into the town, surprised it was so quiet. He stopped at a food vendor along the way and said, "What goes on this day?" Sela had a death grip on his hand as if she feared she'd be discovered and whisked away, so when the man turned to prepare their food, Connor leaned over and kissed her cheek. "All is well. I'll protect you."

She smiled. It didn't quite meet her eyes, but he understood. She'd been under the Channel's control for so long that she likely struggled to believe her ordeal was over.

She was free.

The vendor whistled. "Big news today. English knights went after a group of Highlanders, but the Scots were well over two hundred strong and made easy work of them. Those of us loyal to the Scots are pleased, though some of King Edward's loyal supporters are both shocked and disappointed. It will be a task to bury their dead. I've heard they're to be returned to English soil, though I've not heard who will come forward to do this."

"All is quiet in Berwick?"

"Many are in hiding. All will return to normal this eve, I'm sure, once the ale is flowing again."

The man passed over the meat pies Connor had ordered, and he broke one in two and handed half to Sela. As they walked away, he said, "Where are your things?"

She pointed. "In that inn. When I returned from Grant

land, they said they'd not trust me to stay at the keep anymore. The inn was where I slept alone, although they kept
guards posted outside day and night, not because of me but
because of the wagering going on. Their coin was heavily
guarded. All the men who watched me were at that beach,
so there'll be no guards." She pointed at a door. "We'll not
be noticed if we use the back entrance."

They headed in that direction, circling around the
building. When they stepped inside, Connor said, "Just a
moment." He headed to what was usually the busy part of
an inn—the alehouse.

It was empty.

"There's no one here."

"Good. There rarely is during the day, and my guess is
there won't be anyone here this eve, either. The Channel
controlled it."

She led him up the stairs to her chamber, closing the
door behind them. Once it was shut, she pulled him to her,
turning him so his back was to the door, and kissed him.

She stopped long enough to say, "Make love to me, Connor."

Between her kiss and the thrill of victory, he didn't need
to be asked again. The blood still roared through him from
battle, from knowing they'd won the day, and he didn't
need to be asked again. He wanted this woman more than
he wanted air.

"I can't believe I'm free," she whispered, tugging her wet
clothes off and tossing them on the floor. She reached for
his tunic, pulling it from him and throwing it against a wall.
"My thanks to you and yours."

He assisted her with her clothing as best he could, but
her hands were everywhere on him, distracting him terribly.

"Now, now, now…" she whispered, her teeth nipping at
his ear and his neck. "I want you, Connor Grant. I need
you. I need to feel free…to do what I want…and I want

you."

Connor growled and doffed his plaid, standing in front of her in just his boots, but he picked her up with a roar and his lips traveled all over her skin. He wanted to be rough, to take her hard, but he forced himself to slow down. He set her feet back on the ground and kissed her deeply, tasting her with a voraciousness he'd only felt for her.

Her pull on him was something he could not fight. He dipped his head to take her breast in his mouth, running his tongue all over the full mound before suckling on her nipple. He ran his teeth over the taut peak until she moaned, a sound that drove him to do the same to the other breast.

Her hands locked behind his neck and her small sounds ate away at his control, his need for her, to finish, just insatiable. Picking her up, he settled her against the wall and whispered, "Guide me, Sela. Show me you want me," his voice so deep he wondered if she'd even heard him. He knew from the glazed look in her eyes that she was lost in the depth of her own need.

She reached for him and, after a tease or two, guided him to her entrance.

"Connor, look at me," she whispered, holding him at just the right spot. "Please, I need to see 'tis you."

He locked gazes with her. "Guide me. I need you, Sela. Now."

She spread her legs, allowing him to feel her slickness, and wrapped her legs around his waist. He thrust into her with a growl, pushing in to make sure he was fully seated. He stared into her eyes, and her one word undid him.

"More," she said, her hands now gripping his upper arms.

He picked up his rhythm, banging her against the wall, until he found just the right tempo and placement. She arched against him, trying to take him in deeper, her voice now coming in the lightest of gasps.

"Am I hurting you?" he managed to ask, fearing he was plunging into her too hard.

"Nay, faster, harder…"

He did as she asked, his hands now underneath her bottom, and he was able to hit her just the way he wanted. It must have suited her because she clamped against him with a gasp, climaxing with just a few more thrusts. The sounds she made drove him over the edge and he buried his face in her neck, taking in her scent and everything about her.

Hellfire, he'd never had it like this.

———◆———

Sela clung to him, not wanting to let go. She loved the sensation of his skin against hers. He set her feet down, but just as her heart started to sink—was he leaving?—he reached out and cradled her cheeks.

"That was amazing," he said through his panting.

She tried to calm her breathing, but every time she looked at him, her need seemed to come back. Reaching up to touch his hair, something she had long wished to do, she ran her fingers through the dark locks wet with sweat. "Your hair is curling."

He grinned. "It does that when I cannot handle the heat. Seems you do that to me." He kissed her neck, her ear, and then her lips. "You enjoyed it?"

Enjoyed wasn't the word that came to mind. She loved it, but she wasn't ready to share that thought yet. Uncertain of what to say, she simply told him, "I didn't know it could be like that."

He picked her up and carried her to the bed, setting her down and lying next to her, his arm around her waist. "I don't imagine...never mind. I would prefer to talk about just us."

She had to agree. Her first experiences had been awful, not something she wished to think about now. "Then I'll say that was a fabulous experience, unlike anything I've done before."

He kissed her cheek. "I have to agree."

They stayed like that for a few minutes, each listening to the other's breathing. Sela was still shocked that the building and all of Berwick was so quiet.

"I'm free," she whispered, tears in her eyes.

"You are. Free to do as you wish. Dee and Guy will never control you again." He leaned on his elbow and ran his finger down her jawline.

"What should we do now?"

"We meet with the Grant warriors, hear the story of the battle, and then we head back to Ramsay land. Your daughter is there with my mother. From there, you can decide where you would like to settle."

She took his hand and stared up at the ceiling, hoping it would stop the tears.

"Have you no family at all?" Connor pressed.

She shook her head, still not looking at him. "I'm alone. Just Claray and me. I don't know what to do."

"Not if I have anything to say about it. You'll never be alone."

She cupped his cheek, not knowing what to say.

It was probably too soon to tell him how much she was falling for him.

CHAPTER EIGHTEEN

———◆———

CONNOR AND SELA MADE IT back to the warriors' camp. As soon as they neared the battlefield, Connor whispered to her, "Don't look. 'Tis not a pretty sight."

Even he hadn't seen anything like it in his lifetime. Peering at the sea of dead bodies, of chainmail and blood, of horses wandering and searching for their fallen masters, he understood a little more about his sire's experiences.

Alex and his brothers, Uncle Brady and Uncle Robbie, had taken part in the Battle of Largs, a battle fought—and won—for the return of the Western Isles to the King of Scotland. Connor had grown up on tales of the bloody battle. His older cousins had also fought many battles against Glenn of Buchan and his men.

The gore before him was unlike anything he'd ever seen.

His next thought gripped him tight and wouldn't let go. Had anyone from his clan been hurt? A group of Grant and Ramsay plaids were clustered at the far end of the field, plus a few dressed in black. He tugged on the reins to get Midnight Moon to move quicker.

He had to know.

"Connor, you are all right? Did you see someone you know hurt?" Sela whispered to him.

"Nay, I'm just concerned. My father, Uncle Logan, Uncle Micheil…they're no longer young. I wish to see them with my own eyes."

When they approached the group, his gut clenched a bit

more until he was close enough to hear them speaking. They were cracking light-hearted jokes. Surprised to see his cousin Loki there, he approached the group without hesitation. After helping Sela down, he took her hand and rushed over to the group.

Something inside him loosened when he saw his sire standing at the back of the group. "Papa, you are alive."

"Aye, while my bones will be yelling at me on the morrow, I made it through much better than the wimpy English did. Chainmail and all, they barely made for a battle. 'Tis the good news. The only bad news is over there." He pointed to a group gathered around someone seated on a log. Maggie appeared to be giving medical treatment to someone who was seemingly a poor patient.

"What happened?" he asked.

Loki spun around, clasped his shoulder, and said, "Pleased to see you hale, cousin, but our uncle didn't make it through quite so well." He had the look of laughter all over his face, but he kept it inside.

"Maggie, make it quick, will you not?" The grumbling voice of Uncle Logan carried over to him.

"Logan, don't make her job any more difficult," Aunt Gwyneth scolded from the cluster of people surrounding the patient.

Connor said, "What happened?"

"I'll tell you what happened," Uncle Logan barked, only to cut himself off with a bellow when Maggie's needle pierced his skin.

Loki said, "Rat bastard who got him waited until Uncle Logan charged after a different fool. The man caught his outer thigh as he was going down."

"Right before I cut the bastard down again for daring to touch me... Ow, Maggie!"

Aunt Gwyneth turned around. "I'm walking away before I twist his neck. Poor Maggie."

"No sympathy from my wife, Gwynie?"

"Not when you're acting like a fool," she hollered over her shoulder.

Connor turned because he heard a group approaching. The rest of his cousins joined them.

"Sela, 'twas a fine job you did encouraging those lasses to jump into the sea rather than stay on the boat." Gregor nodded to her, and Gavin joined him. "If you'd waited any longer, they'd be halfway to France by now."

Sela blushed. "I think it was more of a shove than an encouragement, but I couldn't allow them to be become Hord's victims. Were you able to find the other group? Know you where to return the lasses? They were from an abbey, I believe."

"Aye, Maggie found out that many of them were stolen from an English abbey," Daniel said. "They were hosting a retreat for lasses interested in becoming nuns. The poor girls are likely to never step foot in an abbey again, but they've been sent home. When they discovered the truth of the situation, they were grateful for your assistance."

The man she'd once manipulated into fighting in one of her halls in Inverness pulled her into a hug. His acceptance of her was shocking—and liberating. Roddy said, "The other group was found and sent back. The sick lad and lasses Linet tended have also been taken home. Maggie and Will are awaiting the third group. They also wished to stay back to see if Hord attempts to return to Berwick."

David said, "I think we are due a true celebration, and we will do so as soon as we make it to Ramsay land. Papa says we must escort Uncle Logan home so he doesn't kill Aunt Gwyneth."

Connor glanced over at Sela, and he didn't need to ask to know what she was thinking. "Papa, was Mama to stay at Ramsay land? Sela misses her daughter."

Connor's father strode toward him. "Aye, she planned to stay on Ramsay land until this was done. I'll travel with you."

"Aye," Braden said. "As will I. Though I'll not stay long. I wish to be home in time for Yule. One night of celebration, then Roddy and I will return home to Castle Muir. I promised Cairstine and Steenie I'd do my best to be back by the holiday."

"We'll be joining Braden for his first Yule," Roddy said. "Is that not your plan, Daniel? I'm sure Constance will wish to come along."

Connor had told her that Roddy and Daniel and their wives lived together in a castle in a remote part of the Western Highlands.

Daniel said, "Aye, we'll share Yule with you all at Braden's."

Connor said, "'Tis hard to believe, but I think our work in the Band of Cousins may finally be done."

"The only piece still unaccounted for is that bastard Hord, but we'll find that bastard and make him pay. I'll await confirmation from Maggie, but I believe the Channel has been closed down," Daniel said with a grin. "She promises to have a big celebration once she's certain."

Connor said, "I look forward to it."

His sire traveled a path around the group, although Connor could see his movements had slowed. "Aye, I'm ready to return to Ramsay land. I promised your mother we'd be home in time for Yule."

"We'll come with you, Papa." He reached into his saddlebag and pulled out some meat pies, a thought occurring to him. "Where is Thorn?"

A speeding vision headed straight for him. "Do I smell meat pies?"

"Aye, you do. I have enough for all, though we may have to split a couple of them." He handed one to Thorn, and another to Nari who hurried up behind him. "How was the battle, lads?"

"The best ever!" Thorn said. "You should see how the Grant warriors cut those bas...ahhh...men down. They were so powerful. I've never seen anything like it. Is that not so, Nari?"

"We met Loki," Nari said, "and he told us we could come live with him. He has a lad Kenzie and he's nice and he has another son and a daughter, and can we live with them?"

Connor said, "'Tis up to you, lads. You'll be welcome on Grant land or Ramsay land, either. I hope you'll stay close."

"Nari and I wish to stay together. Mayhap after all the celebrations, we'll go stay with Loki for a wee bit. May we?"

"If you're both sure. You must decide for yourselves."

"I'm not sure yet," Nari said.

Thorn grinned. "But we'll tell you after another meat pie."

———◆———

Sela didn't quite know how to feel. They had almost reached Ramsay land, a good number of them traveling together, something she loved. Connor's sire; his uncles, Logan and Micheil; and his cousins David, Daniel, Gavin, Gregor, Roddy, and Braden. Maggie and Will had decided to stay in Berwick for a while to make sure the Channel was indeed done. She prayed they would find Hord and bring him to justice. A part of her would never relax until he was caught.

Traveling with this group brought her hope for a new life. How she prayed she and Claray would be welcomed into either Clan Ramsay or Clan Grant. She couldn't imagine how it would feel to be so accepted, so respected, and so loved. The cousins' back and forth banter warmed her insides, although it also made her feel like she was on the outside looking in. Her parents had been loving and kind, yet it had only been the three of them. She'd never had a family like this, but it was something she wanted for Claray.

Claray. Her gut did somersaults at the thought of seeing her daughter. Had Maddie taken good care of her lass? She suspected she had, and indeed, a more persistent fear was that Claray would love Maddie so much she would not want to return to her mother. The poor lass had spent her entire life under the control of the Channel. She'd not had friends, clanmates, or good food. Ramsay Castle must seem like a wonderland in comparison, and Maddie was the one who'd taken her there.

Connor whispered in her ear and said, "I know what you are thinking, and you need not concern yourself."

She glanced back over her shoulder at him. How did he always know her thoughts? "If you know so much, you can answer my questions without hearing them spoken aloud."

He was a wise man, but was he as wise as he thought?

"My experience has shown me that bairns are resilient, and they love unconditionally. Claray will still love you more than my mother, and she'll be thrilled to see you."

Hellfire if he wasn't right. She simply nodded and changed the subject. "The Highlands are much more beautiful than the last time I traveled through these parts."

"This is West Lothian, barely into the Highlands. Grant Castle will be much different."

"I wonder what Linet will have to say to me. Do you think she'll hate me?" She leaned back against him just a bit, both for warmth and just because.

"Nay, I think she'll be grateful. You saved her from a much more difficult life. That's my understanding. You protected her, did you not?" He nuzzled her neck.

"I tried, though I didn't do well in Berwick."

"She understands why. Merewen talked about how you protected her. Linet trusted you—'twas the only reason she was willing to stay within the Channel."

She took in his profile. The man was devastatingly hand-some. Long dark locks, eyes that seemed to turn color from gray to blue. He looked very much like his sire, though

Connor was taller and had broader shoulders. Still, she could see Maddie Grant in him, too. He had her strong, high cheekbones. More importantly, he was thoughtful and caring—attributes she hadn't seen in many men since Guy and Dee had abducted her from her home—and she knew Alex and Maddie had raised him well.

He smiled at her, that wide grin she loved so.

Loved so. Did she love him? After everything she'd been through, everything she'd done, she hadn't thought she was capable of loving anyone other than Claray.

"What are you thinking? You are deep in thought," he said.

"About your parents. How kind they both are, and how well they raised you. 'Tis not an easy thing to do, raising a child properly. They did a fine job."

He laughed, rubbing her arm. "See if you say the same about my siblings."

"How many are there again?"

"Jake and Jamie, the twins, are the eldest and share the lairdship of our clan. Kyla is my sister, and probably the one I'm closest to. She also looks much like me. Elizabeth, who is the image of my mother, was the youngest for a long while, and might I add that my father lets her do things we were never allowed to do."

She had to chuckle at that thought. "The baby is his dearest?"

He nodded. "Then we adopted Maeve, and she also has a piece of my sire's heart. Her favorite place to sit is in his lap. You'll meet them soon."

They came up over another hill and entered a huge meadow with a large castle at the end of it. "Is this it?"

"Aye, this is Ramsay land. I suspect the bairns will be outside soon. They'll be watching for our group to return. My cousin Lily is the one with the twins, Lise and Liliana. I expect Claray has become friends with both of them. They're busy wee lassies, but sweet as can be."

The castle was surrounded by a tall curtain wall with guards at every corner. Outside the gates sat a small village, well-cared for huts arranged in neat rows. She could tell the fields behind them would be tended in the spring to plant grains and vegetables for the clan. A loch sat not far away, serene and beautiful, since there was little wind in the air. A few cottages sat around the loch, and one end looked quite odd to her.

"What's that at the end of the loch?"

Connor gave a hearty laugh. "'Tis where we swim in the middle of the summer, those who dare. Aunt Brenna always tries to outdo my sire, so she started a rivalry for best loch. She convinced my uncle to set out those logs to give spectators a place to sit and watch the bairns playing in the water. The tables are out there for picnics. Can you see that large tree overhanging the end of the loch?"

"Aye," she said, noticing something hanging from it.

"'Tis a swing Uncle Quade had his men tie to the tree branches. We swing from it and land in the middle of the loch. My favorite competition is to see who can make the largest splash. Loki usually wins."

"But what are the youngest ones doing during this competition?" She couldn't help but think of her dear daughter. Surely it would be dangerous for her to venture out to the loch. "The water must be deep under that tree."

He laughed again, then said, "During the summer, Aunt Brenna ties a rope across the end showing how far the wee ones can go. You can't go past it until you can swim well. My sire used to keep the wee ones busy by playing 'big tree' in the shallowest part at the end. He'd put both arms out and we'd each grab onto an arm and try to hang on, swinging back and forth like a tree in a storm. When we got older, he changed the game and he'd call himself a monster. I used to get scared, but Jamie would giggle so hard he'd always be the first to fall off, many times taking in a mouthful of loch water because he couldn't stop laughing."

"And your sisters?"

"Elizabeth was always too little, but Kyla would grab right on. She'd win sometimes, too, though Jake and Jamie would claim our sire was showing favoritism. They didn't like to admit she was as strong as we were."

"And your mother?"

"Whenever Jamie would go under laughing, my mother would always say the same thing, 'Alex, be careful with the wee ones.' Then Jamie would argue that he wasn't wee. Same thing happened all the time, the only thing that changed was who was hanging onto his arms. Sometimes Roddy and Braden, even Daniel would hang on with one hand. My sire would allow him a foot, too."

She tried to picture herself in the middle of that loving clan, her daughter playing with the other bairns. But where exactly did she fit in? She stood alone. Is that what she hoped for the two of them?

When she brought her gaze back to the gates, she couldn't believe they'd nearly arrived.

Her insides continued to churn with worry—mostly about Claray, but she also feared how the rest of Connor's people would receive her. Although he and his cousins had accepted her, and they were the ones who'd fought the Channel directly, she still felt the pain of what she'd been forced to do.

Connor rubbed her arm, a small gesture that nonetheless filled her with warmth and comfort.

Gavin and Gregor came up from behind them, yelling the Ramsay war whoop.

"Cover your ears," Connor warned, still caressing her arm. She did, but it did little to muffle the sound when he followed with the Grant war whoop, joined by Roddy and Braden. The horses flew across the meadow as if they knew they were home and would be fed soon. Thorn rode with Roddy and Nari with Gregor, their faces split by giant grins. Both waved to Connor, giggling, as their horses raced past. Connor's cousins were good men, too, she'd learned—they were making their horses gallop faster to amuse the laddies.

They reached the gates and the hollering grew even louder if that were possible. The Drummond brothers jumped back and forth between the Drummond war cry and the Ramsay one, since they had the blood of both clans. Connor guided his horse through the gate toward the stables. Some of the cousins followed him, although a few others continued their war cries, riding in circles, to let everyone know how successful they'd been.

A crowd had gathered to greet them, but Sela had eyes only for her daughter or Maddie. She'd just exited the stables and rounded the corner when Maddie rushed by to greet Alex. "Over there, Sela," Connor's mother called out, pointing to a group of lassies in the courtyard.

Sela stood there with a lump in her throat, watching the four lassies as they played with a few young pups. Two of them, likely the twins by the look of them, chased a pup around. Claray's squeal of laughter rang out as a couple of pups chased her around playfully, her red waves flying behind her.

Sela's mind turned to mush at the sweet sound because she'd never heard it before. Oh, her daughter had laughed and giggled on a few occasions, but to hear her overtaken with joy was something different and special. The sight melted the last bits of ice encasing her heart. Tears flooded her face as she stood there transfixed, watching the young ones.

Her daughter had never before played with friends her age.

Claray shouted out "Lise" to one of the young twins, and she and the other lassie both fell to the ground laughing, the sound changing to hysterical giggles as the wee pups licked their faces.

Connor's hand came to the small of her back. "Sela, do you not wish to greet her?" He reached for her hand and stepped in that direction, tugging her forward.

Her hand went to Connor's arm to still him. "Nay. She's so beautiful and carefree. I don't wish to end it yet."

Maddie came along her other side. "She's missed you verra much."

"Has she? I've been so afraid…I feared she wouldn't be happy to see me. Has she been well?"

"During the day, she's fine. She still has nightmares occasionally." Then Maddie called out across the courtyard, "Claray, look who's here."

Her daughter turned to face Maddie, but her eyes immediately found her mother's. Sela swore her heart stopped beating for a few moments as she waited. But then her daughter's sweet voice carried to her.

"Mama!" She jumped up and raced toward her, her wee legs running as fast as she'd ever seen them.

Sela knelt down and opened her arms, catching her daughter as Claray flew into her embrace. The first words out of her wee daughter's mouth were, "I love you, Mama."

Through her sobs, she managed to say, "I love you, too."

"Mama, why are you crying? Are you not happy to see me? You'll love it here. They're all so nice, and they have the best fruit pies." She stood in front of her mother and cupped one of her cheeks with a wee, perfect hand. "Don't cry. I think you will like it here. I surely do. Come see the puppies."

She glanced up at Connor, who nodded. "Go ahead, Sela," he said, his tone gentle. "I'm going inside for a bit. Come in when you're ready."

Sela played with the four wee lasses and five puppies, her own tears dissipating into laughter.

How had she ever become so blessed?

CHAPTER NINETEEN

———◆———

THE EVENING HAD BEEN FULL of good food, revelry, and celebration. Claray had eaten two fruit pies, sharing one with her mother. "Is it not the most delicious pie ever?" she'd asked, as the juice from the sweet apples dripped from her fingers.

Claray's happiness had lit a fire in her soul that could not be doused, and she loved every moment of it. When it came time to settle the wee lassies in bed, Sela followed Maddie and Lily to their chamber. The bed was large, and had a bolster around the edge, likely to keep the wee ones from falling off in the middle of the night. There were several tallows on the walls, and two wee beds off to the side. Claray said, "Mama, the puppies sleep in that one sometimes but the other one is for our bairns."

"Your bairns?" she whispered, having no clue as to what she referred to.

Claray raced to a basket in the corner and pulled out a stuffed bunny. "'Tis my favorite one. I like the bunny best," she said as she gave the bunny a kiss and settled her on the wee bed.

The walls were covered with different carefully woven tapestries. One depicted a rainbow and another was a scene of running horses. Maddie said, "Lily is verra talented. Are they not beautiful?"

Lily blushed and said, "I just wished for it to feel like a bairn's chamber."

"They are lovely. You are indeed talented, Lily," Sela responded. She meant every word, but she couldn't help but wonder whether *she* had any talents.

Besides ordering young women to fight.

"Mama, this is where I'm sleeping," Claray said. "Isn't it lovely? Would you check for spiders before I go to bed?"

Maddie nodded, squeezed Sela's elbow, and said, "I have the broom. The three of us will rid the chamber of all the bugs so you may sleep sweetly through the night."

They only found one bug, in the end, but none of them mentioned it to the lassies. Lily disposed of it discreetly, and the chamber was declared clean and ready for sleep. Claray hugged Lily and Maddie, then wrapped her arms around her mother's neck.

"Mama, you'll not leave me, will you?" she whispered in her ear. "You will be here on the morrow?"

"Aye, we'll break our fast together." She kissed her lightly, then asked, "Where do you sleep, in the middle or the end?"

She pointed to one side of the huge soft bed and flounced onto it. "On this side. Lise and Liliana sleep in the middle and Nellie on the other. Mama, 'tis the softest ever. Look at all the furs and plaids we have." Sela sighed, familiar worry finding its way to the forefront of her mind. Just how had her daughter been treated when she was controlled by the Channel? Vern had always promised her that she was fine, that he watched over her.

But he'd never had a child of his own—would he have known she'd need a blanket?

Had her daughter gone to sleep cold every night?

Sela didn't know. She'd never know.

Of course, it wouldn't help to worry about it now. That was in their past. Claray would always be with her from now on, and if she was not, she would only be with someone she trusted completely, like Maddie, Lily, or Brenna.

She tucked her daughter in, then followed the other

women out into the passageway. "Allow me to show you where you'll be sleeping," Lily said. "We put you right across from her chamber, and Connor will be next to you. Fortunately, we have many extra chambers due to the new towers Papa had built."

The gesture was kind, shockingly so for someone who had experienced so little kindness in her life of late. "Many thanks to you both," Sela said. "I cannot thank you enough for bringing her here." Her eyes darted to Maddie. "What you did…"

"Say no more, lass. 'Twas my pleasure," Maddie said.

Lily added, "She's been a delight. The girls will miss her when you move on." She clasped Sela's shoulder. "I'm surprised you've held up as well as you have, considering all the tales I've heard of what you and the others have been through. I hope you sleep well. If you need anything at all, please let me know. I don't know what you have with you, but we have a few night rails in the chest at the end of the bed if you're in need."

"I must admit I'm exhausted. I'll go tell Connor I'm going to bed. I know he'll probably enjoy the time with his cousins."

She followed them back down the stairs, surprised to see the large number of people gathered in the great hall. The group of cousins stood around the hearth while others clustered around different trestle tables.

To her surprise, two lasses she recognized made their way over to her—Linet and Merewen Baird, although she'd heard both lasses were now wed into the Ramsay clan.

"Sela, may we chat with you?" Linet asked.

"Of course. It would please me verra much." She couldn't help but wonder if they intended to condemn her for what she'd done to them—she'd wronged them both—but if they did, it was their right. She wished to make amends where she could.

They found a few empty chairs off to the side of the

hearth, close enough that they could enjoy the warmth but not so close that the cousins' talk of their final battles with the Channel would overpower their own conversation.

Sela felt her hands shaking slightly, but she gripped them together.

"I just wished to tell you how much I appreciate what you did for me in Inverness," Linet said. "You kept me from what would surely have destroyed me."

Her eyes misted instantly, although she pulled from her experience at containing her emotions to stop herself from turning into a blithering fool. "Leena, I mean Linet, I wish I could have helped you more in Edinburgh and Berwick, but I could not."

Merewen reached for Sela's hand. "Nay, we understand. It was our cruel brother who caused all those problems for us, not you. Please don't think 'twas your fault."

Sela squared her shoulders and folded her hands in her lap. "You are being too kind, although I did what I had to do to protect my daughter. I tried to make a decent life for most of the lasses under my care—" Her gaze shot to Linet, but there was no accusation in her eyes. "—but my biggest guilt is that I turned my head to so many things. I didn't ask questions when I should have. You may not believe this, but I wasn't aware of how many young lasses and lads they sold. I never participated in that part of their operation, and for that, I'm grateful. But still, I turned my head when Fitzroy..." She looked back at Merewen, this time unable to stop her tears. "I'm sorry for what you were forced to endure, both of you. I do apologize for everything I did that involved the two of you. Although I'm not sure how, I intend to atone for my part in the Channel's operations."

"You're forgiven," Linet said. "I know 'twas not your fault, but the doing of those wicked men. Please don't think on it again."

To Sela's surprise, Merewen nodded her agreement. "You're forgiven. All has ended well, and for that we are grateful."

"As am I," she whispered, wiping away her tears. She glanced around the hall to see if anyone was watching their encounter, but no one appeared to pay them any mind. Chatter and laughter echoed in the hall.

"You're both verra fortunate to be part of this clan," she said.

"We both know that," Merewen said. "And we know how lucky we are to have found our husbands. I don't know what has transpired between you and Connor, but I've seen the way he looks at you. We all have. He is a fine man. I suspect you already know that."

"What are your plans now that this is over?" Linet asked softly. "Do you have a home somewhere? I suspect either the Ramsays or Grants would be happy to offer you one."

She shook her head, unable to speak. The generosity of these people, all of them, baffled her. She'd done so little to deserve it. "If you'll excuse me, I'm tired. I'm going up to my chamber. I appreciate your generosity."

The two sisters stood and each gave her a hug. Hesitant at first, she allowed the closeness, pleased to discover that it made her feel better.

Connor turned around and came their way.

"All is well?" He looked in Sela's eyes as he asked, holding her gaze as if to gauge her mood.

"Aye," Sela replied. "We had a good talk, and for that I'm grateful."

Linet and Merewen took their leave to join their husbands, Linet glancing back to smile at Sela one last time.

"Connor, I'm exhausted. I think I'll head up to my chamber. Enjoy your night with your cousins and I'll see you on the morrow."

She hadn't thought he'd accept her excuse and walk away, and he didn't disappoint her. "Allow me to walk you upstairs," he said. "I don't know which chamber you've been given, but I'm in the one next to the lassies."

She said a brief good night to his parents and the Ramsays, then led the way to her chamber. Before opening the door, she grabbed the torch bracketed beside it.

"The torch?" Connor asked, giving her a wide berth as he held the door for her.

"I know you'll think me daft, but I must check for spiders. I sleep much better that way and a torch makes it easier."

"Why don't you let me do that?"

She capitulated, mostly because she was too tired to think of a good reason to refuse him. When he finished, visibly killing two, he took the torch back into the passageway.

"My thanks," she whispered, sitting on the bed.

"In a couple of days, a group is headed to Grant land. You'll join us?"

"Of course," she said, catching his gaze. He looked like he meant what he said. She'd worried that he would leave her behind on Ramsay land, but he had invited her instead. He wanted her with him, and she would go gladly. Connor made her feel safe.

"You are exhausted, sweetling." He leaned over and kissed her forehead, and then her lips. "I hope you sleep well. We can talk on the morrow."

She nodded and followed him to the door, which she closed and locked behind him.

She was free. She no longer had to answer to anyone, and Claray slept happily in the next chamber. Why didn't she feel as wonderful as she should?

She knew why.

Guilt.

———◆———

Connor enjoyed talking to his cousins, but he had a niggling fear in the back of his mind.

What was Sela going to do now that she was free?

He loved her. She was a strong, resourceful woman, and although her ice had melted, he still considered her a queen. Her beauty and the way she carried herself ensured she looked the part, and her heart, now revealed, was surprisingly soft. She clearly loved her daughter, so much so that she'd suffered horrible treatment to save the bairn.

How could he not admire someone with such tenacity?

But he could also see she was lost. The years she'd spent in the Channel's clutches had forced her to create a mask— Sela, the Norse Ice Queen. Now that she'd been stripped of it, she was having trouble figuring out what was left.

He didn't know how to help her.

When their group had thinned, Roddy and Braden moved to a table with him.

"So what is your plan, Connor? What exactly is your relationship with Sela?" Roddy asked.

"I don't know, honestly. I am developing strong feelings for her, but I don't have any idea what's on her mind."

Braden said, "I imagine she's having a difficult time absorbing all the changes. She was under the Channel's control for a long time, was she not? I know it took Cairstine some time to adjust to freedom. But I think repairing Muir Castle helped her. It allowed her to focus on something outside herself."

Roddy asked, "Does she have family or was she part of a clan?"

"Nay, 'tis part of the reason she was in her situation. Her sire was a Scot of Clan Seton, her mother was Norse. The original Dubh men, Granville and DeVere, killed her parents and kidnapped her five years ago. 'Tis the only life she's known since."

"I wish Rose were here. She'd know what to do to help her. It was hard for her to believe she deserved happiness after living under her mother's control for so long."

Connor found himself nodding. "She hasn't said those

exact words, but I can see the doubt in her eyes. She's ecstatic to see Claray so happy, but I don't think she believes she deserves the same."

"You've a tough path ahead of you," Roddy said, "but if your feelings are strong, 'twill be worth it."

Connor pushed away from the table. "I think I'll head up to my chamber. You know where you are sleeping? There's one pallet in my chamber either of you are welcome to use."

"We have two beds, and after all the grounds I've slept on of late, I look forward to a good night of sleep," Braden said. "Unfortunately, 'tis in a chamber with this fool and not my wife, but I'll see her soon enough."

Roddy wrapped his arms around Braden with a big grin. "I'm not sweet enough for you, cousin?" he asked, batting his lashes.

Braden snorted and shoved him away.

Connor laughed as he made his way up the stairs. He loved his cousins. They knew the art of jesting. He crept down the passageway, pleased to hear everything quiet. Peace was theirs at last.

He also loved the woman inside that chamber, but he would give her the space she seemed to need. Once he found his chamber and doffed his clothes, leaving his plaid nearby, he settled onto the bed, knowing he'd fall asleep quickly.

His last thoughts were of a white-haired nymph with ice blue eyes.

———◆———

Connor bolted up out of his bed, grabbing his plaid out of habit and wrapping it around his bare body. What the hell was that noise? The answer came to him in a trice.

Sela was caught in a nightmare.

He crept into the passageway, pleased there was no one else awake yet, and reached for her door. It was locked, but

Sela threw the bolt back and charged out of the chamber, nearly knocking him over.

"Spiders!" she yelled.

"Hush, sweetling," he whispered, lifting her up into his arms and carrying her back into her chamber. He sat on the bed and cradled her on his lap.

The door had barely closed when Connor's sire opened it again, wide-eyed.

"She'll be fine, Papa. A nightmare." He waved his sire away.

"Spiders, more spiders," Sela muttered. "Kill them all, please."

Alex looked deeply concerned, but he nodded and left the room, closing the door behind him. Connor's focus was on Sela, who finally seemed to register he was with her. Resting her head on his shoulder, she whispered, "Spiders, Connor. I dreamed there were spiders everywhere. Will this never end? Is Hord still alive? Will he come after me?"

"Sweetling, I checked the chamber for spiders before I left. Shall I check again? I'll light the tallow and check all the corners, even under the bed."

"Do you mind? I'm so sorry, but if even one crawls on me, I think it awakens me. I know 'tis impossible to rid a castle of all of them, but if they'd just stay away the nightmares might end. Connor, what will I do?"

Connor kissed her forehead and set her down on the side of the bed. He grabbed a tallow and lit it from the torch in the passageway, waving to his sire, who was just returning to his chamber.

Once back inside, Connor checked all the corners. He found and killed one small spider, but he doubted that had set her off. He knew what had caused her screaming.

She'd been dreaming of Hord, the hoarder of spiders.

When he finished his examination, he returned the tallow to its holder then sat down on the bed again. He settled her back on his lap, angling her sideways so she could lean her head on his shoulder.

"Forgive me," she whispered, her voice full of frustration.

"I don't blame you. It's little wonder you dream of spiders. I'd wake up screaming every night had I endured half of the suffering you've been subjected to."

She smiled at him. "Your scream probably wouldn't carry the way mine does. I fear I woke everyone up."

"Only my sire, but he's gone back to bed. I didn't hear anything from the lassies' chamber so I don't think you awakened them."

Her smile slipped. "Connor, I don't know what to do. Will I always have to live with this?"

He sighed, mostly because he wanted to offer her a solution—and yet, he didn't have one. "With time, the number of nightmares you have will probably dissipate. But I'm afraid it will take a while. I suspect the more nights you sleep without awakening, the fewer episodes you'll have."

"But how can I make that happen?"

"I would like to hold you while you sleep. Will that not soothe you?"

She sat up and stared at him. "But if everyone finds out, they'll be upset. Your parents, Lady Brenna. They'll all think I'm…"

He set his finger against his lips. "Do not say that word, and they know you're not. There is naught wrong with comforting you, and you are not a maiden. Besides, I'll sneak out early if 'twill make you feel better."

"Promise?"

"I promise." He kissed her so thoroughly that he couldn't hide his feelings any longer. "I say we enjoy each other whenever we can."

CHAPTER TWENTY

—◆—

"CONNOR GRANT," SELA WHISPERED. "I feel you." She ran her hands across his shoulders and down his arms. "I think you need to remove that plaid and climb into bed."

She stood and removed her night rail, setting it on the chest at the end of the bed. His plaid joined it. He stepped toward her, his hands reaching to cup her breasts as a low growl erupted from him, though he stopped it quickly, not wanting to frighten her. His thumbs teased her nipples until they peaked, causing her to squirm beneath his touch.

His lips went to her neck and he trailed kisses across her fine bone to the pulse under her chin. "Have I told you yet how much I love that you are tall and nearly look me in the eye?"

"Nay," she rasped, her breath catching as she clung to him. "I always hated being this tall."

"No more. I want you to love being this tall because of how nicely we fit together." His hands moved to her back and he tugged her close, skin to skin, and stared into her eyes as he moved his hands over her bottom, caressing her ever so lightly until she wiggled against him.

"That will not help me at all," he teased.

She said, "Then get into bed and I will help you."

He gave her a challenging look and climbed into the bed. He lay flat on his back and clasped his hands behind his head. Still whispering because they wished to keep their movements quiet, he waited until she climbed in next to him to speak. "And what exactly did you have in mind?"

She knelt on the bed and crawled to him, positioning herself over him, then dipped her head until her tongue touched the tip of his manhood.

"Hellfire," was all he could say.

Her tongue teased him a few more times and it was all he could do not to yell out. Then she dipped her head even farther and took him full in her mouth, her tongue still teasing him as she moved, one hand reaching over to caress his sacks.

He allowed her to play for a few moments, then reached for her arms and guided her up to straddle him, his hands reaching to knead her breasts as her breath caught. "No more torture, tall lady. Mount me, please, before I lose it like a laddie."

She reached for him, running her hand up and down the hard surface of his chest, then slipped him inside her with a slight moan, doing it slowly until he was fully seated. Once they were joined, he pulled her down so he could kiss her, their tongues dueling in the same magical rhythm as their bodies. She stroked him just the way he liked it, but after all her foreplay, he couldn't take much more. His hands reached for her bottom, grasping her tightly, and she came with a violence that shook him, his lips still on hers to dampen the sound of her climax.

Then he lost all control, though he bit back his urge to yell as she clenched around him, her contractions milking every last bit of his seed out of him.

They lay in silence together, coming down from their ecstasy, her head on his chest while he rubbed her back. "Heavens above, we are wonderful together."

"Aye, we are." Her finger traced a path around his nipple, across his chest, and up to his jaw. "Is it always like this for you with others?"

"Nay, you are the only one for me."

She sighed, her warm breath teasing him. "What are you thinking?" he asked, his hand running through the silky strands of her hair.

"What's to become of us?"

"Well, this wasn't exactly how I'd planned to ask, but I love you and I'm hoping you'll marry me."

She lifted her head and set her chin in her hand, catching his gaze. "Oh, Connor," she said after a moment. "I meant what I said the other day. I'm not the type of lass you should marry."

His finger moved to stroke her chin. "I think I'm the only one who can judge whom I should marry, and I choose you." He had to convince her that her thinking was all wrong.

"But you should marry a lass who is of noble blood, one who can bear you many sons."

"And I think I should marry the lass of my choosing. My grandmama made my father promise to allow my aunts to choose their own husbands. Think you he would offer any less to his own children?"

She rested her head back onto his chest. Her eyes had shuttered, and he could not read her thoughts. All he could do was speak his truth.

"My family is well-known for loving once and loving powerfully. I will not change my mind. If you need time to adjust to the changes in your life, I will wait for you. And I also promise to love and raise Claray as if she were mine."

Her hand settled on his side. "Do you think I'm capable of loving someone?

"You love your daughter, do you not?"

"'Tis different." She looked down. "A good person wouldn't have done the things I did. I still have much to atone for."

He lifted her chin so their eyes met. "If your parents had not been killed, would you have run away to join the Channel of Dubh?"

She lifted her head in shock. "Nay, of course not."

"Listen to me. Did you give yourself freely to those men?"

"Nay, Connor, of course not. They raped me." He could see the misting in her eyes at the thought of what she'd endured.

"And after you had your daughter, you sacrificed your own moral upbringing, your own definition of right and wrong, so your daughter would not know pain. 'Tis the ultimate sacrifice, in my opinion. You are a victim, naught more, naught less. You need to start recognizing that." His hand cupped her face, his thumb reaching up to wipe her tears.

"I could have fought harder for the lasses. While I ensured they were fed and always had somewhere clean to sleep, I did not speak out enough against the beatings. I...I did not know about the sale of lads and lasses until the end, but I should have figured it out before I did... Mayhap I could have stopped it."

He lifted her chin to look into his eyes. "Think you they would have listened to you? What happened to you when you stood up for Linet in Edinburgh? Do you not understand that they would have found someone else to do their bidding had you refused?"

The tears flowed freely, but he hoped it was because he'd made his point.

She swallowed hard and shook her head. "It would not have mattered. In that much, you are correct. I can only hope the Lord judges me the same way you do."

"Sweetling, if you'd like to speak to an abbess or a priest, I'm happy to arrange that for you. My aunt Jenny married Aedan Cameron and they protect Lochluin Abbey. 'Tis about halfway between here and Grant land. We'll stop there on the way. Spend as much time as you need with them. 'Tis as I said, I'll wait for you."

She rested her head back down on his chest, her tears

leaving a puddle on his skin. "If I'm capable of loving someone, 'tis how I feel about you, Connor Grant. I love you."

His heart soared at her words, only to plummet a second later.

"But I cannot marry you."

CHAPTER TWENTY-ONE

W HEN SHE AWAKENED NEXT, SHE was still lying in Connor's arms, though both of them were on their sides. After telling him that she couldn't marry him, she'd feared he would leave her, but he had stayed. Never had she felt as safe as she did in his arms.

She could give him a vague promise because she thought she might eventually accept his proposal, but then she thought of her promise to his mother. She vowed not to lead him on or accept until she was certain.

It was only right.

He smoothed a few stray hairs off her forehead. "Are you awake, beautiful?"

She opened her eyes and smiled. "Aye, my thanks for staying with me."

"Of course. I love you, and that will never change."

"Never? Are you sure? Even after what I said last night?"

"Even after that. Before I take my leave, I must ask what you would like to do. I accept what you said, although I hope you will change your mind, but I know not where you would like to live. You may stay here if you like, or we can arrange for you to have your own cottage on Grant land. 'Tis your choice."

She'd lain awake for a long time considering exactly that, and her mind was made up. "I'd like to go to Lochluin Abbey with Claray. I think I may like to become a nun."

To his credit, he didn't laugh as she'd thought he might.

Instead, he said, "As you wish. We will take some guards with us and I'll escort you. I know my aunt and uncle would be happy to help you should you need anything."

"That would be lovely."

He got up and put his plaid on, but she couldn't let him go like that. He'd done too much for her.

"Connor," she whispered as she moved closer to him, climbing out of the bed and pulling her night rail on.

When he looked at her, his gaze was full of emotion. For her. He felt all of that for *her*. It was a humbling and terrifying thought.

"I'm sorry, but I'm confused and 'tis the only place I can think of where I might receive the guidance I need. Please don't hate me."

He stood close enough to run his hand down her jaw-line, the caress an aching reminder of all she stood to lose. "Hate you? Never. I will always love you and wish the best for you. But I'm furious at what those Channel men did to you and the rest of their victims. And aye, you were a victim. Not just to Hord but to all of them. The saddest part for me is I have no idea how to help you. I wish I did, but I am at a loss. So all I can say is I support you in this quest, and I will wait for you."

His words gave her a hope she didn't deserve, but she would take it, even if it was only a flickering candle's worth.

"I cannot expect you to wait for me. I can't promise I'll return. I may choose to take my vows." While the words rushed from her mouth, they hadn't come from her heart. She *did* want him to wait for her. She could only pray he would. And she could only pray that her heart and soul would heal enough that she could focus on loving this man, her greatest desire.

"I have no choice, Sela. I know I'll never love another. I'm grateful to have found you, but I would never force you to do anything. You must live your life the way you wish."

He gave her a quick kiss on the lips and left.

Her heart broke into pieces, yet she couldn't bring herself to call him back. The guilt and horrible memories plagued her terribly.

She lay in her bed like an empty shell of a person until Claray came in and hopped in next to her.

***

Sela stopped her horse just outside the abbey. Connor had insisted she be given a horse of her own so she could ride whenever she wished. Since she'd already denied him so much, she'd found herself unable to object. Claray rode with Connor, her new puppy in a small box on her lap. Torrian, the leader of Clan Ramsay, raised most of the puppies himself and had offered the lassie her choice of the litter. Although Claray had been reluctant to leave her new friends, his gift had softened her pain. She'd chose the runt of the litter, male, though she hadn't named him yet.

Before they dismounted, Connor pointed to a place for the guards to go so he could have a private word with Sela. He then lowered Claray from the saddle, handing her down to Sela with a gentleness that made Sela wish to cry.

"I think you better put your puppy down so he can relieve himself," Sela said, kissing her head. Her wee daughter scampered over to a patch of grass and set the pup down, watching his every move.

Connor brushed her cheek. "You're absolutely certain this is what you wish to do?"

Although she was as nervous about this as she'd been about childbirth, she nodded her agreement. "I apologize again for hurting you. But I feel quite strongly that this is right for me. 'Tis the only way I can make it right."

The door opened and a priest waved to them. He was of average height, though his shoulders were a bit rounded, and his dark hair was streaked with gray. His eyes were as kind as any Sela had ever seen. Judging by the way Connor's demeanor brightened, he knew the man. "Greetings to you, Father MacGregor," he said. "I'd like you to meet a friend, Sela Seton. She's come to talk with the abbess about the possibility of taking her vows."

"'Tis lovely to meet you, lass."

"And this is her daughter, Claray, who has brought her new pup with her."

"Will that be allowed? I hope so," Sela said, wringing her hands. She wouldn't be turned away over the pup, would she?

"I'm sure the nuns will love both Claray and her pup. When you're ready, I'll take you inside to meet the abbess." He gave them an assessing look, then said, "Come, Claray. I'll take you and the pup inside. We'll give your mother and Connor a chance to say goodbye." Shifting his attention to Connor, he added, "I'd love to speak with you before you go, lad."

"Of course, Father MacGregor." The priest took Claray inside. Connor touched her hand, his fingers grazing against hers—a gesture subtle enough not to announce their connection to anyone who might be watching. "He married my parents and my sister. I'm sure he'd like to hear how they're doing."

"I cannot thank you enough for all you've done for me," Sela said, turning to him. She wanted to wrap her arms around him.

She could not.

"Always remember this. You deserve happiness, but only you can decide what form that will take. I will always love you. Anytime you need me, send a messenger and I'll be here. If you decide you wish to visit me at Grant land, I'm sure my uncle Aedan would send a group of guards to escort you."

"My thanks to you and your family," she said. "I cannot thank you all enough."

He kissed her forehead and she clung to him for just a

moment before forcing herself to turn away. She turned back to him once. "Promise not to forget me?"

"I promise."

She went inside the abbey, refusing to look back. She couldn't. If she did, she wasn't sure she'd be able to leave him.

———◆———

It took every bit of control Connor possessed not to beg her to stay, but he knew his only chance to be with her was to let her go. To give her the freedom those other men had taken from her. He remembered he had promised to introduce her to his aunt and uncle, but he doubted either one of them could handle it at the moment. He'd stop and see them before he left. Aunt Jennie would be willing to visit her, he was sure of it.

He'd gone over in his mind at least a thousand times how he could help her, but he'd come up with naught. The only thing that might help was to kill Hord, but he had no idea where the bastard had gone. He'd sailed off into the distance to an unknown destination. Maggie and Will were still looking for him, but it seemed unlikely the man would return so soon.

As he mulled it all over again, he made his way to the abbey. She'd had enough time to find her way to the abbess's office, and he'd promised to speak with the old priest.

Father MacGregor was waiting for him at the door. He opened it and waved him in. "Come inside, Connor. Do an old man a favor and sit with me in the monk's section. I'd love to hear about your parents."

Connor nodded and followed the priest down a passage-way that led to a different building, presumably the section where the monks lived and worked. He recalled Aunt Jennie telling him about how hard the scribes worked, writing all day long, transcribing important works and volumes of the Lord's teaching.

The quiet was unnerving for him. Would Sela find it comforting, or would she feel the same way?

The priest entered a small chamber and took a chair in front of the hearth, pointing to the chair next to it for him to sit. "'Tis my favorite place in here. I'm allowed to stay warm while the monks are not."

Connor waited for the priest to sit down before he took his chair.

"Your parents are well, I hope?" the man asked. He respected the priest, especially since he knew how much his mother valued the man.

"Aye, they are doing well. We believe we have put an end to the Channel of Dubh. Papa took part in the battle, but he returned home unscathed. Kyla is carrying her first bairn and due in the spring, as is Jamie's wife, Gracie."

"How exciting for your mother." The priest took a linen square out and mopped his forehead. "Now what would you like to tell me about the lass whom you escorted here? Do I sense stronger feelings than friendship?"

This priest was indeed perceptive. "Father, Sela was controlled by the men in the Channel for five years. One of them got her with child and she raised her daughter inside the Channel. The men used Claray to force her to work for the Channel. I met her in Inverness, where she controlled the women's fighting portion of their operation. While she never stole or kidnapped anyone, she bears a terrible burden of guilt."

"Was she not being forced to do these things?"

"Aye, but she feels she must atone for her part in the travesty. I'm hoping the nuns can help her."

"And your feelings?"

Connor stared into the flames and leaned forward, placing his elbows on his knees. "I'm in love with her. She's a vital, strong woman. If you knew some of the atrocities she's endured, you'd be shocked. I don't know how she's managed to endure it. I asked her to be my wife, but she rejected me, saying she thought it best if she were to become a nun."

"Does she admit to sharing your feelings of love?"

Connor sat up, perplexed by this question. "Aye, she does, but I don't understand how she can walk away if she truly loves me."

"Are you not doing the same yourself?"

Connor gave him a look, confused by this thought, though he knew the words were wise.

"May I share something with you, lad?"

He almost smirked at the priest's name for him. He hadn't been called a lad in a long time, but he would never argue with the man. "Please do."

"I recall having a similar conversation with your sire many years ago. Your mother had been abused terribly, yet she had been raised to obey her elders, and to obey men in particular. She had a difficult time reconciling her beliefs with her life experience, but more importantly..." He paused for a sip from the goblet of water sitting on the nearby table. Once he cleared his throat, he continued, "More importantly, she had a difficult time accepting her own value, and learning to trust your father."

"Truly? I don't think I'd ever heard that. I know my mother was abused, but they've never seemed to have any problems because of it. I'd always assumed they'd married right away."

"Nay, dear Maddie was a troubled young lady. Your father wished to rush her into marriage, but she'd been through too much to be hurried. Perhaps 'tis the same with your young lady. I sense she is troubled, and this could be a good way for her to reconcile those feelings. Do not despair yet, lad. Where there is love, there is still hope."

"Thank you, Father." He stood up from his chair, anxious to leave. "I'll make sure and tell my parents that we had a nice talk."

He had to go. If he didn't, he'd run after her, get down on one knee, and beg her to marry him. And he couldn't handle another rejection.

CHAPTER TWENTY-TWO

"COME INSIDE," THE ABBESS SAID, ushering them into her office. "You may call me Mother Matilda. And what is your daughter's name?" The abbess was a tall woman, although not quite so tall as Sela. Her piercing eyes seemed to reach right down to Sela's soul. She doubted she'd ever be able to lie to the woman. Luckily, this question was easy to answer.

"My name is Sela Seton and this is my daughter, Claray."

"And the puppy?"

Claray sat on the floor with her pup on her lap. "I wish to call him Torry. May I, Mama?"

"Of course. Why Torry?"

"Because 'twas Chief Torrian who gave him to me, and I've never had a puppy before." She giggled as the gray Deerhound shook his head, settling his ears.

"Sister Therese," Mother Matilda called out to a passing woman. "Would you come and take Claray for a bite to eat, please. I'm sure she would love some bread or cheese. Perhaps there is bone for the puppy to gnaw on."

The nun rushed in and ushered the girl and her dog away. Surprisingly, Claray was more than happy to go with the nun.

Once she was gone, Mother Matilda turned to look Sela in the eyes. "Now, please tell me why you wish to serve our Lord. 'Tis not often that we receive young women with a bairn into a nunnery. We also don't keep a nunnery in Lochluin Abbey, meaning we only have a few novices here, but there are others you could join should we accept you. Tell me about yourself."

Sela began her tale, starting with her happy life as a child, moving on to her parents' murder and her life in the Channel of Dubh—the fighting, the whoring, the spiders, everything. She had to give the abbess credit. Her eyes gave away nothing, though she did cluck her tongue and shake her head twice.

"My dear," the abbess said at the end, "that is an atrocious tale, and you have my deepest sympathies for all you were forced to endure. God clearly gave you a strength many of us do not possess. But all of this doesn't answer my question. Why the nunnery?" She moved back from her desk and folded her hands in her lap.

"Because I must make amends for the horrible things I have done. I think my sins have been so great that the only way I can make up for them is to devote the rest of my life to our Lord." At this point, she was so unsettled, she wasn't sure what else to say. If they sent her away, she wasn't sure what she could do to find peace within herself.

"I don't think you have much to make amends for, but I understand how you might feel. You were coerced during much of this, aye? If so, the Lord will not fault you."

"But I can do work for you. I can clean chambers. I could plant a garden come spring. I could work in the kitchens cutting vegetables, washing dishes. I could learn how to cook…"

"Child, please stop." The abbess leaned forward, resting her hands on the desk. "Do you know why I came here in the beginning?"

She shook her head.

"Because my heart belongs to God. Out of my respect for the Grants, the Ramsays, and the Camerons, I'm going to allow you to live and work here. While you are at the abbey, you may speak with the priests and the other nuns, and I also advise you to beg God for guidance. You are so fresh from five years of torture that I would not be one of God's servants if I turned you away. But you must search your heart. Who does it belong to?"

Another nun walked by and Mother Matilda called out to her. "Sister Grace, would you please take Sela here to the chamber at the end of the passageway on the second floor? She and her lovely daughter, Claray, are going to stay with us for a while. She has been through a terrible ordeal and we will help her get past it, if we can."

Sister Grace, a short rotund woman with smiling eyes and gray hair, said, "Of course. Come along. 'Tis a lovely chamber, you'll see. And I'll do anything I can to help you."

"Oh, and Sister Grace?"

"Aye, Mother Matilda?"

"She's going to assist us with cleaning and cooking. You can show her to her duties on the morrow. Her daughter is in the kitchens with Sister Therese. Collect her and you may give them a brief tour before they find their chambers."

Sela turned to the abbess and said, "Many thanks to you, Mother Matilda."

"Bless you, child. May our Lord bring you and your daughter peace."

———◆———

When Connor returned to Ramsay Castle, he was pleased to see that Will and Maggie were there. Everyone had agreed to stay one final eve for a celebration of the Band's accomplishment. The Ramsays threw a wonderful festival with minstrels, trestle tables overflowing with food, and much rehashing of all the Band had accomplished.

Connor enjoyed talking with his cousins, but it struck him that each of them had found their happiness over the last couple of years, and he was alone. He'd found his love, but he couldn't keep her.

Maggie, who'd always been adept at reading others, pulled him aside. Looking him in the eye, she asked, "How are you handling Sela's journey to the abbey?"

He shrugged. "'Tis what she wants, and I want her happiness."

"You're in love with her, are you not? It was hard not to see the attraction between the two of you. She fought it for a long time, but I do believe her heart will belong to you eventually."

"My thanks, Maggie. I hope you're right. I just feel so helpless. What can I do for her? I would help her through this if she would allow it, but she chose to step away from me." He rubbed his chin, reminded of how much he already missed Sela.

"Did she admit to having feelings for you?" Maggie had a way of being direct that he appreciated. She rarely minced words.

"She did, but she believes she'd like to take her vows. I've fallen in love with a nun. How's that for luck?" He couldn't help but grin over that.

Maggie gave him a brief hug. "Be patient. Those men were exceptionally cruel and demented. No matter what she has told you, you have no idea what she was subjected to during her captivity. She'll not tell all, we women are like that. She needs time to heal. The mere story of what that man did to her with the spiders will bother me for many moons. I believe you've chosen a woman much stronger than I would be. Have faith in her if you truly love her."

"I hope you're right, Maggie. Many thanks for your thoughts." He hugged her back. His cousin was truly a strong-minded woman, and her encouragement had given him hope.

She headed off for her husband and Connor felt a sudden, powerful urge to be alone. He moved up the stairs, walked straight past his chamber, and opened the door to the parapets, the cool breeze hitting him in the face.

He didn't care about the temperature. He just wished to be alone.

But it was not to be. He opened the door, surprised to see he wasn't the only one who'd sought solace up there. "Papa? I didn't expect to find you here."

Although mayhap he should have. His sire had always enjoyed spending time in the parapets.

His father gave him a sideways glance. "The view is quite spectacular up here, almost as good as it is at home. But I often come here...you don't." His sire paused, leaning over the cold stone to look at the land splayed out before them. "What brings you all the way up here when your cousins are below stairs celebrating?"

"I felt the need to be alone." He leaned over the parapets in the same position as his sire. "I see why you like it up here. 'Tis peaceful."

His father just quirked his brow.

Connor said, "I had a chat with an old friend of yours before I left Lochluin Abbey. Father MacGregor. He told me something I never knew."

His father, always a man of few words, simply gazed at him with an expectant expression, waiting for a full explanation. He took a deep breath and dove in, hoping he wasn't jumping into a fire pit by bringing up old memories. "He told me that Mama was verra troubled when you first met, and she took her time agreeing to be your wife. I thought you married right away."

A small smile crossed his father's face. "Nay, your mother took her sweet time deciding to marry me. I yelled at everyone but her because I was so upset."

Connor couldn't help but grin at that thought. His father rarely yelled anymore. "Truly?"

"Aye, I went after both of my brothers with my sword, and Aunt Brenna wished to choke me. Even Aunt Jennie, who was only eight summers at the time, called me mean. The only one who could talk any sense into me was the old stablemaster, Hugh."

"Hugh? I thought you'd say Mac. He was our stablemaster, was he not?"

"Mac came with Maddie. He was married to her maid, and they are probably the only reason your mother survived. There aren't many people crueler than her stepbrother, and what she endured... I still know not how she survived it. Women have a stronger core than men do. It took me decades to learn that, but your mother is a good example. I suspect Sela is the same. Many would have succumbed to the torture she endured, but she had a daughter. That alone gave her the push she needed."

"I asked her to marry me, Papa. She rejected me."

"Just as your mother rejected me the first time I asked."

"Mama rejected you?"

He nodded with a grin. "Not in so many words, but I chased her for weeks before she even allowed me near her. She wanted naught to do with me. In fact, I remember the time she sat at our trestle table and told me to take her to an abbey. She wished to become a nun."

"Truly?" He'd never heard any of this before. Why had he not heard this?

"'Tis true." His sire paused, looking him in the eye, then asked, "Do you truly love Sela?"

"Aye, Papa. I don't think I can love another woman. But I don't know what to do. I knew I had to leave her there today, but I wanted to beg her to marry me."

His father sighed and looked up at the moon peeking out from behind the rolling clouds every now and then. "When a woman has been abused, it takes patience, son. Jake will tell you the same. But if you really wish to know how to help her, I would talk to Mama. She went through something similar. If she loves you, too, do not give up on her. Five years of imprisonment and cruelty is not easily forgotten."

"My thanks, Papa." He clasped his father's shoulder, then

turned to go back.

He opened the door, but his sire's voice stopped him.

"Connor?"

"Aye?"

"Women who endure such cruelties are fierce women, and they gift you with strong sons."

How he wished it to be true.

CHAPTER TWENTY-THREE

———◆———

SELA HAD SETTLED INTO A routine. Every morn, she would take Claray and Torry for a walk, then she would head to the kitchens and cut vegetables for the mid-day meal. Claray spent that time with the nuns.

When she finished in the kitchens, she would go to chapel and pray for close to an hour, then gather Claray up and head to the living quarters for her cleaning rituals. She enjoyed cleaning the nuns' chambers because it was her way of ridding the abbey of spiders.

She had twenty different chambers she cleaned, so she adhered to a tight schedule, but it pleased her whenever a nun told her what a thorough job she'd done. It gave her a sense of pride she'd not experienced before.

Each evening, her prayers ended with, "Have I done enough for You not to hate me, Lord?"

Somehow, somewhere, her answer would come, although it had not happened yet.

While Claray's nightmares were improving, Sela often woke up in the middle of the night in a cold sweat, swinging at imaginary creatures. Claray slept on a pallet next to her small bed so she didn't have to worry about striking her.

Torry slept in the box filled with an old soft plaid that Torrian had given her. The pup slept with his nose wrapped inside the plaid, something mother and daughter loved to watch each night when he settled himself just so. After four or five circles, he'd finally plop down with a grunt, then tossed the blanket a wee bit until his nose was in the middle of the folds.

Sela thought about Connor often—his gentle ways, his manly scent, his strong character—but mostly she just thought about how much she'd loved being held in his arms. Would she ever have the pleasure again?

She hoped so. But she hadn't completed her penance yet. Mayhap she never would.

She was cleaning her chamber one afternoon when Sister Grace came inside to join her. "I thought I'd check on wee Claray. This morn I thought mayhap she was taking a sickly turn. How is she?"

Sela turned around and looked at her daughter, quietly sitting on the floor playing with Torry. True, she was usually chasing the puppy in circles, but she seemed fine. "I think she's hale, Sister Grace, but you may be more experienced than me. She wasn't always with me over the last year."

Sister Grace simply smiled—she always smiled, yet it never failed to look genuine—and strode over to Claray. She felt her forehead, then said, "I'm sure she'll be fine."

"My thanks," Sela said. "I'll keep an eye on her."

Sister Grace was about to walk out the door, but she hesitated and glanced back. "Did you not clean your chamber yesterday?"

"Aye, I did."

"But you don't clean all the chambers every day, do you?"

"Nay, I just like to make sure that the chamber is clean for Claray." She turned back to the wall she'd just started to scrub before Sister Grace had joined them. "I'm nearly done."

Sister Grace strolled over until she stood next to her. "Child, what is it you are afraid of? I sense a deep fear in you of something, but I'm not sure what it is."

Sela blushed but kept scrubbing. "'Tis naught, Sister. I'm

fine."

"Mama and I are afraid of spiders," Claray said, all innocence. "I don't like them because they bite."

Sela ignored her daughter and continued to work, hoping the nun would accept Claray's answer and walk away.

A strange look passed through the nun's eyes, but she only said, "Well then, I can see 'tis important for you to clean the spiders away every day. If you need anything, Sela, please let me know."

"Many thanks to you, Sister Grace." She stood up to make a slight bow to the dear woman before returning to her work.

She was surprised that Claray did not wish to go down to the hall for dinner, but since she wasn't especially hungry herself, she lay on the bed and told Claray a story, a tale about a handsome Highlander who spent his time saving lasses from cruel men.

Claray asked, "Is his name Connor, Mama? *He* saved us from mean men."

The sound of his name sent Sela's heart into her throat. "If you like, we can call him Connor." She couldn't decide how to end the tale, but she needn't have worried. They both fell asleep halfway through the story.

She awakened to an odd sound. Rolling onto her side, she glanced at Claray, realizing the sound came from two sources. One was an odd moaning from her daughter, and the second, louder noise was from Torry whining whenever he sniffed Claray. She bolted up and touched her daughter's cheek to awaken her, only to find she was burning with fever.

Claray wouldn't wake up.

Filled with panic, Sela picked her up and ran down the passageway screaming, "Help me, please. My daughter." She didn't know what to do for her, but someone had to know. Claray was everything to her.

Many nuns came out of their chambers. "What is it?"

one called. "What's wrong with Claray?" another asked.

"She will not awaken. Her skin is hot and sweaty, and I know not what to do. Help me, please. Where is the healer?" She searched each face in desperation.

The first nun who'd spoken said, "I'll send a guard for Mistress Jennie. She's a fine healer."

By the time Jennie arrived, Sela was sitting in a chair in one of the receiving rooms sobbing, clutching her daughter to her chest and repeating, "Please don't take her, please don't take her, please, God. She's all I have. Please save her." She rocked in a motion that nearly made her sick, but she couldn't stop.

Claray was her first bairn, so she often felt lost. How she wished her mother were here to help. Claray had only had a fever once before, and it hadn't been this bad. What was she to do?

A woman stepped inside the chamber, and her likeness to Alexander Grant marked her as Jennie. Her brown hair had a few strands of gray in it, but she was still a beautiful woman with kind eyes. "Ah, this must be Claray," she said. "I'm Jennie Cameron. Are you not Sela?"

"Aye, Sela Seton. This is my daughter and I don't know what to do to help her. I've never seen a fever this bad...I don't know...bairns are puzzling...how can I help..."

"Hush. I've been caring for bairns for a verra long time. May I hold her?"

Sela handed her over with a nod. If this woman was Connor's aunt, she could be trusted. Jennie cradled Claray on her lap as she quickly instructed the nuns on what she needed. She then poked and prodded the lassie in what was probably an attempt to awaken her.

Claray did not stir.

"Wee ones often get sicknesses, much more than we adults do. They come and they go, and sometimes there's naught we can do but keep them warm and give them things to drink. The fever burns them dry so we must get her some goat's milk or even water."

One nun said, "I'll get the milk, Mistress Jennie."

Jennie unwrapped Claray from much of her clothing. "I'm going to cool her down a wee bit to see if that will help." She shot a glance at Sela. "Connor told me about you and your daughter, you are aware of this?"

"Aye. He looks much like you, and you look like his sire."

"Alex is my eldest brother. Brenna Ramsay is my dearest sister. I'm sure you have met her. Our mother and grand-sire were both healers. Tell me how you met Connor."

Once the nuns brought her everything she needed, she sent them out and asked them to close the door. "I'd like to hear about you and Connor. Please do tell. He is a dear nephew because he reminds me so much of my brother."

"Connor...I..." What should she say? For some rea-son, she decided brutal honesty would be best with this woman. "I met Connor when I was known as the Ice Queen of Inverness. I worked for the Channel of Dubh. While I wasn't aware they were selling lads and lasses until the very end, I was involved with other parts of their oper-ation. Connor and his cousins fought the Dubh men in Inverness, Edinburgh, and finally put an end to the bastards in Berwick. I'm here to make amends for what I did. I'm deciding whether to take my vows as a nun."

Jennie Cameron assessed her for a few moments as she washed Claray with cool water. "And Claray's sire?"

"He's dead. Truthfully, I'm not exactly sure who her sire was." Sela stared at the unlit hearth in front of them, wait-ing to see if the woman would chastise her. "There were two men, both are gone."

Jennie's voice came out in a soft, compassionate tone that reminded her of her dear mother. "So if I were to guess, you were stolen from your home, raped, and forced into servitude. You gave birth to this beautiful bairn, but they used her as leverage against you. Made you do things to ensure her safety."

Tears flooded her cheeks. Jennie was as brutally honest as she'd been.

And exactly right. How had she guessed? All she could do was mumble, "Aye."

"And I would also guess that you love Connor, but you don't feel you are deserving of his love and all he offers you."

She stared at the ground, unable to speak.

Jennie's voice washed over her, reminding her of the way her mother had spoken to her when she'd woken up in the night, feeling poorly. "You need not say anything, but you've answered my questions. I've seen women in similar situations, and what I'd like to tell you is that you needn't make amends for anything you did while horrible men kept control of you by holding your daughter. You have every right to happiness and should forgive yourself."

"Forgive myself?"

"When people control you like that, it warps your way of thinking, and most mothers will do whatever they have to in order to protect their bairns. I see your actions as no different. 'Tis the way nature intended it. Every bear, every boar, every creature of God acts the same. You did as nature intended for you to do."

That thought had never occurred to her. Were all mothers equally fierce? Her mother definitely had been. She recalled how Mama had tried to hide her from Guy and Dee.

"Mama?" Claray opened her eyes and stared up at Mistress Jennie.

Sela jumped up and knelt next to her. "Sweetling, how do you feel?"

"I'm thirsty."

Jennie sat her up and said, "We have some fresh goat's milk for you. We'll help you drink."

Claray touched Jennie's face and said, "Who are you? I

like you."

So did Sela, and she'd never forget her kind words. Even though Connor had told her much the same thing, Connor *loved* her—it felt different hearing the sentiment from this strong, wise woman who had no reason to stretch the truth to comfort her.

CHAPTER TWENTY-FOUR

———————

CLARAY WAS MUCH BETTER TWO days later. Mistress Jennie had stopped by to see her twice a day, and each time, she and Sela ended up talking for hours. Jennie liked to tell stories about how wee Connor had tried to mimic his twin brothers, grabbing every sword he could get his hands on. He'd given his mother several starts when he was caught dragging men's swords across the bailey at the tender age of three.

But then again, his older brothers had done the same.

She'd also told Sela that Alex had carried each of his bairns around on his chest, wrapped into position with a plaid. Connor had especially loved it when his papa would carry him out to the lists that way, facing outward so he could watch the men practice. He'd bounce up and down in excitement, so much so that Alex would often need to catch him to keep him from falling.

Sela loved hearing her stories, but it seemed her nightmares had gotten worse as Claray's condition improved. More often than not, she woke herself up because she was swinging her fists so forcefully.

When she confided this to Mistress Jennie, the older woman clucked her tongue. "Why don't I take Claray and Torry home with me for a few days? I have two daughters who would love to fuss over her."

Claray was so excited by the prospect of her adventure she nearly jumped on the horse—further proof that she was indeed well. She sat in Jennie's grasp and waved good-bye, her dear puppy in a guard's care. "Bye, Mama. I'll be back soon."

Sela waved back. While she knew Claray was accustomed to being away from her, the way her bairn had left so easily—and with such excitement—had hurt her heart.

So she returned to scrubbing. She cleaned the chambers every day, but still the nightmares persisted.

One night, she woke up and swore Hord was standing on the other side of the chamber. She screamed and two guards rushed inside, but no one was there. During the day, she paced the grounds of the abbey, while at night she scrubbed the inside of her chamber and slept with the tallows lit and her door open.

If she could call what she did sleeping.

She slept less each day.

Hord was here. She knew it.

The group of Grants left Ramsay land. Connor's father had promised Maddie she'd be back in time for Yule, and Braden and Roddy were both ready to head home.

The temptation to turn toward Cameron land and Lochluin Abbey was undeniable, but everyone had advised him to be patient.

And patient he was for nearly a sennight at Grant Castle. By then, his every thought was for Sela. His hope that she would accept his proposal had dimmed, yet he longed to know how she was doing.

If she was well.

He awakened early and went down to the great hall to break his fast. To his surprise, his sister Kyla was already sitting at the dais, munching on an apple. "'Tis quite a belly you're growing there, lass," he teased. "Think you 'tis a lad or a lassie?"

She giggled, her dark hair unbound and hanging down

her back. "I think 'tis a lassie, but if I have to listen to one more of Finlay and Jamie's arguments about who's having the first laddie, I'll tear every single one of my hairs out."

He smiled at his sister. "You're verra happy. I like seeing you this way."

"I am," she said, beaming, but her smile slipped as she looked at him. "*But* you're not. I wish I'd met Sela. Tell me about her."

"She's almost as tall as I am, and her hair is long and so blonde 'tis nearly white. She's beautiful, but I saw the pain in her eyes right away. I knew she was hurting. Although I didn't understand her circumstances at first, I suspected there was more to her than met the eye. I don't know what else to say other than the more I learned about her, the more I started falling for her."

Their mother emerged from the kitchens with a bowl of porridge, her eyes lighting up when she saw them. They were the only ones in the great hall because it was so early. "May I join my children?"

"Of course, Mama," Kyla said.

"Am I interrupting anything?" Maddie asked as she sat beside Kyla. "I don't wish to get in the way of an important conversation."

"Connor was just telling me about Sela."

"Mama," Connor said, "I've been wanting to ask you a question, if you don't mind."

"I'll answer if I can," she said, taking a bite of her porridge.

"Papa told me it took you awhile to accept his proposal. What changed your mind?"

His mother fussed with the stray hairs that had fallen from her plait as she thought. "I was afraid of your father. He had this way of yelling when he got upset that I didn't like."

"Papa?" Kyla said in surprise, leaning forward on her elbows. "He never yells."

"Now he rarely does, but when he was young? Ask your uncles. They'll tell you the same. Age has mellowed him, definitely, but my reluctance to marry him was more about me, not him." She lowered her spoon into the bowl and set her elbows on the table, folding her hands. "Connor, that poor woman was misused for five years. But the worst part of the ill treatment she suffered is she was forced to watch her bairn be misused. I can't imagine going through something like that. Her guilt, however misguided, must be verra powerful. At least, mine would be."

"But why?" Kyla asked. "'Twas not her fault if the men controlled her."

"No matter what, I would wonder if there was something I could have done for my bairn, some way I could have outsmarted them or run away."

A fast scowl stole over Kyla's face. "Oh, Mama. I have to agree with her, Connor. I was awfully mad I couldn't outsmart my captors when I was kidnapped. I was mad at them, but I was also mad at myself for not being clever enough to get myself out of the situation."

"But you did get away," Connor reminded her.

"Aye, but that didn't matter. I'll never forget how hard it was to talk to Papa when I came back. I was so ashamed of what I'd done."

"And Sela's suffering was on a much larger scale," his mother said. "I don't believe any of us can comprehend what she's been through. Watching her parents killed, watching her daughter undergo torture. My heavens." She stared into her bowl of porridge as if transported back to another time long ago. "You have to be patient. And I know this doesn't make sense to you, but she has to learn to love herself again."

"What?" Connor asked.

"She's angry with herself for all that transpired. She may even believe that she could have prevented either of her parents' death. She has to love herself before she can love another."

Kyla nodded, taking another bite of her apple. "Our mother speaks wisely. Heed her words."

Connor's twin brothers burst in through the front door, full of energy and vigor despite the early hour. "Get your lazy arse out in the lists, brother," Jake bellowed. "I'd like to see how you beat those Dubh men."

"Nay," Jamie said. "I want him to go to the butts with me. I heard Aunt Gwyneth worked with you for a time."

He nodded. "And Gregor. What better teachers could I have? I'll visit the butts with you, Jamie. They gave me some special arrows I've not seen before."

He got up from the table, leaned down to kiss his mother on the cheek, and said, "My thanks to you both."

Connor spent several hours working with his brothers, taking the occasional break for ale and conversation. It was a good distraction from thoughts of Sela—until Jamie mentioned her.

"Are you worried about Mama and Papa accepting Sela?" Jamie asked.

Connor thought about his recent conversations with his parents. "At first, aye. But they both told me they don't judge her for what she did under the control of the Dubh men. Do you feel differently?"

Jamie shook his head. "Nay, she's a brave lass for certes. I hate spiders." He shuddered dramatically as he said it.

Connor looked to Jake. "Your thoughts, Jake? How hard was it for Aline?"

His brother sighed. "I'll warn you 'tis verra difficult to watch someone heal. Aline cried out in her sleep for a long time, but she's healed a wee bit more with each passing moon. Patience, brother. It takes patience, and control."

"Control?" Connor asked.

"Aye. Else you'll be tempted to punch the wall and pretend 'tis the bastard who hurt her. If you give in to anger, you'll end up with a broken fist and no satisfaction."

"How is she? I haven't seen her around."

"She's been sick."

"Carrying?" Jamie asked, his eyes lighting up.

"Nay, she's not carrying. You worry about your wife and I'll worry about Aline."

Connor didn't know what else to ask his brothers, so he just shrugged—the gesture as helpless as he felt. "Would you like to see what Gregor gave me before we left Ramsay land?" He reached into his quiver and pulled out four arrows. "Interesting, aye? When he went off to rescue Linet, he feared his arrow skills weren't enough to protect them both. He started practicing with his sword more, but he also thought of ways he could make his arrows more deadly."

"Why do they look like that? I've not seen those before," Jake asked. "Though I'm not a skilled archer. You are better than I am at this, Connor."

Jamie sputtered out a laugh. "You'll not hear him say those words often." He turned one of the arrows over in his hand. "Quite unusual, I agree. Why change the edge?"

"'Twill light with fire, if I wish."

Jake had turned away from them but jerked back around in an instant. "Fire? For what?"

"There's no harm in making something twice as deadly," Jamie said. "Besides, haven't you been in a situation where you can't make a direct hit to man's heart or his head? A fiery arrow to the arm might still be deadly. Or you could use one to light up any building made of wood or with thatched roofs. Ingenious. Leave it to Gregor to think of such a thing."

"Aye," Connor replied, pulling the new arrow out and aiming it to test its weight. "Jennet creates all manner of things, so I wasn't surprised to hear Gregor had done some inventing of his own."

He let the arrow loose and hit his target on the first try. His face shifted into a scowl as he imagined Hord on the receiving end of that arrow.

"Who were you pretending that was, brother?" Jake asked, giving him a knowing look.

Connor shrugged. "Hord. The man had an obsession with Sela. Am I the fool for believing that he'll return for her after everyone's given up on him? Was that not the way Mama's abuser did it? Hord is shrewd, I'll give him that much."

"Don't doubt your instincts," Jamie said. "If you're prepared to face him, he'll never catch you completely off-guard."

"And as for Sela, stay patient," Jake said, clasping his shoulder. "You'll have no regrets."

Jamie snorted. "'Tis about time, brother. We were starting to wonder if you'd ever choose a lass."

"Aye, we were going to choose for you this summer if you hadn't."

"My thanks, but I'll choose my own wife." Connor didn't even want to think about what they may have planned for him. "I think I'll not trust my dear brothers to choose for me, based on past experiences."

Jamie took a swig of ale from his skin. "Why would you say such a thing?"

"Och, I don't know. Mayhap memories of the time you tried to match me with the one who was in love with me? The one who couldn't even talk to me because she was so busy staring at me and petting my hand?

Jamie spewed his ale across the ground in front of him, then burst into laughter.

Connor crossed his arms in front of him, staring at the two. "That was at one of the Ramsay festivals. And I did what I had to, but when she tried to climb up behind me on the rope swing, I had to finally put an end to that match."

Jake bent over at the waist and roared unlike he'd heard in a long time.

Jamie sputtered, "We didn't really know the lass. We just noticed how she stared at you. You must admit she was pretty."

"I'll agree with that. She was a beauty, but 'tis not all that matters. Laugh as you like, you two, but I am bigger than both of you now," he said with a grin, turning back to the target and shooting off a few more arrows.

Jake asked, "What makes you think we had anything to do with that?"

"Mayhap because the year before you tried to attach me to a lass who was older than our mother," he muttered, firing off two more arrows.

"Now, Connor. We were just teasing you back then. We thought you'd gain some experience from the woman," Jake said, moving up to stand next to Jamie, clasping his shoulder. "'Twas part of our duty as older brothers. This time, we'd find you a nice lass your own age."

"Sure you would," Connor said, finally stopping to stare at his two dear brothers. "The woman whispered things in my ear that I'd never heard of before. She scared me when she described all that she wanted to do with me. I was only five and ten at the time."

Jamie took another swig of ale, still chuckling a wee bit.

"And I mean explicit detail. Things I don't think you knew anything about back then. I should have sent her back to the two of you."

Jamie spewed his ale again, breaking into gales of laughter. When he was finally able to calm himself, he said, "Our apologies, but 'twas funny."

Jake said, "The one you've found, I noticed, is a wee bit different. Sela's quite stunning."

Connor crossed his arms and gave his brothers a smug look. "Aye, and as I said, if you ever have a mind to attempt anything like that again, remember I'm bigger than you now."

"Aye," Jamie said, always conniving. "But 'twill be two

against one."

Loki came up behind them and said, "Nay, two against two. I'll stand with you, Connor."

Jamie and Jake made disgruntled sounds.

"My thanks, cousin," Connor said. "Didn't hear you sneak in."

"Just thought I'd check on the standing of the Dubh men before Yule. I'll be staying put for the rest of the winter, but curiosity has me wondering..."

"No news of any Channel activity. 'Tis done as far as we know."

"Good. Now, let's see who's the best archer, shall we?"

They continued working at the butts. Shortly after the sun was at its highest, Connor noticed two horses headed their way. His heart lodged in his throat.

"Are those Cameron plaids, Jamie?" he asked.

"I think they are."

He mounted his horse and rode out to intercept the messengers. One guard asked him, "Connor Grant?"

"Aye, I'm Connor."

"Your presence is needed immediately at Lochluin Abbey. Mother Matilda's request."

Shite.

CHAPTER TWENTY-FIVE

S ELA DID HER MORNING CHORES, chopping the vegetables for the main course, but she couldn't erase the feeling that Hord was hiding somewhere near or in the abbey. How could she prove it? She surely did not wish to find him.

Sister Therese came along to check on her progress, something she usually did once a day. "My, but you've cut those vegetables mighty fine this morn, Sela. Are you all right?"

She dropped her knife, just then noticing what a tight grip she'd had on it, then wiped her hands on the apron she wore over her wool gown. "I'm fine, Sister. And you?"

"Aye. Fortunately, I will enjoy the diced vegetables that size, but you needn't have cut them so small."

"My apologies, Sister. I'll do better on the morrow. Allow me to step away and put them in the pot on the fire."

"Aye, then you may go to chapel."

She loaded the foodstuffs into the pot, then headed to the chapel after cleaning her spot. Normally, she made her way to the altar and knelt, saying her prayers for forgiveness and guidance.

This morn, she stood at the back, unable to move forward.

He's here, Lord. He's here, Lord. Please help me. Please don't allow him to hurt me again. Protect Claray. Please teach me how to protect myself.

After chanting her prayer at least ten times, the answer came to her.

She needed a stout stick to fight back.

Thank You, my Lord.

She hurried toward the back door, hoping not to run into anyone. There was still plenty of time to clean the chambers later. She had to find a big stick first.

Several guards milled about outside. She greeted each one politely, then moved on.

"Where are you off to, my lady?" one asked.

"I'm headed to the forest. Would you mind escorting me? I don't wish to run into any reivers."

Or Hord. But she kept that thought to herself, sensing no one else would understand.

Two guards followed her as she moved through the trees, checking next to the fallen logs for the exact stick she needed. It took her ten minutes to find one that was big enough to do the job.

She wrapped her fingers around the thick branch and swung it through the air as hard as she could, picturing Hord's laughing face in front of her.

She liked it.

"What do you need that for, my lady?" one guard asked.

If she told him, he might take it away. The guards were there to protect them after all, and they likely wouldn't understand why she'd want something to protect herself.

"Yule is coming, as you know. 'Tis going to be a decoration," she lied. "I thought I could hang some berries and ribbons from it to pretty up the warming room and the chapter house."

He didn't ask any more questions, instead moving along with her and looking for more.

She found another.

And another.

And another.

Each one was bigger than the previous one.

"My lady, are you sure you need all of these? We can carry a few more, but then we may have trouble getting them back to the abbey."

She looked at the guards' heavily laden arms and said, "My apologies. I think one more should be enough."

Her breath caught when she found exactly what she was searching for. It was so large that she'd barely be able to swing it. But she'd practice until she was stronger. That was what Connor had told her about archery and sword skills. It just took practice.

She could barely lift it, but it was perfect.

"Here, my lady, I'll carry that one for you."

"Nay!"

She hadn't meant to shout at him, but she strongly felt this was the one. She needed to be the one to bring it back to the abbey. "I'll pull it behind me. I think we have enough. We can return now and many thanks for your help."

Both guards beamed. They were used to dealing with nuns and priests and monks. She supposed they enjoyed talking to a regular person for a change.

She yanked the large branch behind her. It took perseverance, but she made it back. "You can put those branches right there and I'll take care of them."

After the guards left for their original posts, she took a stroll around the periphery of the abbey. She needed a plan. She had enough sticks that she could spread them around. Carefully measuring out the distances, she found a place to hide each weapon around the outside of the abbey, each one perfectly positioned so she'd always be able to reach one.

No matter where she was when Hord found her.

Wouldn't he be surprised when she hit him on the side of his head, knocking him over? When she was finally satisfied, she went inside, taking the largest stick with her to put in her chamber.

Mother Matilda stopped her in the passageway. "My, my, but what have you there, child?"

"'Tis a large branch that I'd like to break up to use in decorations." She thought carefully, begging the Lord's forgiveness for lying to an abbess. "'Tis a surprise so I cannot tell you any more than that."

She gave the abbess her best smile, then headed toward her chamber. Grabbing all of her cleaning supplies, she moved on to complete her chores for the day. The last chamber to be cleaned would be her own, just before she went to sleep.

If she could sleep. She kept trying, but she lay awake most nights—worrying, planning, strategizing how she would beat Hord this time.

The more chambers she cleaned, the more concerned she became.

There were more spiders than usual.

Most days there were only one or two per chamber. Today, she'd found four in one, five in another, and three in the third one.

Hord was here. She was certain of it.

She hurried to her chamber to clean it, but then she had second thoughts. It was paramount that she prepare herself for the bastard. Dusk was upon them, but there was enough light for her to see. She traced her earlier steps and found each of the sticks, taking them one by one back to her chamber.

She'd only just finished when Sister Grace entered the chamber. "More sticks, Sela?" she asked.

"Aye, 'tis a surprise. I cannot tell how I plan to use them." She smiled and wiped the sweat from her brow.

Sister Grace rushed down the passageway toward the abbess's solar, but Sela didn't have time to consider why she was in such a hurry. She had to clean.

Kill more spiders.

She cleaned every space in her chamber. She'd found six

spiders. How could that many have found their way into her chamber? There was only one answer.

Hord had put them there.

Sitting on the edge of the bed, she allowed the tears to come, flooding her cheeks.

Where was Connor? She needed him, but she'd sent him away.

She blew her nose into a linen square when the abbess entered. "How are you this eve, Sela? I hear you've been quite busy."

"Good eve to you, Mother Matilda. Please come in and have a seat on my bed." The abbess sat next to her. "My chamber is clean. I just finished it, though I've been busy this day. I saved mine for last."

"What is it that keeps you so busy?"

She smiled at the abbess, mopping her tears with the linen square. It was comforting to have someone else with her. Hord wouldn't come for her if she wasn't alone, would he? "I'm killing spiders."

"There are more than usual? You always keep your chamber spotless."

"I try my verra best. Excuse me, there's another." She bolted up from her seat and used a cloth to squash the beast on the wall.

"Oh, another right there." She slapped the wall with her bare hand.

"And there's another."

Mother Matilda had gotten up, too, and stood slightly behind her. "I don't see any spiders. Are you sure your eyes aren't deceiving you?"

"Nay, see? There's another." She jumped to another spot, slapping the wall with her cloth. "And that one, too. How could you not see it? And there's another yet. And another."

Sister Grace came to the door, concern on her face, though Sela had no idea why.

"Mother Matilda, the person you sent for this morn has

arrived."

Sela didn't care who was here. She had three more spiders to kill.

She had to do it. Before they got her.

———◆———

Connor had ridden Midnight Moon so fast that he gave him an apple as soon as they arrived. Nodding to a stable lad, he said, "He needs water."

He rushed inside, not surprised to see a nun waiting for him, kneading her hands. "She's in her chamber. Mother Matilda is with her. She's seeing things now."

"Where is Claray?" he asked. "You will keep her overnight?"

"Mistress Jennie took Claray to her keep."

He wasn't quite sure what to do, but he followed the nun to the chamber and stood in the doorway, his eyes finding Sela in the dark. She moved from spot to spot on the wall—smashing, slapping, and squashing at will. He doubted there was anything there.

Mother Matilda greeted him and said, "I know not what I can do for her."

"My thanks for calling me. I'll probably take her to my aunt Jennie's keep to calm her down. We'll likely return on the morrow."

The abbess patted his arm and stepped away.

Sela hadn't even noticed his presence. "Sela? What has you so busy?" he asked.

Her head spun around, her eyes lighting with recognition, but the initial spark of joy left them and she whirled back to face the wall. She stood in one of the corners, sobbing. "Connor, have you not heard? Hord is here."

He could tell she'd lost control so he chose his next words carefully. "Where is he?"

"I haven't seen him for certain, but I know he's here. Look at all the spiders in my chamber. Usually there's only one or two. I've killed over a score, and there are so many more. Look at this corner. The webs hide their true number, but I must kill them all. I have to protect Claray."

He slowly moved over to her, not wanting to upset her. "What are all the sticks for?"

"To hit Hord when he finds me. I remembered what you told me about practicing. He won't find me defenseless. But these stupid spiders keep coming," she said, her voice breaking as she sobbed. "These spiders, Connor. I cannot stop them, they keep growing bigger, they keep... Help me put an end to them, please."

He came up behind her and wrapped his arm around her waist. "Hush, sweetling. I'll take care of the spiders." He brought his hand out to take the cloth from her, noticing there wasn't a spider or a web in sight. "Watch me kill them." He took the cloth and swept it up the corner, then down again. "See? They're all gone now. I won't let them harm you."

She pointed to the right. "There's one over there."

He didn't see anything, but he pretended to kill one.

"And one over there." She pointed to the left. "Connor, I can't keep up with them. I know not what to do." She broke away from his arms and started slapping at different spots on the wall. "Look at them down here," she cried, kneeling on the floor to kill the spiders she believed to be in the edge between the floor and the wall. "Help me kill them, please."

She slapped and hit and slapped and hit until he could stand no more. He wrapped his arm around her waist and lifted her away from the edge. "Why don't you let me kill them for you? Do you not recall that I said I would protect you forever?"

"Will you? Can you? There's so many that we will both need to kill them. I cannot allow them to get to Claray. Please help me." She pushed away from him and placed her hand on his chest.

The fear in her gaze was more than he could handle. How was he to help her? "Why don't I take you to Aunt Jennie's and I'll come back and burn them out of the chamber."

"You will? For me? 'Tis a wonderful idea. They'll surely all be dead then."

The haunted look in her gaze was too much for him. He had to calm her, convince her that there were no spiders there.

"I promise. As soon as we get there, I'll turn around and come right back."

"My thanks, Connor. Make sure you check afterward to be sure they're gone. Under my bed, behind the chairs, in the corners, even the ceiling. They can hide anywhere."

Her body wrenched with sobs and he picked her up in her arms. "I'll take care of you. I love you, remember?" He kissed her forehead.

"Aye, I love you, too. I'm sorry I hurt you."

"I understand. I will wait for you."

"But Hord. You must find him." She rested her head on his shoulder and continued to sob.

"He'll not touch you. Do you trust me?" He kissed her again, hoping to distract her from the chaos in her mind. He'd do anything to help.

"Aye, I trust you. You'll protect me." Her hands gripped his arms so tightly that he wondered if she'd ever let go.

"I will." He carried her down the stairs and through the passageway. Mother Matilda nodded to him as he carried her outside. By the time they reached his horse, she'd fallen sound asleep. The stablemaster stepped forward to gather her into his arms so Connor could mount and then handed her up to him.

Cradling Sela on his lap, Connor spoke to the two Grant guards who'd traveled with him. "I want you checking the perimeter for strangers. I'll send some Cameron guards to assist you."

He doubted they'd find anything. She'd imagined all the spiders. He hadn't seen any in the entire abbey, and he'd looked on his way down the passageway. The bastard frightened her so that he continued to torture her from afar.

Even so, he knew better than to ignore a woman's intuition. Gavin had told him how Merewen could feel Linet's presence. Could this be similar?

When he arrived on Cameron land, he carried Sela inside. Aunt Jennie had been informed of his arrival and rushed out to meet him. "Is she hale? Did she hurt herself? Does she have a fever?"

He glanced down at Sela to ensure she was still asleep, then said, "She thinks the man who tortured her, the one who loves spiders, is back. I suspect 'tis all in her mind, but to be safe, I sent the two guards who accompanied me out to search the perimeter of your land. Would you be able to have Uncle Aedan send a few of his guards out, too?"

"Of course. I'll speak with him. Claray is staying with us and she's doing verra well. Why don't you take Sela to our hideaway? That way Claray will never see her in this condition. I can send food and ale out for you."

"My thanks, Aunt Jennie. She fell asleep as soon as I picked her up."

Jennie led him out of the back of the keep, and he followed her down a path until they reached a cottage hidden in the brush.

He recalled hearing about this cottage from his brothers, but he'd never been inside before. Nestled in the middle of carefully-tended flowers and trimmed bushes, it consisted of two chambers. The front chamber was small but cozy, with a table with four chairs in the middle and two larger, cushioned chairs in front of the hearth. Vases of dried flowers on the mantle above it gave the place a pleasing scent of lavender. The only other furnishing was a chest covered with thick furs and a couple of books resting on top. Jennie loved books, so it was no surprise to find them inside the cottage.

Jennie moved to the back chamber, waving her hand as she spoke. "Aedan loves it so much that he added the front chamber. Sometimes we like to sit and read out here where 'tis so quiet."

The back chamber held a large bed, piled high with furs and pillows, but his gaze caught on the unusual ceiling. He couldn't help but stare at it as he followed his aunt into the back.

Aunt Jennie said, "It opens to the sky, but you'll not be using that his time of the year. Aedan had it built so we could look at the stars in the summer. He has the rectangular part connected to a rope outside. He can lift the roof and tuck it away for the night, though you must do it from outside. 'Tis one of Aedan's favorite things, to gaze up at the stars on a clear night. 'Tis far too cold this time of year, and Sela needs you close."

He wasn't sure what to do for Sela and said as much. "How can I help, Aunt Jennie?"

"Set her down on the bed so I can examine her before I go."

Connor did as Aunt Jennie asked, watching her skilled fingers travel across Sela's body without disturbing her. "Hand me the tallow, please."

Connor gave it to her and she held it up close to Sela's face. She did not stir or even twitch. "Look at the dark circles under her eyes. She hasn't been sleeping much at all if I were to guess, which is probably why she fell asleep in your arms right away. She knows she's safe." She handed Connor back the tallow and covered Sela up with a plaid.

"What do I do for her, Aunt Jennie?"

"Let her sleep. She'll probably sleep the night away and wake up with little memory of the tricks her mind played on her. Exhaustion can do odd things to a person. I'll return with a basket of food and some ale. Let's hope she's fine in the morn, but I would suggest keeping her away from the keep and Claray for the time being."

"Are you sure seeing Claray won't help her?"

"That all depends on your answer to this question. Could she be right? Could this man be watching her? Because if so, I'm sure she wants Claray far, far away."

Connor had no idea, but he intended to find out.

CHAPTER TWENTY-SIX

WHEN SELA OPENED HER EYES, she thought she was still dreaming for a moment. One of her good dreams, where Connor was with her, not a nightmare full of spiders. They were in a strange chamber, and he lay next to her on the covers wearing naught but a plaid. It had to be a dream, and yet, she was wearing her gown from the abbey. She climbed out of bed, careful not to awaken him, and shed her clothing.

He did not disappear.

Could this be real?

She could look at him all day long. He looked peaceful, sound asleep as he was. Then, to her surprise, one of his eyes popped open, followed by the other.

"Are you really here, Connor Grant?" She ran her finger down his jawline. "Why did you come? Are you growing a beard? You look quite scruffy."

"Three questions are too many at once. Aye, I'm here. I came because I love you, and I didn't have the chance to trim my beard first."

"Where are we?" she asked, her finger still traveling over his body, over his ear, down his chin, to his dark chest hairs. She could go on touching him forever.

"We are in a cottage on Cameron land."

"How did you know to come?"

"Mother Matilda was concerned about you."

"I turned daft, did I not? I saw things that weren't there.

I thought Hord was outside the abbey, setting his spiders loose on me. What is wrong with me?" She stopped the movement of her hand and locked gazes with him.

He took her hand and brought it to his lips for a kiss, then cradled it against his chest. "My aunt, the healer, says exhaustion can breed illusions. You fell asleep as soon as I picked you up in my arms. You had dark circles under your eyes."

"Connor, will this never end?"

He sighed, pulling her closer. "Aye, someday 'twill end for you, but 'tis too fresh."

"Make love to me," she said, feeling his hardened sex underneath his plaid. "I need you."

"Sela, we are not married. I could get you with child. 'Tis wrong for us to keep doing this, but I'll tell you that you are impossible to ignore when you lie in my arms with naught on. Have you decided to accept my proposal?"

She chewed on her bottom lip before she answered. "How can I marry you when I fear I am losing my mind? I sent Claray along with Mistress Jennie because my night-mares were becoming worse, and I feared I would hurt her in the middle of the night." She paused, considering the matter—if she got with child, would it be a sign?—then said, "If I am with child, I will marry you. Otherwise, I will not subject you to my maladies." She reached down underneath his plaid and gripped him lightly, moving her hand up and down. "I need you. Please?"

He growled and took her lips in his, ravaging her mouth with a desire that she shared. She pushed him away enough to say, "I do love you, Connor."

"All right, but this will never happen again until you agree to be mine," he said, moving his hand down to the thatch of light curls in the vee of her legs, teasing her folds with his finger before he plunged into her slick wetness.

"'Tis not the part of you I want." She reached for his hand and removed it.

He stood up and dropped his plaid to the ground, then settled himself between her thighs and said, "Guide me. Show me you want this."

She spread her legs and grasped him, bringing him to her entrance, playing with the head a bit before positioning him to enter her. "Your turn."

He plunged into her, moaning when he was deeply seated, and dropped his head to her shoulder. "Sela, you drive me to daftness. Do you not know it?"

He pulled slowly out and then moved back into her, waiting until the last second to thrust in completely. She gasped.

"I love you. Tell me you love me again," he whispered against her ear, his warm breath heating her even more.

"I love you, Connor. I need you."

He thrust and withdrew, thrust and then held, pulsating in the deepest part of her.

She gasped, each one coming in a higher pitch. "Connor."

"You'll be mine someday, will you not?" He brought his lips down to the silky skin of her neck, caressing every spot where he could feel the beat of her heart.

"Aye, I am yours now. I'll never want another."

He pulled out again, propelling himself in and out until she feared she was loud enough to be heard in the abbey. Her need built inside her, deliciously painful, but she wanted him to set the pace. "Again," she whispered in a husky tone.

He continued to move slowly, in and out, in a rhythm that was sweet torture. When she could take no more, she pressed against him. "More, faster, please."

He sped up the rhythm, driving into her with a force that she needed. Clutching his shoulder, digging her nails into his skin, she cried out his name as she teetered on the edge, finally going over into a convulsing state of pleasure as he called out her name and joined her.

They lay there quietly, bodies still intertwined. "Sela, I cannot live without you," Connor said at last. "Please marry me."

"When I am convinced I will not be a burden to you, I will consider it. I can't say any vows to you until I trust myself. Can you understand that?"

He nuzzled her neck, taking in the sweetness of her scent, and kissed her shoulder. "You need more time. I will be patient."

He rolled to the side and she rested her head on his shoulder. "Tell me something else. What made you think Hord was back? You must have had a reason."

She thought back on the last few days. "It was just a feeling—that I was being watched, judged—that he was lying in wait for me. Instead of cowering like I used to, I vowed to fight him. I searched and found several stout sticks that I could use to defend myself. But I know I imagined the spiders in my chamber last eve. I did find a few more than usual around the abbey, but that truly means naught. I know that."

"Aye, it could be just the weather," he said, lightly rubbing her back. "Do you want me to take my leave again?"

"As much as I love having you here, we cannot live like this without marriage. I know that. The only thing I ask is that you might search the area a bit before you leave. Would you be willing to do that? I know the guards at the abbey have looked for signs of Hord, but they're not like Grant guards."

"My men are already searching. Why don't you dress and return to the abbey when the sun is up, and I'll talk with Aunt Jennie and Uncle Aedan. Tell them more about the possible intruder."

"I would appreciate that. Will you stop to see me before you go? Please?" She played with his bottom lip and his teeth came out to nip her lightly.

"I promise." He stood up, giving her a full view of his

body, the planes and crevices of his muscles begging to be touched, but she controlled herself.

"Someday, when I'm able, I plan to kiss every spot on that big body of yours. Just looking at you pleases me."

He spun around, a blinding grin on his face. "And how I look forward to reciprocating."

She watched him grow hard in front of her, chuckling because she was so happy that she could incite such a reaction in him.

"Keep staring at me, lass, and see what happens," he taunted.

He would be hers if she would just say so, and oh, how she wanted to say so, but he deserved better than a woman who couldn't control her own mind. She tore her gaze from his fabulous body and grabbed her clothing.

Donning her chemise and gown first, she stretched before she walked over and peeked out the door.

She swore a shadow crossed in front of her and hid behind a tree.

Now she knew she was turning daft.

———◆———

Sela was back inside the abbey, waiting in the front receiving room for Connor to return. The men he'd sent out the previous eve had found nothing, but he'd gone out again with a larger group, including a few Cameron guards. They'd been gone nearly three hours. She'd gone through the motions, completing all of her chores, but now there was nothing to distract her.

She wanted to see him.

She wanted to know what he'd say about Hord.

Fortunately, she didn't have to wait much longer. Connor stopped Midnight Moon in front of the abbey after waving the Cameron guards on to their keep. The two guards he'd brought with him continued to patrol the area as they'd done since he arrived.

Rather than wait for him to come inside, she rushed outside. "Did you find anything?"

He dismounted and took her hand. "Nay, naught. We found one place a short distance away that appeared to be a reivers' camp, but they'd moved on. There was no evidence of a single traveler anywhere."

So she *was* losing her grip on reality. Somehow, she would have preferred it if they'd found him, or some sign of him. It would have meant she was okay. "My thanks for checking. It must be my imagination. I'm so sorry to have brought you here for naught," she said, tears misting in her eyes.

"Naught? I'd gladly come to see the woman I love anytime. All you need to do is say the word, and I'll come to you." He glanced up at the skies, gray clouds moving in. "But I must go. We wish to be home before nightfall. Send a messenger anytime," he said. He gave her a brief kiss on the lips, then mounted his horse.

He turned away, but she stopped him. "Connor?"

"Aye?"

"Remember me, please? I...I don't want you to give up on me after all. I have this fear you'll forget me when you are around all the lasses in Clan Grant. I'm sure there is a line of beauties hoping to catch your eye."

"That could be, but I don't notice them. Only one lass has ever caught my eye, and she stands in front of me. I'll remember you forever."

He gave a short wave and took his leave. The skies were beginning to look fierce, so she hugged herself and hurried back inside. Mother Matilda was waiting for her.

The older woman gave her a shrewd look. "You are better?"

"Aye, forgive me for whatever I did last eve. I don't recall much, but I know I was not making sense."

"Sela, when you came here, I asked you to decide who your heart belongs to. I told you mine belongs to God. I don't know if you've figured it out yet, but I'm quite sure your heart belongs to Connor Grant."

Her head dropped and she fought to hold back tears. "Mayhap you are right, Mother Matilda, but I still have many sins to atone for. I'm working hard on that, and I pray every day."

"Good. I'm glad you are. Your answers will come soon."

She had visited with Claray earlier, while Connor spoke with his aunt and uncle. The wee lass was having the time of her life with the Cameron girls, Tara and Riley. Jennie had invited Claray to stay for a few more days, and Sela had heartily agreed. Riley was twelve summers and Tara ten and six, old enough to watch over her although not so old that they wouldn't want to play.

Although she missed her daughter, Sela did not want to burden Claray with her problems.

Talk was quiet that eve after the last meal, as if the nuns were afraid she would break in front of them.

Sister Grace asked, "Are you sure you're hale?"

"Aye, I was exhausted, and I don't recall most of what happened. I feel much better today." Another white lie. Much of the night had come back to her, but she didn't feel ready to discuss it with anyone.

When the meal finished, she stopped to say her evening prayers, thanking God especially for Connor, then went straight to her chamber. She searched it thoroughly and didn't find even one spider, to her delight.

She'd almost fallen asleep when a huge boom of thunder awakened her, so loud that she sat straight up in bed, reaching for an extra plaid due to the sudden chill in the air. The storm continued, but she was so exhausted, her eyes fluttered shut again.

Another loud bang rent the air and she bolted up again. Something wasn't right.

Someone was in her chamber.

Hord.

"I wondered how long you'd sleep through the storm. I grew weary of waiting for you. I've spent much time in the cellars of both abbeys, collecting my friends," he said, holding up two bags containing his wicked creatures. "We had a wonderful time until the Grant fool came along, and you whored your way into his bed. Did you enjoy that little bit of fun last eve, Sela?"

It took her a moment to find her voice, but once she did, she shouted, "Get out, you bastard. I'm not going anywhere with you." Climbing out of bed, she raced toward the door, yelling for help, but the thunder drowned her out. Hord grabbed her by the arm, hard enough to leave bruises.

"You'll shut your whoring mouth, or I'll take Claray instead of you. Make your choice."

"Nay, nay. What do you want?"

His finger brushed her cheek. "Why you, my sweet. 'Tis all I've ever wanted. If you'd only accepted my proposal, you would have had a wonderful life. You are mine, and if I cannot have you, no one will. Do you understand?"

She nodded, looking up into his crazed eyes. His brown hair was wet from the rain, hanging in strings around his face. The dirt under his fingernails made her wish to vomit. "Where are you taking me?"

"Eventually, I'll take you to our verra own home, but I do not wish to travel in the dark, so I have other plans for you this night. You need to learn to obey me."

Keeping hold of her arm, he dragged her down the stairs at the end of the passageway. She knew what awaited them—the dark cellars. He picked up two bags from the bottom of the steps and headed toward a door that led outside. "No one will see me. They haven't noticed me all week, and I doubt they're patrolling in the dark. But be forewarned, if you scream, I will let you go and head straight to the Cameron keep. I've already found my way into their cellars. It will be easy for me to find wee Claray in the middle of this storm."

CHAPTER TWENTY-SEVEN

SELA DID AS HORD ASKED, following him quietly as he yanked her through the mud and the trees. The sheeting rain continued to pound down around them, drenching her thoroughly in the cold. He'd allowed her to get her mantle, but it did little good.

She fell and screamed, hoping the sound would be heard, but the din of the storm was too loud. Even the openings in the stables had been bolted shut. The horses were all under cover and the area was empty.

Hord dragged her to her feet and yanked on her arm. Tears threatened to drench her cheeks, but she refused to give into them, not wanting to let the bastard know she feared him. He finally stopped tugging on her when they reached a clearing in the woods. She didn't like what she saw in front of her.

Ropes tied to two trees.

"What are you doing? Leave me be! Connor Grant will return and kill you."

Hord just laughed. "He left in a hurry. You think he cares for you? He comes to lie between your legs and you let him. He took what he wanted and left. He'll not be back."

He pulled her to the trees.

"Nay, you'll not tie me up. Nay, you won't." She fought with all her might, but he was stronger. If only she had one of the sticks she'd collected, but she'd moved them back outside, thinking Hord's return an illusion. A large stick sat a short distance away, so she kicked and fought her way to it. Grabbing it up, she swung it into his cheek with all her might. He roared, letting go of her.

She took off back toward the abbey, but he followed and caught up with her, slapping her and throwing her to the ground. Before she could recover, he flipped her over and sat on top of her. All her squirming did naught to budge him.

"You bitch. You will pay for that."

When he climbed off her, he grabbed her plait and yanked her behind him, her scalp screaming with pain. Back at the tree, he threw her to the ground and sat on her, tying her arms to the tree one at a time before he climbed off her.

Sitting up, she yanked on both arms, but he'd tied her tightly. She couldn't move them.

He disappeared, to her surprise. She tried her best to slip her wrists out of their bindings, hoping the wetness from the rain would help her, but to no avail.

She was bound and at his mercy.

Hord returned with his two bags of spiders. "This time, there'll be no killing my pets with your hands."

Another bolt of lightning lit up the sky, giving enough light for her to see the crazed look in his eyes.

He set the two bags inside a hollow log to protect them. "Unfortunately, I'll have to wait until the rain stops. I want to watch." His evil grin scared her more than anything.

She prayed and prayed and prayed that the rain wouldn't stop, but of course it did. Hord reached into the log, pulling out the two spider bags and another sack. From that one, he drew out a dry tunic, which he used to replace his sodden one. "I plan to watch you for a long time. I have two lovely bags of my pets, and I'll release them slowly. I wish to be quite comfortable."

She just couldn't stop herself. She bellowed with everything she had, "Connor!"

Connor was only a couple of hours from Cameron land when something caught him—Sela's voice saying his name.

"Connor!"

It was impossible he'd heard her, and yet, he felt certain she needed him. That he should go back for her.

He turned his horse around and said to his guards, "We're going back."

"Why?" one asked.

"I can't explain it, but something is wrong."

The guard surprised him by saying, "Suits me. I could feel something wasn't right there. As much as we searched, we turned up naught, but there was something in the air."

Had he not already decided to go back, the guard's words would have decided the matter for him. If there was even the slightest chance Sela was in danger, he needed to see to her.

They hadn't traveled far when they reached a meadow. Heading across it, he was surprised to hear a whistle off from the side. Stopping his horse, he glanced back over his shoulder. A lone rider headed straight for them. Holding his hand up to his guards, he waited to see what the man would do.

An ally would greet them.

Hord would not.

Rather than turn tail and run, the man headed straight for them. Connor couldn't identify his plaid, so he didn't ride forward to meet him, but turned his horse to face the man.

Recognition dawned as the man came closer. He'd seen him in Inverness. And Berwick, too.

"Connor Grant?" he called out.

"Aye. Who's asking?"

The man stopped his horse directly in front of Midnight Moon. The beast looked lathered. Why had the man been pushing him so?

"My name is Vern. I was Sela's protector, of sorts. I worked with Guy and Dee before they started selling lasses and lads. They would have killed me if I'd left, and I didn't want to abandon Sela and Claray. So I stayed even though I hated them and all they did. I'm grateful for you and yours."

He paused to catch his breath.

Connor said nothing. While he recognized the man, he didn't recall much about him other than the fact that he'd come up to Sela and asked her if she needed help.

That memory was the only reason he allowed the man to speak.

Vern took a deep breath and said, "Hord. He's back. Found a different ship to drag him back to shore before he was too far out. He said he's going after Sela to finish what he started. The man has always been daft for her."

"How long ago did he leave Berwick?"

"He left a few days ago, after hearing she was with the Ramsays. I've been searching for you ever since. I'd heard talk Sela was in Lochluin Abbey, but I didn't tell Hord. Whether he heard on his own, I don't know. But she needs protection."

"Where are you headed now?"

"I'm returning to Inverness. 'Tis where I belong, but I'd hoped to catch up with you or one of your clan to help her. My injury will keep me from being of much help."

Connor noticed the blood-stained section of his trews. "My thanks to you and Godspeed."

He turned his horse around and retraced his path, heading straight back to the abbey. That convinced him. He'd had a strange inkling that Hord was there and Sela needed him, but Vern's confirmation would have convinced even the strongest naysayer.

They hadn't traveled far when the sky opened up and dumped rain all over them. He couldn't let it stop him, though it definitely slowed his travel.

He had to get to her before Hord did.

Lightning forked from the sky as they reached the abbey, lighting up the building in seconds' long bursts. He paused his horse and scanned the area.

The stables were all closed up due to the storm and no one was out.

He had to get inside to see if Sela was there. To his advantage, the rain stopped as he rode toward the abbey. Dismounting his horse, he shook the wetness from his hair as best he could and made haste for the door. He entered the receiving room of the abbey, not surprised to see three guards waiting out the storm.

"Grant, did you not just leave?"

"Aye, but I heard someone was headed this way. Have you seen any strangers in the last few hours? Or the last two days?"

"Nay. We searched with the Camerons' guards after you left, but we found naught. We quit when the rain drenched us. Who the hell would go out in this storm? 'Tis brutal, though it seems to have let up. We'll take up the patrol again."

"I'm going to check on Sela."

"We'll wait for your instructions."

He moved as quietly as possible down the passageway, saying a quick prayer he'd find her sound asleep in her bed, but it didn't surprise him when he found the chamber empty.

She'd been right. The bastard had been here for two days, waiting for the best moment to attack. Hurrying back outside, he said to the guards, "She's been stolen from her bed. I could use your help."

"The lass was daft last eve. Are you sure she didn't just run off on her own?" one of the guards asked. He shifted in his chair, clearly reluctant to leave his comfortable surroundings.

"If she is, I could use your help finding her, you arse." He spun on his heel and returned to his horse to grab his sword and his bow. The perimeter was heavily wooded, so Midnight Moon would have to be left behind.

Three other guards joined him, and he said, "Bring a torch. It could help us find tracks."

"The rain would have washed any tracks away," the lazy one said.

"Just bring a torch, if you please." He was done listening to foolishness. He was about to turn in one direction, toward a clearing surrounded by trees, when he heard a scream from the opposite direction. Spinning on his heel, he raced off, doing his best to keep from falling on the slippery ground.

Hellbent on following the sound he'd heard, he didn't stop running until he was deep in the woods. He heard the men following him, and one had clearly brought a torch because he could see a brief distance ahead of him.

He held his arm up halting the men behind them. He *saw* her. The bastard had tied Sela to a tree, but he was nowhere in sight.

He turned to the man with the torch and said, "Stand next to me in the clearing. I'll do all the talking. Don't do anything unless I tell you to."

Connor charged into the clearing, allowing himself to lock gazes with Sela for a mere second, hoping it was enough to show her that he loved her.

As soon as Hord saw him, he darted behind Sela and put his dagger at her throat.

Connor assessed the situation, his peripheral vision taking in everything. Hord only had two weapons, the one he held and his spiders. Two bags much like Sela had described sat off to the side on top of a hollow log. He knew how much Hord loved his spiders.

Sela was bound to the tree, so she'd be unable to move, which was not helpful. He didn't even know if she could bend down to give him a clear shot.

He pulled out his bow and his sword, but Hord yelled, "Drop the weapons to the ground. All of you."

Doing as instructed, he and the guards dropped their swords, the motion holding Hord's attention enough for Connor to quietly reach for the special arrow Gregor had given him. In the span of a single second, he lifted the special arrow up to the torch and it caught the flame, just as Gregor had said it would.

He nocked the arrow carefully and shot it straight at one of the bags full of spiders.

Hord bellowed as he dropped his knife and ran to the bag, trying to smother the flames. "Nay, I need them. They were chosen especially for my wife, my Sela!"

Connor set another arrow to the torch, and the moment Hord turned to face him, his eyes furious and his mouth open, he fired the second flaming arrow into his chest. His clothing caught fire, spreading slower than usual because they were damp.

Connor raced over to Sela with his dagger, ready to throw it at the man if need be, but Hord ran to his other bag of spiders, grabbing it and clutching it to his chest as they all went up in flames, the bags sizzling oddly.

Connor cut Sela's bonds and tugged her behind him, worried the blackguard would still run at him. He had to admit he'd taken a chance. The flames might not have worked because of the rain.

Hord fell to the ground, his clothing still burning, while the bags of spiders hissed with flames.

Hord, the hoarder of spiders, was dead and would never bother Sela Seton again.

CHAPTER TWENTY-EIGHT

SELA HELD A DEATH GRIP on Connor as Hord fell to the ground. An awful crackling sound echoed through the trees, but the guards seemed oblivious as they offered him their congratulations.

"Took that bastard out, did you not?"

"I can't believe the flames got him in the rain."

His attention was only for Sela. He turned around, taking her hands, but she launched herself into his arms, burying her face in his neck and sobbing. He said to the men, "You take care of putting the flames out and handling the body. I'm taking her back inside." He lifted her into his arms, tucking her against him, hoping that the death of the bastard would put an end to her nightmares and all her torture.

Probably not completely, but...

"Connor, how did you know to come back?" she asked as they cleared the woods.

"I cannot explain it, but I had this feeling. You cried out to me and I heard you. 'Struth is I didn't wish to leave because everything felt off, but I didn't know what else to do because I had no proof that he was here. But I heard you when you called out to me." He passed a bench and sat down, doing his best to push the wet strands of hair back from her face. "Thank the Lord for that. I also ran into a past acquaintance of yours after I turned around. You had a man who watched over you in Inverness."

"Aye, Vern. I'd so hoped he hadn't died. I never saw him after Berwick so I guessed he'd stayed when the Dubh men moved."

"Apparently not. He was in Berwick when Hord returned. He came to warn me, said Hord had set out from Berwick a few days ago. You were right. He was here waiting for the right moment."

"I know. He told me he'd hidden in the cellars. He was angry you'd come to see me. I was so frightened. My thanks to you." She kissed him, suckling on his lower lip for a moment.

He forced himself to pull away. "I don't expect this has changed your mind about marrying me, but I hope it will help you heal. He can never harm you or Claray again."

She rested her head back against his shoulder, wanting to relish these last few moments together. She would never tire of this man, but Hord was not the only reason she struggled so. "I know. For that I'm so grateful, I don't know how to describe it. Connor, I wish I were ready, but I'm just so confused right now."

He stood up and set her feet down, wrapping his arms around her and kissing her forehead. "I'm going to walk you inside. You need to get out of those clothes."

"Can't you find a change of clothing before you go back?"

"I have one in my saddlebag, but I can't stay any longer."

"Why?" she asked, her voice hitching. "Cannot you wait a while?"

"Because it hurts to be this close to you and know you're not mine. I'm sorry, but I must leave." He couldn't explain it any other way. The longing he felt was so keen it hurt. All he wished to do was take her inside the chapel, marry her, and take her home.

He walked her to the door and kissed her deeply. "Remember I will always love you."

With that, he walked away.

Sela couldn't put into words how she felt as she watched the man she loved walk away from her. But she knew, with all her heart, that she had to let him go.

Would Hord's death stop her nightmares?

Had she atoned for all the pain she'd caused the lasses in the Channel?

Would she ever be able to make amends for her sins?

So many questions, so few answers. She needed to do better before she pledged her troth to him.

She stood rooted to the ground, sobbing with all her might.

A few moments later, Connor mounted his horse in his dry clothes, waved to her, then motioned to his guards to move out.

She watched him go down the path away from her and her heart broke into so many pieces she couldn't hold still. Even though nothing had changed, her feet raced after him, and she shouted his name over and over again.

When he stopped and turned to face her, she said, "I love you with all my heart, Connor Grant."

He smiled that beautiful smile of his and then turned back again, pulling on the reins.

She couldn't let him go yet.

"Connor, please!"

He stopped again and she ran up to his horse, leaning against it, and said between her sobs, "Promise you'll never stop loving me?"

"Always and forever."

And Connor Grant rode out of her life again.

She stood in the same spot for a long time, sobbing so hard her breath hitched. She had to watch him until the last signs of him disappeared. When he was finally gone, two sisters came on either side of her and reached for her elbows, turning her around and pointing her back toward the abbey.

A fortnight later, Sela sat in her chamber on the floor, watching her daughter. Claray was such a beautiful child. Thank goodness she'd brought the puppy along as a companion for her. Watching the two play together was one of her rare pleasures.

Sela had spent the time apart from Connor working toward her goals. But all her prayers, all her work did nothing to relieve the guilt she still dealt with on a daily basis.

She'd only had one nightmare since Hord had died. And even that one had been mild. It had been the day after the incident. She'd awoken shaken up, but the feeling dissipated as soon as she recalled the bastard was dead.

The dreams had never come back, for either her or Claray.

The only recurring dream Sela had now was about a handsome man with dark hair just below his shoulders. Normally straight, it curled whenever it got damp, something she privately loved. Every time she thought of her Highlander, her heart smiled.

Yet she hadn't gone to him yet.

She didn't feel worthy of such a man. Only one thing that Hord said stayed with her.

Whore.

Sister Grace knocked her hand on the side of the open door and stepped inside the chamber. "Good afternoon, my dears. Sela, Mother Matilda would like to speak with you. I'll stay with Claray."

"My thanks to you, Sister. I'll go right away."

As her slippers echoed down the passageway, she couldn't help but wonder what this was about. Had the abbess decided it was time for them to leave?

She stepped into the woman's solar and bowed her head. "Greetings to you, Mother Matilda."

"Sit down, Sela. 'Tis time for a wee chat."

Sela took the chair in front of her desk and folded her hands in her lap. She took a deep breath and waited for the abbess to speak.

Mother Matilda leaned back in her chair and asked, "So who does your heart belong to?"

Sela hadn't expected the woman to be so direct. She could feel the blush crossing her face and her neck. While she wished to tell another lie, she'd promised herself she was done lying.

She whispered, "Connor Grant."

The abbess nodded with a smile. "I'm glad you recognize that. I can see it in both of your faces. Has the man proposed marriage to you?"

"Aye."

"But you turned him down?"

She sighed, wondering how to explain herself. "I haven't directly rejected him, but I've asked him to wait. I'm not ready yet."

"What holds you back, child? This is no place for a wee lassie to grow up, nor is it a place for you. Don't you feel you've healed? Your nightmares have ended."

Tears slid down her cheek. "Aye, in some ways. But in other ways…" How did she mention the word "whore" to an abbess?

"What holds you back?" the woman persisted.

"Noble blood," she blurted out, pleased the words had popped into her mind. "Connor should marry a lass of noble blood. I'm no one special. I'm not deserving of him."

"Lass, I'm not going to subject you to this interrogation any longer, but I wish for you to listen to me. Many marriages in this world take place because one powerful family wishes to unite with another, and most of them are unhappy marriages. You have a man who loves you, and if I were you, I would run into his arms."

She tried to speak, but the abbess held her hand up. "Nay,

I don't wish to hear about the fact that you had a child when you were unmarried. That was forced on you, as were many other things. You need to let that go. Connor doesn't care, so why should you? You have a purpose in this world, as does every person born. God decides your purpose. He will let you know what that purpose is, but you need to listen to Him. For me, it's serving our Lord. Yours is not serving God, so what is it? You need to think hard about that. Sometimes a person's purpose is to love and care for another. What is yours?"

Her purpose? She had no idea.

"Go and think on that. And pray for an answer from God. You need to move on with your life."

Sela forced herself to stand and take her leave, again with a short bow. She headed directly to the small chapel used by the nuns. While the abbey contained a larger place of worship they all attended to say mass, this one suited her perfectly.

She knelt and prayed exactly as the abbess had suggested she do. Then she waited, hoping for a quick answer, just like the one she'd received about the stout stick.

Her heart sank when nothing came to her. After a while, she rose and padded down to her chamber, watching Claray giggle with Torry.

"Mama, I miss my friends," her daughter asked. "May we visit them again soon?"

Unable to speak because of the tears lodged in her throat, she just nodded.

Her purpose?

She was more lost than ever.

CHAPTER TWENTY-NINE

IN THE MIDDLE OF THE night, Sela bolted up in bed, something that had happened too often in her life. But this time it wasn't because of Hord or spiders. Her gaze darted around the chamber in search of what had awakened her. Claray and Torry were sleeping with Sister Grace this eve because Sela hadn't wanted her daughter to see her cry herself to sleep.

A woman stood in the doorway.

She blinked three times, but the figure remained. This nun was new to her. There was no wind, yet the woman's gown billowed around her. It was white with a blue band around the middle, so long it seemed to cover her feet. She had a strand of pearls around her neck and hair almost as light as Sela's.

"Good eve, my dear," the lady said, her smile warm and welcoming. "I see I've surprised you." Her eyes actually sparkled in the dark, something that shouldn't be possible.

"Who are you? I've never met you before." Strangely, although Sela knew nothing about this woman, she trusted her completely. There was something about her…

"My name doesn't matter, but my purpose does. I see you're confused about *your* purpose, so I thought I'd assist you, if I may."

"What is *your* purpose?" she hesitated to ask, especially since she suspected this was no normal nun, but she wished to know everything about this woman.

"I'm the guardian of innocent lasses. One of many. I've been called to this area twice before. In fact, Connor has seen me, although he's not quite a believer yet. I'm working on that."

"Why are you here?"

"Because you are so lost. You must stop feeling guilty for your involvement in the Channel. You were put there to protect those you could, and you did. The rest of what you did was what you had to do to survive. God forgives you for all. You've done your penance. It's time for you to move on to fulfill your second purpose in life. Once you fulfill your purpose, you will live a wonderful life of happiness."

She moved closer to the woman, surprised to see that the closer she moved, the more translucent the woman appeared. Was she a spirit?

"Aye, I'm a spirit of a sort." Her light laughter filled the chamber with warmth, another oddity.

The woman knew what she was thinking. Was that possible? While not necessarily convinced, she wished to hear her answer to the problem that plagued her. "What is my purpose? Please."

"You've had two, but you already fulfilled the first. You have one left. Why, your purpose is one of the noblest. You are a mother, and you are a wonderful one. In fact, Claray has siblings waiting to be born, but you are a little slow understanding what is meant for you. You must accept this and move forward. Your loving husband-to-be awaits you."

Her eyes widened, stunned at this revelation. A mother? That was her purpose?

The spirit began to disappear, so she moved closer. "Wait, please. How can I be good enough for Connor? I had a bairn out of wedlock. Does not that make me a—" she shuddered before she said the word, "—whore?"

"Nay, child. Your heart is pure." She smiled and gave her a small wave. "Tell Connor my work here is finally done."

And with that, she was gone.

———◆———

The next morn, Sela began to pack her things as soon as she awakened. Sister Grace came in a few moments later and asked, "You're leaving?"

She nodded. "Aye. The abbess is correct. 'Tis time for me to move on. I'm going to say goodbye to the Camerons, ask for an escort to Grant land, and I hope to marry Connor Grant."

Claray tugged her arm. "Mama, are there lassies who I can play with there?"

"There certainly are. Find your toys and Torry's things." Then she turned to Sister Grace, "Would you mind waiting here for a moment while I go talk with the abbess?"

"Of course. I'll help the lass collect her things."

She hurried down the passageway, feeling a new bounce in her step. She nearly knocked Mother Matilda over when the nun stepped out of the chapel just before she passed it. "Forgive me, Mother Matilda. It was careless of me."

"You seem quite happy this morn. Have you come to tell me something already?"

"Aye, I have. My purpose is to be a mother. I'm going to marry Connor." She let her breath out, so pleased she was able to explain everything.

"What changed your mind so quickly?"

Did she dare admit she'd seen a spirit? No, she thought it best to think of it as a dream. "God's answer came to me in a dream."

"Congratulations. I'm pleased to hear it."

"Many, many thanks. You have my gratitude for your patience."

"Child, you deserved it. You've been through too much. 'Tis time for you to enjoy some happiness. I'm glad you finally understand you deserve it."

She turned to head down the passageway, but then stopped and whirled back around. "Is there a new nun here? One with hair just a shade darker than mine?" She had to ask. It could have been a nun who'd visited her. The rest might have been the product of an overactive imagination.

"A new nun? Nay."

She nodded and turned around to leave, but the abbess's voice caught her.

"Believe in God's spirits. They have unusual ways of getting what they want." She walked away without another explanation.

They said their goodbyes to the Camerons a short time later, and Sela gave Jennie Cameron a special hug. "My thanks for everything."

"You're welcome. You and Connor will make a wonderful couple. I look forward to seeing my brother watch his youngest son marry. He'll be so pleased. Alex was like a father to me for many years, so his children are special to me."

Sela chewed on her lip, trying to think of exactly the right words to tell this wonderful woman what she meant to her. "I owe you for so much, but especially for watching over Claray when she had the fever. I cannot tell you how much it meant to me to know she was well-cared for. And Tara and Riley are such sweet lasses…"

"You need not say any more. We will be family soon. Remember that. You must hold on to your beloved memories of your mother and father, but allow yourself to forget everything else."

"Do you think your brother and his wife will accept me?"

"Absolutely. We parents want our children's happiness first and foremost. And you make Connor verra happy. Godspeed to you."

CHAPTER THIRTY

CONNOR HEADED OUT TO THE butts alone in the middle of the afternoon. He had to admit he'd hoped Sela would come back to him before now. But he'd heard nothing since Hord's death, and each day was a little bleaker.

Many people had reminded him to be patient, but he felt as though his patience was about to run out. It had been a fortnight since he'd last seen Sela, and he'd vowed she would have to come to him next.

He fired ten arrows, hitting the center of the target ten times.

He sighed, settling onto a log to think. That was when he saw her.

The ghostly woman he and Roddy had seen at Sona Abbey many moons ago stood at the opposite end of the field, smiling and waving at him. He'd seen her with Daniel, too, but that time she'd worn a heart-shaped red stone around her neck. She wore the same white gown with the same blue band around the waist.

He hurried toward her, but her billowing white form began to fade to nothingness. Her hair was waving in the wind, the color red, and a necklace of pearls hung around her neck.

He whispered, "The pearls are back this time. I remember. But your hair color changes, doesn't it?"

"Goodbye, Connor Grant. You've earned a happy life.

You'll be a wonderful father."

She disappeared in a second.

He dropped his bow and rubbed his eyes. Blast it all, he was turning daft. He wished Roddy were here so he could ask him about her. He'd seen her a second time, too, and her hair had been different then. Had that been with Daniel or Braden?

He bent over to pick up his things, but he heard his name.

"Connor!"

It was a voice he thought he recognized, one he'd ached to hear, but it couldn't be, could it?

He moved out into the meadow, glancing one way and the other until he found a group of ten horses galloping his way. Then he heard it again.

"Connor!"

A woman jumped down from her horse and broke into a run, headed straight for him. He caught sight of a thatch of red curls on the horse behind her. A child riding in front of a guard.

Had Sela come to him?

Hope bloomed in his heart, sending warmth down his limbs.

He hurried closer, not wanting to run in case he was wrong, but the closer she came, the more he was sure it was her. She was almost to him when she shouted, "Connor Grant, I love you!"

He held his arms open and she leapt into them, twining her arms around his neck. "Sela?" was all he could get out.

"Aye. I love you and I accept your proposal, but only if you can answer one question."

"What?" He was so elated, he would have granted her whatever she wanted.

She gave him a saucy look and asked, "Do you remember me?"

He laughed, lifted her in the air, and said, "Forever."

EPILOGUE

———◆———

A FORTNIGHT LATER, CONNOR AND SELA crossed onto Cameron land, and that small movement hit deep in Sela's belly. It felt strange to be so close to the place where she'd been attacked, but it had been part of the journey that had brought her back to Connor, and she had never been happier.

Connor's mother had been incredibly understanding of her plight. She understood why Sela had waited so long to agree to be Connor's wife, and her sympathy and encouragement meant more than anything.

Sela didn't care if anyone else judged her unfairly as long as Connor and his parents could see her for what was in her heart.

Claray had enjoyed every minute on Grant land. Maddie had fussed over her every day as if she were her own. Connor's youngest sister, Elizabeth, had taken Claray everywhere with her, even to visit a cousin named Ashlyn. Her wee daughter, Ishbel, had a litter of puppies, so Claray and Torry had spent hours playing with them.

Sela glanced over at her dear daughter riding horseback in front of Connor, whom she now referred to as Papa.

His family had made them feel at home, something she cherished. She was actually starting to feel as if they belonged there.

They were returning to Cameron land so she and Connor could be married at Lochluin Abbey, along with

Gregor and Linet. She was a wee bit unsettled about seeing the abbess and the sisters again, but she knew they wished the best for her.

Connor, Claray, and Sela rode with his parents and his siblings, though the pregnant lasses were traveling in a large cart covered with thick furs.

Claray's face lit up as they approached the stables at the Cameron keep, her wee finger pointing to the cluster of people outside the building.

Connor glanced at her and said, "My cousin Loki and his cast of bairns. I'll explain later, but he and his wife, Bella, offer their home to many young ones who have lost their parents." Thorn, who'd been riding with Alex, jumped down and scurried over to join the group.

Loki stood in the middle of a cluster of lads. The only ones Sela recognized were Nari and now Thorn. A lass with hair the prettiest combination of gold and red stood off to the side of them with two younger bairns, and from the looks they were giving each other, she had to be Loki's wife.

A wee pony stood off to the side of the group, bucking like a wild horse.

Brodie Grant, Loki's adoptive sire, stood next to Braden and Cairstine. Sela had met Cairstine and their boy, Steenie, on the family's visit to Grant land. "Paddy wants to have a special entrance," Steenie whined.

The lad's grandmother, Celestina, placed her hands on his shoulders and said, "Now please remember, Steenie. Horses cannot speak. Paddy will have a fine spot in the wedding procession. He'll not be forgotten."

"Paddy has a different way of telling me things," Steenie said to his grandmother.

The pony reared up as if to agree.

"He wishes to be special, 'tis all he wants, and I do, too." Steenie stared up at his grandmother with a hopeful gaze.

"Greetings, Connor," Loki said, lifting his gaze to them.

"We're just trying to arrange the processional. Do you not wish to arrange it yourself? After all, you are one of the grooms."

Connor shook his head. "Nay, you're doing a fine job, Loki." He helped Claray down and she made her way over to the group of lads, although she stood off to the side, observing their antics.

"What's wrong?" Thorn asked.

"Steenie and Paddy want to ride alone and be special," Nari said. "I told him that I should have an extra special role because I helped save Gregor and Linet."

Thorn, looking quite indignant, said, "But I saved all the lasses because I told Connor about the ruse!"

Nari said, "Nay, you didn't know what a ruse was. Connor had to tell you."

"I *did* know. And I helped save all those lasses because I heard about the ruse. I should be special, too."

Steenie moved to stand between the two and said, "I'm special because I found Paddy the Pony and he took me to Grant land to find Braden to save my mother from those bad men. And we saved other lasses, too."

"Aye, but I'm the most special," Thorn said.

"Nay, me," Nari added.

Paddy reared and started making strange noises.

Loki threw his hands in the air, indicating he didn't know what to do. "Is there anyone here who can control a wee pony?"

Alex said, "I can, if you'd like." He dismounted and assisted Maddie down.

"Nay!" Brodie said. "Steenie has tender feelings for the wee beast."

Alex just quirked his brow at his brother as he made his way past the group, toward the keep. "You all enjoy yourselves. I'm looking for an ale and one of my sister's meat pies."

Sela wasn't sure what to do—sometimes it still overwhelmed her to be part of such a large and loving family—so she edged closer to Connor, who wrapped his arm around her shoulders and tugged her close. She noticed he was grinning from ear to ear at Loki's troubles.

The lads bickered, the pony fussed, and the rest of them stood around the outside giggling at the antics. Sela's heart dropped into her belly when Claray ran over to stand in front of the wild pony.

"Connor, the pony might hurt her," she said, pushing on his shoulder to urge him to intervene.

But she didn't need to worry. To the amazement and surprise of the rest of the group, Paddy leaned down to Claray and nuzzled the wee hand she held out to him. She stood up on her tiptoes and kissed him just above his nose.

Steenie hurried over to them and stared at his pet in shock. Then he broke out into a grin and turned to the group.

"Paddy said he'll do whatever Claray wants."

Claray giggled as Paddy dipped his head toward her. "Mama, may I have a pony, too?"

———◆———

Two days later, Connor stood in the Cameron courtyard in his leine and the finest red, green, and black Grant plaid he owned. His sire stood with him, along with his brothers, Jamie and Jake, all four dressed identically.

Jamie clasped his shoulder and said, "I have to admit, I didn't think I'd ever see it, Connor."

"You've chosen a fine woman," Jake added.

Connor glanced at his father, pleased to be looking down at him just a bit. "You, Papa? Did you believe it would happen?"

"I never doubted it for a moment. When a Grant lad finds the one, he doesn't change his mind. 'Tis for life."

"Mount up, Grants," came the call from Logan Ramsay. "These blue Ramsay plaids sure are the finest ones here, are they not?" He grinned and mounted his horse.

Jamie wasn't the only one who'd doubted this day would come. Connor had wished for it with all his heart, but he'd worried naught would come of it. It was still winter, but it wasn't snowing, and the sun had managed to peek out a few times.

The actual wedding would take place inside the beautiful abbey, although the elders had insisted on including a fine procession in celebration of the end of the Channel of Dubh. There'd been no more sign of Dubh activity anywhere since Hord had met his fiery end.

The portcullis lifted and the procession began. Connor looked over the land between the Cameron gates and the abbey, and a lump formed in his throat at the throngs of people who'd come to see the couples wed.

The group was led by Aedan Cameron, his brother Ruari, and Drew Menzie.

Will and Maggie followed, holding hands as they made their way to the abbey. Behind them came the rest of the Band and their wives:

David and Anna

Daniel and Constance

Braden and Cairstine

Roddy and Rose

Gavin and Merewen

Gregor and Connor came last, their brides waiting to join them inside the abbey, although both lasses were positioned to watch the processional.

Flanking the group came another very distinguished group:

Micheil Ramsay and Diana Drummond rode their horses next to their sons.

Logan Ramsay rode next to Gavin, and Brodie and Robbie Grant also rode next to their sons.

Gregor was flanked by Quade Ramsay and Chieftain Torrian.

Alexander Grant held back, riding next to Connor, and Jamie and Jake had fallen in beside their sire.

Halfway across the field, the procession slowed as a wee horseman joined them.

Steenie darted across the field riding Paddy the pony, who put quite a show on for the group. Two falcons and an owl followed him, swooping through the air in what looked like a dance. Two other ponies followed, carrying Thorn and Nari, both beaming with pride to be part of the big event.

The throng of guests, proudly wearing their plaids, parted for the procession and cheered their clansmen.

When they reached the abbey, men came out to hold Connor's and Gregor's horses, while they dismounted and headed into the abbey, their immediate family members following. Other guests were allowed in until the seats were filled.

All was quiet.

The abbey was full, decorated with ribbons and dried flowers. Connor and Gregor stood together at the back of the church. Father MacGregor was already behind the altar. Connor glanced at his cousin, wondering if Gregor was nervous, too. His hands were so damp, he felt the need to wipe them on his plaid.

Gregor quirked his brow at him. "'Tis finally here, Connor."

Two processions of lasses entered the church, one side led by Steenie and Thorn, the other side led by Loki's adopted son, Kenzie, and Nari.

The lasses sang hymns as they met in the middle and proceeded down the center aisle of the church, each carrying a bouquet of flowers. Connor couldn't believe how many they'd gathered. As soon as they began to walk, many of the guests started to cry. The audience slowly rose to their feet.

The procession consisted of many of the lasses who'd

been rescued from the Channel, dressed all in white, marching and singing. Looking at them, Connor couldn't be prouder of the work the Band had done. Their group might have disbanded, but their work had changed lives.

The last lass member of the processional was Claray, who gave everyone a big smile, giggled, and whispered, "Greetings, Papa," before she strode down the aisle. She carried a large basket of flowers.

At the end of the procession, Sela came from one side of the chapel and Linet from the other.

Linet wore a pink gown adorned with an array of embroidered flowers, sewn carefully by her sister. Her dark hair flowed down her back, woven with ribbons and flowers carefully placed by Gregor's Aunt Avelina.

She looked lovely, but as soon as Sela entered the chapel, Connor noticed no one else. She wore an ice blue gown, the exact shade of her eyes. She stepped out with her head held tall, shoulders squared, and a beaming smile. Connor could barely keep himself from gasping. The gown was unadorned but sleek, flowing a distance behind her. Her white hair was bound in two braids along the side in the Norse fashion, then pulled back to join the rest of the hair freely flowing down her back. She was the most beautiful woman he'd ever seen. But today she was no Ice Queen. Her smile lit up the abbey.

She joined him and took his hand, then leaned over and whispered in his ear, "Now do you remember me?"

———◆———

Two nights later, Connor and Sela stood under the night sky in his aunt and uncle's favorite spot on the hill behind the abbey. They'd had two days of celebrations for two weddings, and while they'd enjoyed themselves, they were both exhausted and looking for some quiet time. Sela took his hand and squeezed as they stared up at the stars. It was a cloudless night, perfect for stargazing.

She hadn't mentioned the spirit she'd seen on her last night in the abbey, but she did remember that the spirit had mentioned visiting Connor. This had to be the best place to broach the subject. "Connor, do you believe in spirits and faeries?"

He spun his head to stare at her so quickly that she thought it may have hurt his neck. "Why do you ask that question?" His gaze narrowed.

"I didn't tell you before, but I dreamed of a woman the night before I returned to you. She was a beautiful woman in a white dress."

"With a blue band around her waist and pearls around her neck?"

Her mouth fell open. "So you do know her?"

He grabbed both of her hands. "Aye, I first saw her with Roddy at Sona Abbey. I made him promise not to tell another soul. It was in the middle of a thunderstorm. What did she say to you?"

"She said she was the protector of bairns and told me my purpose was to be a mother."

"I saw her just before you returned. It was only a moment, but she said I deserved happiness and her work was done." Connor stared up at the stars above, as if seeking clarity. Then he kissed her cheek and said, "She also said I'd be a wonderful father. I hope she's correct."

"Mayhap she was the one guiding you and your cousins to follow the Channel. To save all the lads and lassies you did."

Connor sighed, wrapping his arm around his wife's shoulders. "My sire believes in faeries and spirits. My grandmother did, too. Why should I not? Aunt Avelina is connected to the other realm in some way, or so Papa tells me. Says he saw the heavens above respond to her. Still swears he's never seen anything like it. 'Tis why he doesn't question Paddy the pony."

A star shot across the sky, leaving a trail of light behind it.

Sela pointed. "Look. What do you suppose that means?"

Aunt Jennie and Uncle Aedan crested the hill just in time to hear the end of their conversation. "'Tis said a star like that is a bairn finding its way to the womb," Jennie said.

"A bairn?" Connor asked.

"A tale of the stars. One of many," Aedan said. "Believe whatever you choose."

They talked a bit more before they decided to head back to the keep as a group.

They'd almost made it back to the keep when Sela realized she'd dropped a linen square and went back to retrieve it, Connor following her. She picked it up off the ground and glanced up at the stars one more time.

"Connor, do you think we'll have a bairn together? The spirit said we will."

A billowing shadow of the spirit they'd seen crossed in front of them, her smile luminous. "Your aunt was correct, Connor. That shooting star was your first-born finding its way to its mama. Congratulations!"

———◆———

Nine months later…

Connor paced the great hall in the middle of the night, his sire and brothers chuckling while his mother and sister grinned. "This is taking too long," he declared, looking at them all as if they could do something to hurry up the process.

The door he'd been watching abovestairs finally opened, and Aunt Jennie stepped out of the chamber. "Connor, do you wish to do as your sire and sit at her side? The bairn is almost here."

"Aye!" he shouted loud enough to wake the entire clan.

He bolted up the stairs, taking them three at a time, ignoring the teases and taunts of his brothers, both of whom had already preceded him into fatherhood.

Aunt Jennie opened the door for him and he bolted inside. His wife's face was as red as a ripe apple. Whatever pain had her in its grip must have eased, briefly, for she let her breath out with a whoosh and leaned back against the pillow.

"Connor, if your bairn does not get out soon, I'm going to reach up, find a leg and pull it out." She gritted her teeth and glared at him.

He'd heard about this, about wives yelling at their husbands before they delivered a bairn, so he ignored her comment.

He sat on the stool next to her and asked, "What can I do to help you?"

"Why are you here? Men do not attend these things," she said, grasping his hand tightly while he mopped her brow.

"True, but my sire was at each of our births. I'd prefer to stay if you'll allow it," he said.

Aunt Jennie, fussing with her supplies, said, "Every single one. My brother would not be moved, and my nephew is even bigger. I'll not be pushing him out."

Sela met his gaze and held it. "Aye, I would like you to stay. My first time was not the best. It would comfort me to have you here." She reached up to cup his face, but then her eyes widened with pain. His dear wife leaned forward and pushed, hooking her hands around her knees as she let out a fierce growl.

Aunt Jennie checked her progress, Aunt Caralyn behind her. "I can see the bairn's head, and 'tis quite fair, I think." Aunt Caralyn peeked and said, "Aye, a wee Norse bairn. We've not seen many of those."

Connor asked, "Do you think 'tis a lassie?"

Aunt Jennie smiled at him. "You've three nephews now,

Connor. I'm surprised you don't wish to have a lad first, like your brothers and sister, but I hope 'twill be a wee lassie for your sake. She'd have a time teasing all the laddies, would she not?"

Sela leaned back and whispered, "I care not whether 'tis a lad or a lassie, I just wish for the babe to be born. Please, Aunt Jennie."

"I think the babe may come with your next push," Aunt Caralyn said, patting her knee.

Connor kissed his wife's forehead. How happy their new life was together. The two of them, along with Claray, lived in their own cottage inside the bailey. Sela fussed over every detail to make it warm and cozy. They'd spent quite a bit of time learning how to fish in their loch, Claray laughing as she chased about the flopping fish. The wee lassie had become a favorite in the clan with her red curls and sweet giggle.

Sela let out another growl and leaned forward, pushing so hard Connor wished he could help her. A loud shout erupted from her lips as their bairn burst into the world, slipping into Aunt Jennie's capable hands.

Aunt Caralyn had linen ready to clean the squalling bairn up while Aunt Jennie finished with her tasks, both of them talking in soothing tones to the new life they held in their hands.

Connor forced himself to avert his eyes from the babe to attend to his wife. He squeezed her hand and kissed her forehead. "You did a fine job with our wee one, Sela. I love you."

"What is it?" Sela asked, peering at their new bairn in awe.

Aunt Jennie held the bairn up for them to see.

"Congratulations to both of you. 'tis the wee lassie you wished for, Connor, and she has the white hair you hoped for, too. Have you a name yet?"

Connor smiled, his heart brimming with happiness, and

kissed his wife again. "I'd like to call her Dyna, after your mother."

Sela burst into tears and hugged him. Then she turned to Aunt Jennie and said, "Aye, Dyna."

~ THE END ~

DEAR READER,

Thank you for reading Connor's story!

Is it the end of the Grants and Ramsays?

Absolutely not. It is the end of The Band of Cousins because, though I am putting the finishing touches on a Christmas novella tied to the Band, the Channel of Dubh has finally been destroyed! There are still many tales to tell of the remaining Grants and Ramsays: Jennet, Kenzie, Brigid, Elyse, Elizabeth, Steenie, Riley, Brin...and so many more. My present plan is to package them a little differently. Some will be stand-alone novels, others will be presented as trilogies or duets. One that will definitely come to fruition is a trilogy about the healers in the group—Jennet, Brigid, and maybe Elyse.

We'll see! I go where my muse goes.

Happy reading!

As always, reviews would be greatly appreciated. Sign up for my newsletter on my website at *www.keiramontclair.com*. I send newsletters out with each new release.

Another way to receive notices about my new releases is to follow me on BookBub. Click on the tab in the upper right-hand side of my profile page. You can also write a review on BookBub.

Keira Montclair

www.keiramontclair.com
www.facebook.com/KeiraMontclair
www.pinterest.com/KeiraMontclair

Novels by

Keira Montclair

———◆———

THE BAND OF COUSINS
HIGHLAND VENGEANCE
HIGHLAND ABDUCTION
HIGHLAND RETRIBUTION
HIGHLAND LIES
HIGHLAND FORTITUDE
HIGHLAND RESILIENCE
HIGHLAND DEVOTION
HIGHLAND BRAWN

THE CLAN GRANT SERIES
#1- RESCUED BY A HIGHLANDER-
Alex and Maddie
#2- HEALING A HIGHLANDER'S HEART-
Brenna and Quade
#3- LOVE LETTERS FROM LARGS-
Brodie and Celestina
#4-JOURNEY TO THE HIGHLANDS-
Robbie and Caralyn
#5-HIGHLAND SPARKS-
Logan and Gwyneth
#6-MY DESPERATE HIGHLANDER-
Micheil and Diana
#7-THE BRIGHTEST STAR IN
THE HIGHLANDS-
Jennie and Aedan

#8- HIGHLAND HARMONY-
Avelina and Drew

THE HIGHLAND CLAN
LOKI-Book One
TORRIAN-Book Two
LILY-Book Three
JAKE-Book Four
ASHLYN-Book Five
MOLLY-Book Six
JAMIE AND GRACIE- Book Seven
SORCHA-Book Eight
KYLA-Book Nine
BETHIA-Book Ten
LOKI'S CHRISTMAS STORY-Book Eleven

THE SOULMATE CHRONICLES
#1-TRUSTING A HIGHLANDER

THE SUMMERHILL SERIES-
CONTEMPORARY ROMANCE
#1-ONE SUMMERHILL DAY
#2-A FRESH START FOR TWO
#3-THREE REASONS TO LOVE

STAND-ALONE NOVEL
FALLING FOR THE CHIEFTAIN-Book Three in
Enchanted Falls Trilogy

ABOUT THE AUTHOR

KEIRA MONTCLAIR is the pen name of an author who lives in Florida with her husband. She loves to write fast-paced, emotional romance, especially with children as secondary characters in her stories.

She has worked as a registered nurse in pediatrics and recovery room nursing. Teaching is another of her loves, and she has taught both high school mathematics and practical nursing.

Now she loves to spend her time writing, but there isn't enough time to write everything she wants! Her Highlander Clan Grant series, comprising of eight standalone novels, is a reader favorite. Her third series, The Highland Clan, set twenty years after the Clan Grant series, focuses on the Grant/Ramsay descendants. She also has a contemporary series set in The Finger Lakes of Western New York and a paranormal historical series, The Soulmate Chronicles.

Contact her through her website, *www.keiramontclair.com*